sweet & sultry

SERIES

someone
LIKE YOU

PAX SINCLAIR

ISBN 978-1-7336445-0-1 (ebook Edition)
ISBN 978-1-7336445-1-8 (paperback Edition)

Printed and bound in the United States of America
First printing July 2019

Published by Red Kettle Ink
2010 El Camino Real #1151
Santa Clara, CA 95050

www.paxsinclair.com

Book Cover by Uniquely Tailored, www.uniquelytailored.com

Dedication

To Garry who patiently waited for me to tap out one more sentence even when it made us late. P and M, you always believed in me.

Acknowledgements

Writing is a solitary adventure, and it can be difficult to ask others to be a part of the process. I am grateful for the help and support I received from these beta readers. You made this a better story, Katia, Maureen, Jennifer, Oxana, Deborah.

Special thanks to Ash. You know what you did.

Table of Contents

Prologue

Bexley Winston was studying me over the top of her large-frame glasses, waiting for my answer. I shifted uncomfortably in my chair, hoping to disappear. Her frustration with me had reached her fingertips. The tapping of her perfect nails on her spotless desk was sending my nerves into overdrive. She glanced at the clock. "You know I've only got twenty minutes. We promised we would let them know today at one."

We sat in her small contemporary office in downtown San Francisco. The soft gray haze of the city filtered in through large windows behind her. The view was a row of dingy gargoyles perched on a 1920s office building across the street.

Bex, my best friend, marketing guru, and wrangler was waiting for my decision on a new hire. As usual, I was fraying her last nerve ending. I pushed the sleeves of my cardigan to my elbows, then grabbed my mug from the edge of her desk to buy some time. I wrinkled my nose at the white stuff floating in my cold tea. Had we been sitting here that long?

"Emma Antonia Benton Cameron!"

I looked up at the mention of my full name. Bex placed her hand on the phone.

"Why do I have to decide now? Can't I put this off? I'm sure a few more months won't make a difference."

"No, this is already in motion. I don't see why it's a hard decision, you've had more than enough time."

"True, but…"

"I can tell them we've moved the deadline. Maybe they'll wait for your decision a few more days. But if you want this project to be finished in time for the Passion Moon event; we've got to start recording no later than next Monday."

We'd planned the Cooper Flynn book, *Danger Dance: Passion Moon*, to release on the night of the total eclipse of a blood moon. We've been pushing hard with the advertising despite the various myths surrounding these kinds of celestial events. We reclaimed it for love, instead of buying into doomsday predictions. A few romance authors saw the same opportunity and scheduled book events for Passion Moon.

Knowing we had a hard deadline made me want to jump out of my seat. What would Luke do? Forget it. I wouldn't be in this gigantic mess if he were here.

"Fine, I'll go with William Kaulder."

Bex raised an eyebrow. "I thought you liked Austin?"

CHAPTER 1

Coffee Morning

One month earlier

After three years, I still had a problem waking up in the morning. I'd roll over to rest an arm on an empty cold space that lacked a warm body. For those brief moments, my hazy, sleep-induced mind imagined Luke had forgotten his phone or keys and was just outside the room. Or he was lacing up his runners getting ready for a pre-dawn jog. I half expected my husband to slip back into the room just before he left to kiss me goodbye.

Sitting up, I swung my legs to the side, intent on getting up. But instead, my fingers clutched the edge of the mattress. It had been a long time since something triggered the sadness. I lowered my head as if in prayer.

Centering was the only way. It was a technique I'd learned from my grief and loss group. They'd helped me through the rough patches after Luke's death when I didn't understand what was happening to me.

The dark mood began to subside enough for me to push out of bed, stretch and refocus. I smoothed the duvet and arranged the pillows. Settling on the foot of the bed, I closed my eyes and took in a long relaxing breath of coffee aroma. The automatic coffee maker had kicked on, and it was brewing my first cup.

I needed to stop thinking about my morning coffee and meditate. Before I could begin to center, a large lump of black fur landed next to my thigh. Intelligent golden eyes looked up at me.

"Good morning, Daisy," I sighed, stroking my cat. She meowed back a greeting, then rubbed her head against my thigh. Spending time with Daisy always readjusted my mood. "I'm hungry too. Let's get something to eat."

Mug in hand, I padded down the hall to my home office. As I tapped on the lights, Daisy raced ahead of me for my desk.

One wall of the room was painted hot pink. At the center of this pink explosion hung an oversized inspiration board that occupied most of the space. Pictures of actors and models were pinned three deep like a careless afterthought. Lost among the sea of faces were tacked notes, quotes, even pictures of scenery. I collected these bits and pieces as resource material for my stories.

Moving closer to the board, my hand ran along the top right corner. Our family photos were arranged here in a more orderly display. Camerons and Bentons, all the way back to a faded photo of one of my ancestors who was rumored to be a raider in the Old West, kept me company while I weaved my stories.

My gaze settled on my favorite photo of Luke. We'd taken an impromptu week-long vacation to Aruba about five summers ago. It was literally 'get your tooth brush and passport and let's go.' Our guide had taken this picture in front of an open-air restaurant. Luke's pushed-back straw fedora allowed a few brown ale locks to touch his forehead. The intense hazel eyes squinting from the sun. His arm around my shoulder, my arms around his waist, we'd looked happy and in love.

The guide caught Luke's dimpled smile looking straight into the camera while I gazed up at my handsome husband.

My fingers brushed my lips, then I gently placed my kiss on his face. "Good morning, my love," I said, completing one of my morning rituals.

Daisy danced the perimeter of the desk, avoiding most of my papers and accumulated writing paraphernalia. She took a long epic feline stretch before plopping onto her pillow, then stared at the office phone. The red caller light signaled two voicemails were waiting. Taking a sip of coffee, I leaned forward to press the play button.

"Hey, Emma," came the excited voice of Bexley, my excellent marketing guru. "We need to nail down an MN."

MN was code for male narrator. I rolled my eyes.

"Don't roll your eyes," she said, busting me.

Coffee almost shot through my nose. Good thing I had cooled it with cream.

"You always do that when I bring up this subject. Seriously, you are losing revenue on the Cooper Flynn series because you haven't released an audio version. Not to mention your audio fans are getting restless. They've started an online poll on who should be the voice of Cooper. William Kaulder is polling off the charts."

Kaulder would be. He was the rock star of narrators since he hit the scene about five years ago. He could voice anyone, including women and children, with alarming accuracy. He even voiced a crying baby, although how he nailed that, I was still wondering.

With his legion of fans, and my cult following, we could push the Cooper series into bestseller territory, and a lucrative movie deal could follow. I'd seen it happen to a couple of authors from my critique group. His voice somehow had this magic touch.

"Call me soon, don't forget. I have something exciting to share with you. Bye, bye."

I pushed the pause button and looked at Daisy. Her golden eyes stared back at me with concern.

3

"I know," I said to Daisy, "He would be the perfect choice for this project."

Luke and I had decided we needed a fresh, unknown voice for Cooper. But this was William Kaulder and I was in love with him. I meant; I was in love with his voice. I had every book he'd ever narrated, including two horror stories that scared the shit out of me. I was so anxious for two weeks I didn't want to be alone. Luke had to convince me not to take a knife to bed because I thought aliens were coming for me. But I sucked it up and listened to those creepy stories because it was Kaulder who had the voice of the hero.

Halfway through my emails, I remembered there was a second message. I pushed play.

"Hi, Em girl, it's me," came a low, lazy male voice. I dropped into my chair, almost spilling my coffee. "I'm back in town. I was hoping to see you soon. I've some loose ends to tie up, then I'll be free. I'll find you when I'm finished. Today, tomorrow, I'm not sure. But I'm looking forward to catching up." He was humming something just before the phone clicked off.

This couldn't be real. That was Parker, or at least a very good facsimile. He was my husband's younger brother. My infamous brother-in-law was fun, adventurous, and unbelievably sexy. The kind of man that left a trail of quivering hearts in his wake. I'd known these brothers since high school. I'd bet five bucks the loose end was female.

Why was he showing up now? Out of instinct, I grabbed my cell to go through my contacts. I put the phone back down. There wouldn't be a number there, and nothing showed up on my office phone. I hadn't seen him for almost three years. After Luke's funeral, he was just gone. I'd gotten cards with brief notes for my birthday, Christmas, and Valentine's Day. But other than that, nothing. I gave up thinking about his motives. I would know soon enough when he showed up. In the meantime, I decided to invite Bex to my house for mojitos. I figured it was the only way I was going to get through the MN conversation.

CHAPTER 2

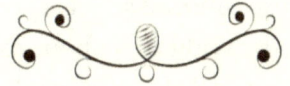

Mojito Madness

I balanced a tray with a pitcher of mojitos, a couple of tall frosty glasses, and food. I'd made the mojitos from scratch, thank you very much. I also arranged an artful assortment of nibbles on a plate. I figured if our session lasted all afternoon, I would treat Bexley to dinner and pay for a car ride home.

"What's this news you wanted to share?" placing the tray between us on the table. My friend looked appreciative, sizing up the pitcher. I admit the limes and mint looked refreshing. I had used a heavy hand with the rum, so the refreshments were lethal. I slid into the lounge chair. It was warm for November even by Northern California standards. We sat in my backyard like two ladies who did liquid lunch.

Bex moved her chair closer to the table. "Before we talk about my news, we should discuss the MN. You've been putting it off for way too long. You should have done it with the release of the first book. But I get it. You wanted to make sure it was a success. But here we are about to release book three..."

I poured a glass and handed it to her. "You need to take a breath. I get it. I understand. I'm ready to start the process."

She beamed and accepted the glass. "Goody, I thought you might be agreeable. So, I brought a binder full of men."

I grabbed my glass and poured to have something to do. I didn't want her to see I still wasn't ready.

She pulled a blue plastic binder from her over-sized bag and pushed it across to me.

"So, these are the candidates?" I asked, staring at it as if something from the underworld was about to leap out and drag me off. Luke had always managed this part of the business. He was the one who interviewed and hired Nancy Mueller, who narrated the Molly Dixon series. The Cooper Flynn series continued the adventures of Molly Dixon but through the point of view of her love interest Cooper Flynn.

"The men aren't actually in there," she snorted.

"I know," still not pleased.

"The book contains bios, samples of work, and even pictures. We can begin scheduling interviews at anytime."

I frowned. "You know my rules."

Bex put her glass down and placed a hand over her heart like she was about to pledge allegiance and dutifully recited my creed. "I won't meet actors, and I'm not Molly Dixon,"

I took a sip and shook my head. "Words to live by."

"I thought this time you might make an exception. I understand about the Molly Dixon part, but why won't you meet actors?"

I sighed. "When an actor is really good at what they do, you fall in love with them. When you meet this amazing person, and they're nothing like the wonderful character you love, you're heartbroken. It's like dating an impeccably dressed guy. You think something might be wrong after months of dating because he never wants to hang out at his place. You drop by one day thinking you might find out he's married with three kids. But you discover he's a hoarder. He has a foot-wide path through all his junk in his apartment. And if that wasn't enough, he has to move every two years because he has so much stuff. You almost wished you had found another woman. It might have been easier."

She seemed to be working hard to follow my logic. "Yeah, right, that's a concept. I now see why you're almost a best-selling author. You can make a story out of anything." Bex grabbed her glass. The ice clinked when she took a sip. She made a yum sound, replacing it back on the table. "Anyway, they're not actors," she shook her head, "What am I saying? Most of them are veteran stage, film, and TV actors with training from places that have Royal Academy in the name."

"You know my rules. But on second thought. I'd like to amend my credo. I'd like to think I'm the kind of person who can evolve."

Bex looked hopeful.

"I think it's only fair to include all celebrities."

She rolled her eyes. "Look, you're not meeting Gerard Butler or Idris Alba."

I grinned. "Hmmm... now those men would make an exciting story."

"Many are working actors. You might have seen their faces. Maybe not know their names." She grabbed a piece of cheese and waved it for emphasis. "You know, I tried to interest Brad Pitt in your project, but he refused, because you won't meet him."

I pushed the book forward. "I changed my mind. We can table this a while longer."

She put the cheese down. "Okay, okay. Let's just put it to the side for now. I'm ready to talk about my news." She jumped to her feet, addressing an imaginary musician. "Drum roll, please. My news is I've received an email from William Kaulder's agent. He's a huge fan and is interested in narrating the Cooper series."

"We can't--"

"Wait, let me finish. He's willing to waive his ginormous fee for a small doable retainer and a percentage of the sales," she grinned.

"Oh my God, Kaulder. The man of my… I mean the narrator of my dreams. Wait a minute. He's a fan? He knows my work?"

"I would say that is a giant yes." She plopped back into her seat.

We stared at each other for a heartbeat. Then we screamed and stomped our feet like two tweeners getting concert tickets to see their favorite boy band.

She placed a large, unopened envelope on the table. "He submitted a bio with a picture."

As far as I knew no one had seen a picture of William Kaulder. He was a recluse. I could relate to a decision to be anonymous. I wrote under the pen name of Angela Stryker. I sometimes gave written interviews. Or on a very rare occasion, a phone interview.

"I know his agent, and I had to promise her the photo would not be given to anyone, and that it would be returned. He's serious enough about this job to let you see him."

True, we could hire Kaulder through his agent, he'd work in a studio, and I'd never need to meet him.

"This is not like meeting a celebrity. Think of Kaulder as another member of your team, like your accountant or me."

"Have you seen the information in the packet?"

"No, I received it by FedEx. I thought we could review the contents together. When I responded to his agent, I told her we wouldn't consider working with him without a full bio, and a demo sample of material we'd chosen. A meeting too if it goes that far. She agreed to all of it. It looks like they made an exception with you."

I held the envelope in my hand. It felt weighty. "If you didn't open it, how do you know there's a photo in here?"

"The agent told me what to expect in the packet. Oh, by the way, there's also a contract included. Are you going to keep talking, or are we finally going to see what the mysterious William Kaulder looks like?"

I grimaced. My fingers found the tab. My hands unsteady with anticipation, I pulled out the sheets of paper. The bio was on top. I glanced at it. It was a who's who of the New York Times bestseller list. Bex walked around to seat herself next to me. Daisy appeared from nowhere and wedged herself between us.

I pulled the photo from the stack. It was a head shot. He had thick dark hair, mischievous dark eyes. He was very handsome, a strong jaw and a mouth that smiled often. He was a heartbreaker and at least twenty years older than me. Age wasn't a big deal for me, but there needed to be a spark. He would be a fascinating man to meet for dinner.

Bex moaned. "I was hoping he was Zac Efron and this was his other secret job."

"You don't have to be in your twenties to be hot. Besides, we're not hiring him for his face."

This could be a quick solution to all my problems, but no, Luke and I decided it should be a new voice. I was an indie author that published my own books. We tried to support our fellow independent writers and narrators that didn't or couldn't go through regular publishing houses. We wanted to give a chance to an unknown narrator to breathe life into an established series.

"No," I returned the photo to the table. "We won't go with Kaulder." I glanced at the binder. There had to be fifty people to sort through. "How about this, why don't you go through the book and select three, and I'll look at them. No photos of the final candidates, just bios and samples."

She returned to her seat. "You're sure you're up for this?" Daisy bounded off after her, deciding to sit with my friend. The ungrateful little traitor.

It would be hard because I was doing it without Luke.

I sighed. "I'm sure. You know what we're looking for, and three shouldn't be overwhelming to review. Please email Kaulder's agent and let her know we've decided to go with someone else."

Bex was stroking Daisy. The cat's purr of contentment could be heard from where I was sitting.

"I have a suggestion," she said, looking up from the cat. "Why don't we hold off on me talking to Kaulder's agent until you're sure.

Why not let him think he's still in the running? You never know, you might want to work with him someday."

"Okay, fair enough." I picked up my glass for a toast. "To hearing Cooper speak." We both smiled and clinked glasses.

CHAPTER 3

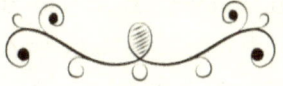

Austin City Limits

I checked the text from Bex again. After reviewing the three candidates she submitted, I'd decided to meet with Austin Santoro, someone who had limited narration experience and wasn't an actor. The samples he sent were promising, but what caught my eye was a recommendation from William Kaulder.

Bex arranged a lunch at the Waterline in Campbell. She thought it might be better for us to meet in the South Bay where we both lived instead of making the trek north to her San Francisco office.

The text said to meet Austin at 11:30 a.m. I arrived ten minutes before and confirmed the reservation with the hostess. I snagged a seat near her podium facing the door. I hadn't seen a photo of him. Bex said to look for a 'tall guy.'

I took out my cell and ran through my messages, then started to play a game. I was losing badly to a bunch of birds when I noticed the restaurant was filling up. I checked the time. I'd been waiting for forty-five minutes and I hadn't received any more texts. I usually gave someone about ten minutes before I'd start checking on their arrival time.

I was about to text Bex when a man appeared at the door. People around him stirred nervously, discreetly giving him space. He stood unaffected, searching the room.

It was difficult not to stare at him. The man's face exuded menace like a sexy super villain. I studied him for a few moments, not sure if this was the man I was meeting. Now I wished I had insisted on a description from Bex. He was impressive, with a powerful body, handsome face, and dark hair that swept to his broad shoulders. I could almost see him clad in leather and armor standing with his commanders searching the valley below for his sworn enemies as the wind whipped wildly through his dark tendrils.

My imagination was working overtime, but I had to admit if he was the narrator, he should be starring in a novel instead of reading it.

Bex did mention he was tall, and he looked well over six feet. I began to weave a path to him, parting the small crowd as I walked. When I finally reached him, I looked up with my best howdy smile.

"Hi--"

He looked down at me and arched an eyebrow. "I'm not interested."

My cheeks grew warm. I mumbled an apology, stepped back, and turned. I bumped into another man who was tall but had no doom swirling around him. I produced another big smile, and he returned a huge grin.

"Are you Austin?"

The man looked me up and down, "No, that's not me. My name's Bill. If that guy is stupid enough not to show, I'd be happy to…"

A voice boomed behind me. "I'm Austin. Is this man bothering you?"

Pivoting, I looked up at Mr. Doom again. His expression hadn't changed, but at least the eyebrow wasn't arched. He looked at the man now standing next to me and scowled. The man took a step back and left.

Great, rude and protective. Wonderful combination.

"Are you Bex?"

"No." Why did he think I was Bex? "I'm Emma, good to meet you."

"Yes, you as well," his voice barely above a whisper.

More diners crowded into the foyer, and Austin began surveying the room again. The hostess approached us, glanced up at him, and suggested a table on the patio. I walked in front of him. People were staring as we moved between the tables. I threw a quick glance over my shoulder to see him in full scowl mode. He looked like an enforcer walking in back of a mob princess.

When we got to our table, the hostess dropped the menus then scurried away. I was about to grab my chair when a big hand clasped it and pulled it out.

"Thank you," I said surprised at the polite gesture.

He nodded and pushed the chair in as I sat. He found his seat facing out to the restaurant.

Now that we were seated, it suddenly became awkward. We picked up our menus. It seemed an easier way to engage in conversation. "Have you been to this restaurant before?" I asked.

"Yes," he said, looking over his menu.

"Is this your favorite restaurant?" It was a silly question, but maybe he'd crack a smile or give me more of an answer.

"No."

I glanced back at my menu. As I suspected, I was going to be peppered with monosyllabic words for the rest of the interview. The man probably didn't speak unless he was about to do a narration. Maybe it wouldn't be too unprofessional to order a double scotch. I looked up to catch the waitress's eye and found him studying me.

"I apologize for being late," he said, putting his menu down. I bit my lip to suppress a giggle. The dark gaze he settled on me was from an evil villain. "There was an accident on 280, and I wasn't given your number."

His rich baritone voice caught me by surprise. "Oh, it happens." I smiled.

He didn't smile back. He just looked less formidable.

The waitress arrived and placed two glasses of water on the table.

She beamed, running her hands down the sides of her apron. "How y'all doing? My name is Veronica, and I will be serving y'all today." Veronica was pretty with predatory eyes and what grandmother would have called buxom.

She turned to Austin, and I was treated to a side view of those C cups almost in his face.

"They call me Roni for short," she breathed like it was an effort. He continued to look at his menu without noticing her blatant come-on.

Roni remembered I was also seated at the table and threw a glance at me. Then her attention snapped back to Austin.

"You know, I think this is a good time to tell y'all about the specials." She pulled out a small notebook from her pocket.

She read from the book with an animated delivery. I half expected her to describe herself as one of the specials, but she stuck to crab legs and shrimp. She did take extra pains to sidle up to him when he asked about an item on the menu. To his credit, he was polite and unfazed by her attention.

"Do you need a few minutes to decide what you really want?"

I had no proof, but I'd bet the comment was some kind of back-handed reference to me.

"I know what I'm having," I offered. Our waitress turned to me, her face questioning why I was still there. I should have been annoyed, but this episode of 'how to get a man's attention: 'Roni style' was bordering on hilarious. Losing interest in me, her concern trailed back to Austin. She continued as if I hadn't spoken.

"I would suggest the Captain's appetizers if you still can't decide. It's a sample of our most requested items."

"We'll have that. Thank you," Austin replied without consulting me. I almost said something, but this was a business meeting, not a date. But still.

"That's decided," she said, trying to get a reaction from him with her erect posture. Austin continued to look at his menu without looking up. "I'll leave the menus so you can choose your main course." She left, swaying her hips way too slowly. I smiled to myself. She was going to be sorely disappointed when she found out I was picking up the check.

Something about him was tugging at me. Bex said he was not an actor, but he looked familiar. I shrugged. I might have seen him profiled as a narrator in an industry magazine. I shot another glance at him over my menu. He was wearing a light jacket, a black long-sleeved T-shirt, and jeans. I was wearing something similar. This was Silicon Valley. It was kind of our uniform around here. Tats were peeking out from under his right sleeve, the design extending to his hand.

He rubbed his goatee and looked over at me. "You're staring."

"Sorry, but has anyone told you that you look like that wrestler?"

"Yes," and he resumed looking at his menu.

"The one that did the cute commercial with the little girl. I think the little girl was his daughter?"

"Look, I'm not a wrestler. I'm not him," he said, his jaw tight.

He could have been a doppelgänger for that wrestler. The one whose name I couldn't remember.

"Sorry."

"Please don't say sorry."

"Okay, sorry..." I grimaced.

He frowned at me. I leaned back in my chair and threw a look at him. We stared at one another until some disturbance behind me caught his attention. The meeting was not going as planned. Maybe I could still order that scotch.

The noise in the restaurant increased as more people took seats on the patio. Austin began searching the crowd, fingers drumming the table.

Bex thought he was worth a meeting. She wouldn't be happy if I didn't at least attempt to interview this man. I tried to catch his eye. "Your bio didn't list an acting background. How did you become a narrator?"

He picked up his water and began downing most of the liquid. I waited for an answer. Apparently, at this moment, hydrating was more important. He returned the glass to the table and began his story. "I was injured while working construction..."

It sounded like he had given this story a few times. He recited it like a caller at a bingo hall. I fought an urge not to yawn. He continued to drone on.

Austin leaned in, looking at his audience of one. I sat up straighter. Did I really nod off? "Then what happened?" I asked.

"What happened next is I listened to audiobooks for several months while recuperating. I was reading too, but more and more I gravitated to the spoken story."

I caught the well-modulated voice of a narrator. The man and the story were getting interesting.

"Listening to these readings was extraordinary," he said. "I'd experience novels I'd already read in a new way. It was like hearing a new artist cover an old song."

I was awed by the change. I thought at first it was a performance, but the story didn't sound rehearsed. It was possible he was attempting to make a connection, but I wasn't sure. He rubbed his chin, considering. "I thought for a long time I..."

He stopped abruptly, his attention turned to something in the restaurant, then anger flashed across his face. I was about to turn around to see what the cause of his irritation was when he bounced up from his seat. His bulk jostled the table, knocking my water glass over, and a river of liquid poured onto my lap. I grabbed a napkin and pushed away from the table, blotting the water from my jeans.

"What the...?" I said. But he was already digging into his back pocket. A wad of bills flew out and landed on the soaked surface.

"I can't do this," he said, still pissed at something. "I've got to go. This will pay for our lunch."

I watched his broad back as he retreated to a side entrance. I turned to see people staring at me. Great, we were the entertainment.

I grabbed my purse and checked the money on the table. A hundred dollars was more than enough to pay for appetizers and a very hefty tip. I saw our waitress approaching with our food. She glanced at the wet, empty table and me heading out.

"Hey, wait, this is your order."

"Sorry Roni," walking past her, "He left money on the table; the rest is your tip." Then I disappeared through the same side door.

CHAPTER 4

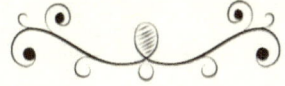

Who Let the Cat Out?

The spinach smoothie was helping me calm down as I talked to Bex between gulps. She was on speaker, and I had just given her a blow-by-blow of my lunch with Austin, including the part where I had to walk through a crowded parking lot among people who were either snickering or horrified at the wet stain on the front of my jeans. I sat on the cool granite kitchen counter looking out into my front yard.

"I don't know what happened," Bex said. She was the one who had recommended Mr. Doom Wrestler Austin. "I've put a call in to him, but I haven't received a response. There's got to be an explanation for his behavior."

"Yeah, that he's a psycho." My irritation flared again as I took another gulp of the green drink.

"What do you want to do?"

I slid off the counter to rinse the glass in the sink. "I'll look over the other two candidates again and let you know if I need to see more."

"There is something else. It's about the audio version of the Cooper series."

I tensed. The release was to be the night of the blood moon eclipse. The third book was the last one Luke and I had worked on, and I wanted it to be a tribute to him.

"It's about the studio. A fire destroyed most of the equipment. They can't honor our agreement. I've tried to find another place, but the local ones are booked. You might have to consider going out of state or even the country if you want to make your deadline."

I braced myself against the sink. This project seemed to become more difficult by the day. A meow drifted up from near my feet. Daisy was looking at me. "Do you want to go out, girl?"

"Excuse me?"

"Sorry, Daisy wants to go out. Please keep working on it, and let me know what you find. I want to avoid missing our deadline. It's bad enough we still don't have a voice for Cooper."

"Will do." She clicked off.

I walked the length of the kitchen into the foyer. The door had been sticking lately. I tugged at the handle with two hands until I jerked it open enough for Daisy to make a dash outside. I pulled the door open wider to inspect the lock when I saw a man dressed in a uniform leaning against the porch post with his back to me. I cleared my throat to get his attention, and he turned toward me.

My breath caught. My heart bounced. "Parker!" I ran out and launched myself into his open arms. He caught me, his strong arms tight around my waist, lifting me up a few inches from the ground.

"Hi, Em girl, long time no see." He gave me a chaste kiss and breathed in deep. "Still using that lavender soap? You do smell like heaven." He squeezed me a little too tight, then released me.

I slipped my arm around his waist. He took his captain's hat off and slipped it on my head. "Now you're part of my flight crew."

We laughed.

"Come on inside. I'll make us coffee, and we can talk."

Parker squinted at me. "I know you've got something stronger than coffee in there."

I chuckled. "I seem to remember you're a scotch drinker."

"Oh, aye lass, that I am." He winked at me.

"I think I have a bottle with your name on it. And by the way, I'm wearing Love and Luck. Does that 'You smell like heaven' line work?"

He shrugged. "Usually, but I've got to follow it with my devastating smile." He demonstrated. I lost all reason for a few seconds.

I brought a bottle and two tumblers into the living room. Parker shrugged out of his coat. I took it from him and placed it and his hat in the hall closet. He was pouring the scotch when I returned.

"How long are you staying?"

He handed me a glass. "To reunions," he said.

"Reunions," I repeated, and we touched tumblers.

He picked up my TV remote and handed it to me. "Could you find some background music?"

"Jazz, right?"

"You read my mind."

I tapped the remote. Joshua Redmond's sultry sax filled the space, and I was treated to a half grin of approval.

"I've left my job with Eos," he said, settling on the couch. "In February I'll be flying for Cubago."

That was news. He'd been working for Eos since he left college. He'd been flying even before he received his pilot's license. Their dad was a commercial pilot and taught Luke and Parker to fly, but it was Parker who pursued it through college, landing a job with a major airline.

"Why the change?" I really wanted to ask why he had left so abruptly after Luke's funeral, but we would get to that.

He took a sip. "I guess the short answer is I'm tired of the European run and think I'd like the change working Down Under will give me. Their hub is in Mascot, a suburb of Sydney, and I plan to move there."

"So, you're just stopping to say goodbye on your way to Australia? That's more than I got the last time you left."

He looked down at his glass. "I know I was an ass for leaving like that. With Luke's death--it was, too much."

"I could have used your help. Your parents were a comfort, but they couldn't stay with me forever. They had their life in San Diego."

"I've come back to make up for what I did. Maybe it can be a new start for us?"

Parker was the doted-on golden boy of the family. I understood. I'd lost my husband, but he didn't have his big brother to lean on. Luke's passing tore a gigantic hole in all our lives.

"Where are you staying?" I asked.

"I'm still technically an employee of Eos. I'm staying with the flight crew at a hotel downtown."

Luke would never have forgiven me if I allowed his brother to languish in a hotel while I was living in this large house with Daisy. Besides, it would be nice having family stay with me, and I could use help with this audio launch. It might be a very good idea.

"Why don't you stay here? You know the guest room is more than comfortable, and you'd have your own private entrance."

"Are you sure it would be no trouble?"

Why do people always say that? "Yes, Parker, you're always welcome."

He sprang to his feet. "I'd hoped you'd offer. I'll go back to the hotel to get my cases and check out. I should be back in time for dinner."

I handed him his coat, hat, and the key to the side entrance. He reassembled himself, dropped the key into his pocket, and straightened his tie. I admit my heart skipped a beat looking at him. He slipped his arms around my waist, pulling me close. I looked up into those emerald eyes, and for a minute I thought he was going to kiss me. My face grew hot, and I put my arms around his neck.

"Goodbye, Mr. Parker," I said in his ear. "I'll see you soon."

He laughed. "I'll see you tonight, Ms. Emma."

Daisy shot back into the house as I watched Parker stride down the path. I was already starting to have second thoughts about having him stay. It had been a long time since I shared this house with someone. I had created routines to get through the days. I wasn't sure how he was going to fit into my days or nights.

Time was slipping away. I needed to re-review the two narrators' bios Bex had sent over. At first glance they didn't appear to be suitable for the project, but that was based on a cursory review. I returned to my office and had just sat down to search for the files on my laptop when the doorbell rang. Parker must have forgotten something. He probably didn't want to startle me by coming in the side entrance. I grabbed my phone and pushed it into the front pocket of my sweats. I padded down the hallway. Midway down, I heard banging. Oh no, Parker, you did not just start beating on my door. "Okay, okay, I'm almost there," I yelled.

I yanked on the front door with both hands, but it refused to budge. "You'll have to push," I called out. But before I could get a grip on the handle, the door flew open. I was knocked off balance and fell on my behind with a painful thump. Daisy skipped over my lap to get outside to freedom. Why was she running like a demon out of hell? I peered around the door to see Austin looking down at me with an interested expression. He held out his massive hand and pulled me up.

The phone rang.

I checked the name. "Hi, Bex," I groaned.

"I've spoken to Austin. He wants to talk to you about the lunch today. I think you should listen to him. I wanted to warn you he's going to drop by in case you want to pretend you aren't at home."

That cork had already been popped. My behind ached. I wondered if it was possible to break something back there. I refrained from rubbing it.

"Thanks for the heads up. He's already here." I clicked off.

He was standing on my threshold, with sad eyes like a forlorn basset hound. I sighed. "Come in," sweeping my hand toward the kitchen. I offered him a glass of water. He took his drink and we sat at the table. Austin's shoulders were hunched. He looked down at his water, managing to look sheepish.

"I can fix that," he said to the water.

"Excuse me? Fix what?"

"Fix your door. You'll continue to have problems until you shave it."

Why would a door need to be shaved? I guess he might be an expert. He did say he worked construction.

"Okay, fine," still irritated.

"I'll go get my tools; they're in my truck."

He spread out a clean tarp and placed his toolbox on the surface. He evaluated the door, running his hand along the frame. "You could bring a chair over, and we can talk while I work and maybe you could hand me tools?"

I wanted to start yelling at him, but he'd asked nicely, although he hadn't made eye contact. I lugged the kitchen chair over next to the toolbox and waited. Wait a minute, he needed to give me answers as to why he ruined my lunch. I crossed my arms. "Why did you throw money at me like it was for services rendered and leave?"

He gave no reaction to my question, just looked like he had made a decision. He started to take his jacket off. If I thought he was impressive before, just from a peek at an open jacket, I was seriously wrong. I'd never seen anyone so perfectly built other than actors in a movie. He folded his jacket, placed it near the box, then flexed his shoulders.

"I was afraid there was going to be an altercation," he said, still looking at the door.

"From that guy I bumped into?"

"No, from four women."

"You've lost me."

"Remember you said I looked like that wrestler?"

"Yes."

"You're not the only person who thinks that."

I was beginning to follow his logic, but it seemed far-fetched.

"Your back was to the restaurant. You didn't see the four women who were about to approach our table. If it was just them, I could have handled it, but it looked like most of the restaurant was about to mob us."

"This has happened before?"

"A few times, but lately it's gotten worse. Ever since that guy did a commercial with his daughter, they think he's approachable... or I am. Remember our waitress Roni? That's the kind of reaction I get when they think I'm a celebrity."

"Maybe, if you didn't dress or wear--"

The side of his mouth pulled down and the fixed stare he threw at me said he didn't appreciate my suggestion. I stared back unafraid of his bluster. He caught my reaction and softened.

"Sorry," he shook his head. "He's messing up my life. I'm just wearing jeans and a T-shirt. I'm not going to wear business suits to look different, and my face is my face."

It sounded like he'd had this conversation with someone else who had offered the same advice.

"Seriously, I've been mobbed. It's not fun, and when you tell them they have the wrong guy, it gets even uglier. There was no time to explain; I had to get out of there," he said, looking at me. "I've eaten at the restaurant before. If I'd gotten there on time, we could have gone to the patio and had lunch with no problems." I guess it was a plausible answer. He appeared sincere. He leaned against the door. "I'm sorry about what happened in the restaurant. If you don't mind, I'd like to finish the interview now. I want to answer your questions." This time his face approached a pleading smile but somehow didn't get there. "I'm trying to remember where I broke off our conversation."

I still needed a narrator, and his tape did sound promising. He even apologized.

"You read audiobooks while recuperating from an injury," I reminded him.

He exhaled his relief. "Yes, I remember now. Could you hand me the plane? He gestured toward the tool box.

I hesitated, not knowing what to choose. I was out of my comfort zone.

"It's this big," he said drawing his hands out about six inches apart, "It's made of metal with a knob on top. Be careful, it has a blade on the bottom."

I handed the odd-looking device to him.

"I admired their skill," he said, making long strokes on the side of the door with the tool. "I was able to do voices and accents too. I thought I'd like to try--"

"Is that when you met William Kaulder?" I interrupted him.

He hesitated in mid-shave. "Yes, it was about that time."

"I love William Kaulder," gushing more than I should, "I mean I'm in love with his voice."

That was stupid. I was interviewing this man to be my narrator. I needed to shut up.

Austin was staring at me.

I pulled it together. "How did you meet him? I noticed the recommendation from Kaulder in your bio."

"We have a mutual friend," he said, resuming his work and offering no more information.

He didn't want to talk about the relationship. Fair enough; this was an interview, not an opportunity to dish about Kaulder.

He was sanding the door with a lot more concentration than it deserved. I guess he was waiting for another question. We talked about the books he had narrated. He joked a little with his deadpan humor. He even had me giggling at some antics at his studio when a skunk slipped in while he was recording. He was funny, engaging, and sexy in a dangerous way. Maybe he didn't even know how hot he was. When he finished, my front door opened easily.

"Will you give me another chance?" he asked, putting away his tools.

"Do you always have tools in your truck?"

He shrugged. "I was helping a friend. I normally don't carry them around." He threw his jacket over his shoulder, then picked up the toolbox and tarp. "I'd like to make up for this afternoon, if you'll let me. I want to invite you to my house for lunch and to see my recording studio. We can talk about Cooper. I can also prepare another sample if there is a passage from the book you want me to work on."

"I think I'd like that."

"If you have any background on Cooper, that would help me with creating his voice."

I did have information about him that hadn't made it into the books. "I'll email it to you later today. Should I send the file to the email address on your bio?"

"That would be fine." He began to move toward the door.

"Austin?"

He turned, and I caught up with him. "Let me give you my cell number. You can call me if you have a question."

He put the toolbox down and fished in his back pocket. Taking a step forward, he handed me his phone. If he was surprised by the offer, he didn't show it. He was standing too close, his large body near enough to touch. I wasn't uncomfortable, just very aware of him, of his maleness.

Maybe that's why I punched in my computer password and had to start again. I finally handed it back. His fingers brushed my palm as he accepted the cell. The interaction sparked something deeper in me that was probably not his intention. He nodded his thanks, holding my gaze. I searched his face, but I don't know what I expected… there was nothing to read, this was just business. "Oh, by the way, I also gave you my office number just in case."

He slipped the phone back into his pocket and retrieved the toolbox. "I'll call you about a time to meet for lunch." Then he was out the door.

I watched him walk the path from my front door. Not sure why I offered myself as a contact when I usually refer everyone to Bex. I gave a deep sigh; time was growing short, and if he could nail the voice, we might meet the deadline. What harm was it to give a hot guy my number?

CHAPTER 5

Riverwood

y office phone rang. The sound gave me an unpleasant jolt of reality that I would rather not have right now. I was writing a particularly difficult part of a scene and I didn't want to slow the flow of words. Whoever was calling, unless they were bleeding from the eyes, would have to wait.

The phone continued its tinny sound, begging me to answer. I was too deep into the action of the scene. Cooper Flynn was bare-chested, standing in the middle of a courtyard, and was about to slam his fist into a very ugly guard. Something snarky was about to come out of his mouth when my caller started speaking to the voicemail.

"This is Betty from the Riverwood Lexus dealership. This is the third and final reminder that your car is scheduled for an all-day maintenance service today at 10 o'clock. Please call to confirm--"

I snatched up the phone. Betty, the longtime service desk receptionist, had stopped in mid-sentence. "Hello," I gasped into the receiver.

"Emma? Is that you?" came the amazed voice. "You forgot your appointment again."

I shut my eyes and swore under my breath. I'd been going to this dealership since Luke and I came to the valley. Everyone there knew me. "Guilty. What's the chance for a reschedule?"

She snorted, "You've got two chances... What am I saying? The answer is hell no. You left it too late. We're too close to the holiday... or did you forget about Thanksgiving? We're booked solid. Unless someone dies, you're looking at February, maybe. But with your spongy brakes I wouldn't chance it. If you want to cancel, there's always Antonio's Garage."

That was a real threat. Antonio's always had time, because anyone that knew better went to Riverwood. If I didn't take this appointment, I'd be royally... "I'll be there at ten. Is the courtesy van available? I'll need a ride back home."

"Yes, it's running today, but it might be a wait. We have an unusual number of cars to service today."

"Thanks for the warning."

I replaced the phone on its cradle and sat back. Maybe I'd use an app to arrange a car ride when I got back home; I had other errands and appointments I'd completely forgotten. Parker had sent me a text earlier. He would be flying the Pacific Northwest run up to Vancouver, but he would be back late tonight. He had a rental and if he was here, I could have used it. It would take most of the day to finish my to do list, but I couldn't put it off. I'd spend the evening writing. There wouldn't be any distractions until Parker showed up.

I was turning onto the highway when my phone rang. An unfamiliar number appeared on the screen of the car console. Normally, I wouldn't answer if I didn't know the caller. Since I had put my number on the 'do not call' list, I got more unwanted calls. I wondered if the government was selling our numbers to shady advertisers? I pushed the talk button. "Hello," sounding a tad bitchy. I almost added 'I don't want whatever cheesy thing you're selling.'

"Hello?" a deep voice rolled through the car, "This is Austin. Austin Santoro... we met a couple of days ago."

Now I felt like an idiot. "Hi, Austin, yes, I remember. Sorry about the attitude. I get edgy answering calls from numbers I don't know."

He chuckled. "I do it too. It sounds like you're driving."

"I'm on my way to the Riverwood dealership to have my car serviced." There was a long pause. I almost thought I had lost the connection. "Austin?"

"I'm here. I just finished going through the file on Cooper you sent over. I'd hoped we could meet to go over it today. I have questions."

"I would, but I have errands to run and an appointment I can't get out of after I drop off the car."

"How are you getting home?"

That was personal? Or maybe he was curious?

"I don't mean to get into your business, but if you need a ride, it was my clumsy way of offering. I'm working on the Cooper series today. We could talk while I drive you around."

How long would that conversation last? I didn't know him. That was an imposition even if we'd known each other for years.

"I'm not a stalker; I'm trying to prepare a demo for you to review. This would help me. You did say you were up against a deadline?"

And he just said the magic words.

"If you feel uncomfortable, you can drive my car and I'll be the passenger. If you still need the car after you've answered my questions, you can keep the vehicle and leave it at the dealership when you're done. It won't be a problem; they know me there."

See, anyone who knows better has their car serviced at Riverwood. That was a generous offer. I'm the one that gave him my contact numbers and encouraged him to call me if he had questions. Did it matter if it was in a car or my office? I'm sure we'd be talking for only an hour and my deadline was looming. "Okay, I'll accept your offer." I swear I heard a relieved exhale.

"I'll meet you at the dealership. I'm leaving now."

"Hey, Betty," I called, pushing the glass door open. She raised her head, acknowledging me while she handed a customer a key. They had remodeled the reception waiting room and the service area in glass. I personally didn't care to watch the servicing of my car, but I'm sure there were enough people who did enjoy that activity. I walked toward the counter; there were only a few people ahead of me. I pulled out my phone to check messages. Parker had sent me another text asking me to throw the clothes he'd left in the washer into the dryer. I shook my head. When did I become his maid? I'm sure it killed him not to ask me to fold his laundry. He did say please and signed it with the emoji that had two crazy eyes and its tongue lolling out. I giggled.

I pulled the key off my ring and handed it to Betty.

"Do we have the car for the whole day?" she asked.

"Yes."

She folded the service estimate and slid it to me across the counter. "The courtesy van is gone. It might be awhile before it comes back… it just left."

"That's fine, I'm waiting for a ride."

She squinted and looked past me. "Okay," her attention absently drawn to something behind me. "By any chance is your ride Austin Santoro?"

I turned to follow her gaze. Across the lot, leaning against a black truck, stood Austin, a baseball cap pulled low, dark glasses, arms folded. He did a slow nod when he saw me looking at him. I stupidly gave him a wave. "I guess he is."

Betty came around to stand next to me. Giving him an enthusiastic wave. Her smile turned into a smirk. "You know I hate you, you lucky, lucky girl."

I started towards the door. I guess we're going to do this. She called after me before the door swung closed, "Let me know if you guys can't make it back here before closing."

Why did he bring a truck? Maybe he didn't own a car. I wasn't about to steer a candidate for a monster truck rally.

Austin saw me heading for the passenger side and scrambled there before me opening the door. I hoisted myself into the cab, landing in plush leather. I took a look around as I attached the seatbelt.

"To tell you the truth," he said, pitching his cap in the back seat, then sliding behind the wheel. "I walked by the sedan and didn't think. My offer to drive still goes. This truck looks like a bruiser, but it's fun to drive."

"This cab is huge. Your backseat could easily sleep two people, I mean, accommodate more passengers."

The dumb comment went over his head.

"I take a lot of trips, dirt biking mostly, camping or fishing sometimes." He put his key in the ignition. "Last chance to drive."

"Thanks, maybe another time."

"That's settled. Where do we go first?"

I know he offered but... "Are you sure you want to do this?"

He tossed a serious look at me. "I'm in if you are?"

"Alright." I took a few seconds to go over the to do list in my head. "I need to pick up my dry cleaning."

I thought he was going to wait in the truck but he followed me inside. The young woman, who was the owner's daughter, gave Austin furtive glances as the clothes whirled around the gigantic rack until it stopped at the right garment. It was beginning to get cold, and I needed my coat. She was just about to ask him if he needed help when he followed me out of the shop.

Austin placed my dry cleaning on the back seat. "Where do we go next?"

I looked around the tiny shopping center. "I have some time before our next stop; it's only a few blocks down the street. I haven't eaten anything today. I'll treat you to a coffee. We can walk it. It's only a few doors down."

The funky coffee shop was inhabited by locals, the kind that didn't need to be in an office to do their 9-5. I came here when I needed a break from my work. It was independently owned by Charles, an ex, well, he was an ex everything, marine, priest, CEO, firefighter. I'd asked him several times to sit down with me and tell me his story. But he'd always give me this devilish grin and ask which life.

They were having a class or meeting at the far end of the shop. Lots of groups met here on a regular basis. We were only getting a couple of coffees to go, so the additional crush of people was no big deal. Austin was standing close at my back on the right. I called to him over my shoulder. "How do you like your coffee?"

"Hot and black."

Figures.

"Hi, Em." Charles was placing a cup down for a customer. "What will you have?"

I finally had him in my sight as the couple in front of me walked away. "My usual, a large black coffee and two scones." Austin moved to my side. "You're going to love the scones," I smiled up at him, "Lucy makes them."

Charles bagged two of the pastries. "Lucy's my current wife. I married her because she could bake, among other things," he winked at me, handing me the bag.

The crowd hovered close around us. Every available spot was occupied by a body. We took a couple of steps away from the counter to clear enough of a path for other customers to order. Austin stood in back of me, his warm body close, his lips at my ear as he asked questions about the shop. His low, rumbling voice forced me to lean back, almost resting on his chest to hear him.

"Em, this is your order."

My head jerked up, and I moved away from Austin.

Charles slid the scalding cups of coffee towards me. My cup would be half full because I needed to douse it with cream to make it drinkable. Austin, on the other hand, grabbed his cup, took a considerable gulp, and grinned. His mouth must have been lined with flame retardant.

People tightly maneuvered to the side station to get lids, stirs, and napkins. Austin allowed me to go forward. I placed the bag down and poured in cream and picked up a lid. We switched places, his intense gaze on me. Neither looked away as our bodies brushed in a careful dance. My heart quivered at the guarded touch and the faint spice from his skin. The spell finally broken when he turned to the table. I took a shallow breath and stayed about two steps behind him, needing to keep some distance. Glad that he couldn't see he had affected this lonely widow.

The bustle of the crowd was relentless. I wanted to escape this shop, but it was Austin allowing others to grab items ahead of him that kept me a prisoner in this zoo. I was about to nudge him to move it along when I spied the white bag of pastries I'd left on the station. I took a step forward to reach to his side as he whipped around to face me. A woman at my back stepped into me, shoving me forward into Austin's chest. His hands flew into the air like a bird taking flight, "What the f--?" his expression wild as my coffee vomited out of my unlidded cup. A huge unsightly brown stain covered most of his white shirt and some of his jeans. The woman threw a mumbled 'sorry' over her shoulder and continued to weave her way through the crowd.

"Em," Charles shouted over the noise, "Sorry about that. I'll replace the coffee and scones. Why don't you wait outside? I'll bag the order and bring it to you."

"Thanks, we'll be in a black truck out front."

Charles handed me the coffee with extra scones and napkins. He apologized again.

"Where do we go now?" Austin asked.

My companion looked like someone had thrown up on him, but he was enduring his ordeal. The coffee wasn't hot, but he had to be a sticky, uncomfortable mess. I handed him the extra napkins. "Do you have a change of clothes in the truck?" He'd said earlier he used the vehicle for trips.

"Usually I do, but I moved all my equipment out to clean the cab, and I haven't had time to repack my essentials. Don't worry about it, I'll be fine." He maneuvered the vehicle to the edge of the parking lot.

I took a sip of my coffee.

He threw me an expectant look.

"Oh, right, you don't know where you're going. Make a left. About four blocks take a right on Cedar Lake… it will be at the end of the street in a cluster of shops… drive all the way to the back, and the building is by itself."

When he pulled in front of Georgia's Day Spa, I hoisted my bag on my shoulder. Austin cocked his head, looked at the sign, then back to me.

"I did say I had an appointment I couldn't get out of. Everyone knows mani-pedi appointments are sacred. You're welcome to bail."

"But we haven't talked about Cooper. Can we talk inside?"

"I don't like to discuss my books in front of strangers. They don't know I'm Angela Stryker. I'll be done in an hour and a half. We can talk then if you're still here."

Bewilderment traversed his handsome features. I almost wanted to hug him to tell him it was going to be alright. Offering to drive me was a sweet gesture, but I knew he was uncomfortable. It was nice having a hot guy trailing behind me all day, but it wasn't practical.

"Why don't you go home, shower and change, and we can do this another time. I'll call you later." I pushed out of the truck and headed for the spa. The door tinkled as I entered. Mary, the receptionist, glanced up from her screen as I walked to her desk. I inhaled. Georgia's was like bathing in a fragrant tranquil stream. My tension was already slipping away as I anticipated spending time here.

The door tinkled again and Austin appeared, looking like he'd just emerged from the coffee wars.

"Can I help you?"

"He's with me." Why he was still here was beyond comprehension.

"Oh, alright. Did you want a service as well? We could do a couples mani-pedi; Regina is available..."

I tossed a glance at Austin; his horrified face was comical. "We're not together exactly; he's driving me around today while my car is being serviced."

Mary looked at us, trying to figure out something. "You could be in the room during her service. I stepped between them and shook my head no, narrowing my eyes that this should be the last of her suggestions.

She smiled her understanding. "Darlene is finishing up with her last client. I'll take you to the waiting room."

She escorted us to a long room filled with chic flea market furniture. Surprisingly, the couches and chairs worked well together. A beautiful worn antique mirror and botanical prints hung on the pale mint green walls. Soft music drifted in from speakers mounted on the ceiling. Before Mary left, Austin requested the restroom and excused himself. We both watched him trail down the hall until he stepped inside a door.

"Mary," I said, nudging her out of her stupor.

"Sorry," her attention returning to me, "What can I do for you?"

"Does Georgia still sell apparel?"

"Not anymore. She stopped a few years ago. Why?" Then awareness crossed her features. "We do have promotional items. I'll show you. Storage is over here."

When I returned to the room, Austin was reclining on a couch, eying the reading material on the table. I didn't think he'd pick up something on fashion to read but he did appear to be studying a woman's magazine with the title *Ten moves that will make your man go wild in bed* splashed across the cover. He looked up. The thin cotton of his shirt had dried, and the stain appeared lighter. I handed him the T-shirt. "Mary said this was the best she could do on size. It was a long-sleeved black tee with *Do It All Day at Georgia's* written in pink across the back.

It was hard to say what registered on his face as he looked at the offered garment, but instead of taking it from my hand, he stood and pulled his shirt over his head.

The action was so unexpected I just stood there dumbfounded, staring at the smooth muscles of his broad chest. Thinking he shouldn't be taking off his shirt in front of a woman who'd only had sex with small vibrating objects for the last three years. A slow smile crossed his lips. He was enjoying my reaction. I angled my gaze away, embarrassed that I didn't have more control.

I concentrated on the mirror behind him. My flushed face peered back at me, looking more affected than I realized. I tore my gaze away from my image, feeling strong enough to look at him. But something else in the mirror caught my eye. I blinked and stepped back. I reacted without thinking, not believing what I saw. Austin's back was a mass of ugly scars that cut deep into his flesh. It was a brutal landscape of ridges and valleys that made him look like an alien species.

Austin's grin disappeared. He turned, seeing the mirror. Several emotions whipped through his features until his hurt settled on me. His back in full display, I took a sharp breath, the reality starker than the reflection. He turned back and avoided my gaze as he retrieved the shirt from my hand and pulled the garment on.

Darlene entered with an apologetic smile. "Sorry for the wait. I can take you now." She glanced at Austin and said, "Regina is still available if you've changed your mind about a service..."

I stood there not knowing what to say. He wouldn't look at me. All Austin's attention was on Darlene. "No thanks. I'll be outside," he said as he moved past us. The hot pink *Do It All Day at Georgia's* on his back flashed at me as he walked through the door.

CHAPTER 6

A Side of Fries

Austin lifted his gaze from his phone when I approached the driver's side. His sunglasses hid his eyes, but there was noticeable tension in his shoulders. It was difficult to know what he was thinking. I couldn't imagine what I would do if someone looked at me with revulsion. A hard knot in the pit of my stomach told me I'd hurt, even embarrassed him. I wasn't looking forward to the next few minutes.

The driver's side window lowered, and Austin's face turned toward me.

"I've rescheduled the appointment," I said. Trying not to sound nervous.

He leaned forward, arms on the steering wheel. "I thought mani-pedi appointments were sacred?"

"They are," I said, conspiratorially, "But if you give them a hefty tip as an offering, your sin can be forgiven. I'm hungry, so I'd like to talk over an early lunch?" The door locks clicked open. I jogged over to the other side and slid in.

"Where do you want to go?" he asked, not looking at me. I couldn't read his mood, but at least he hadn't decided to bail.

I adjusted my seatbelt. "The last place I chose was a disaster. Why don't you choose?"

He tapped his fingers on the steering wheel a few times, thinking. "I know where we can eat and it's not too far."

A food truck was not what I had in mind. We were in an industrial park on North First Street in San Jose. To be exact, we were in line in the Drachen Technology parking lot queuing up with their employees to sample fare from the Grilled Cheese Rebellion. The enormous truck was decked out in socialist graffiti. They even had a cheese manifesto tacked next to the menu.

I leaned into Austin. He lowered his head to listen. "You don't look like one of those guys that would chase food trucks," I whispered.

He straightened up, face wary. "Really, what do they look like?"

I couldn't see his eyes, but he was doing that thing with his voice again. Pushing meaning into every word, like he was stroking the strings of an instrument. "I don't know, but they don't look like you."

He chuckled.

Good, he doesn't completely hate me. I was afraid he was going to brood for the rest of our time together. I was beginning to relax and study the four menu items listed on the truck.

"We're almost at the counter. You'll have to decide what you want to order soon," his voice less tense. "

I gave it more consideration.

"Have the Italian Rising," said a female voice behind me. I turned to see a tall, striking, dark-haired woman smiling at me.

"Don't pay attention to Kellis," said her younger companion laughing by her side, "it's her favorite."

"Excuse me if I know what's good," she quipped.

We moved to the counter. Austin chucked his chin toward the women, acknowledging their suggestion, then looked at me, "Do you want an Italian Rising? It's good,"

All agreed like a trio of bobblehead dolls.

"Fine," giving in to peer pressure.

"Fries?"

"No fries, but I'll have a bottled water."

Austin ordered, then we stepped to the side to wait for our food. The two women took our places at the counter.

The women came to stand beside us after placing their orders. "Are you new employees? This is Kellis and I'm Haley."

"No," Austin said, "Don't tell anyone but we're Cheese Rebellion groupies. We're actually the head of their fan club." I agreed, nodding my head, making an effort to keep the same deadpan expression.

Obviously, Kellis wasn't buying it. "No problem, we're going to the lunchroom to eat. But if you're looking for a place to picnic and don't mind this nippy weather, there's a nice park at the end of this road about a mile."

Our order was called. I thanked them and we moved to pick up our food. "Oh, by the way," Kellis called out, "I just love Georgia's spa." Austin's shoulders tensed, but he kept walking. I had to jog to keep up with him.

The picnic table was drier than the bench. We sat on the table, our feet on the seating, and spread the sandwiches, drinks, and his fries between us. I was in my coat; the women were right... it was chilly today. I watched him pull his sandwich from the container and take a bite. We munched in silence for awhile taking in the nearly bare trees and empty scattered benches nestled in the landscape. It was one of those parks that the employees used. A team might do some informal meetings here, but it was also designed for walkers and joggers with a groomed path and parcourse.

I wanted to broach the subject of his scars, but I didn't want to appear insensitive. He seemed scary a few days ago when we met in the restaurant; I never would have imagined we'd be here eating grilled cheese sandwiches.

"You're staring at me again," he said meeting my gaze. "What's going on in your head?" He set his sandwich down and slipped onto the bench, leaning back, his elbows on the table. "Are you mulling over what you saw at Georgia's?"

I didn't respond.

"Maybe you're thinking I'm a freak, or a masochist that likes to inflict pain on myself?"

I looked down on my companion. He'd turned his attention to the landscape. "You have no idea what I'm thinking and freak would be the last thing I'd use to describe you."

He gave a grunt of disdain. One of those noises men make that are supposed to embody everything they're feeling at that moment. He's hurt, I get that. If he wants to push, I can push back. He might look like a villain, but then again, I didn't think he might be into self-flagellation. Did he have more cuts and scars on his body? If that's how it happened, then this conversation was going to be something way above my vanilla experiences, but I was willing to listen.

He moved his shades onto his head, his dark eyes regarding me. "You're wondering how it happened, how I could be damaged. I can see you're dying to find out... You're thinking maybe there's something sinister like abuse... Maybe you're one of those bleeding hearts that wants to throw out some pity to the damaged guy."

I bit down on my sandwich, chewing slowly, watching him. He needed to talk, even if he was trying to bait me into some kind of reaction so he could lash out. When I was in pain, I was lucky to have my group. He might not have anyone that would listen, but it was fine with me; I'd been where he is now. I'd been down Anger Road before.

"Reality is much more boring," sounding uninterested in the subject. "At our first meeting, I told you I was injured on a construction site. I was a general foreman. The job was working on a small commercial building in the valley. I managed my crew and the subcontractors. We were due for an inspection later that day. I had climbed the scaffolding to check some electrical work. Luckily, none of the others on my crew were with me. The last thing I remembered was descending. The rest of what happened was a blur. The scaffolding was faulty. It gave way, and I fell. My back took most of the impact. It was cut up pretty badly, and then there were the surgeries."

He must have glossed over that part in the restaurant. He stretched then twisted his body toward me. He looked past me into the distance, his voice still indifferent when he continued. "When we were in the waiting room at Georgia's and I was facing you, I pulled off my shirt on a whim. I'd cleaned up in the restroom, but I was tired of smelling like coffee. I didn't plan to give you a show, but I'll admit I enjoyed the look on your face when I was shirtless until you saw my back. I'd forgotten I was in front of that mirror. What I saw in your eyes is the same disgust I feel, even now after all this time. Normally, I wouldn't have done that, exposed my ugliness to you, or to anyone. It's okay, I know you think I'm a freak. I saw it in that unguarded moment."

I tossed my sandwich into its box. The sound brought his attention back to me. "I didn't cancel my appointment and ask you to lunch out of a lurid fascination of what I saw in the mirror, and I'm fresh out of pity unless I'm throwing myself a party. The truth is, I'm human, and I was caught off guard. I can't help my reaction, but I can say I'm sorry that it was insensitive."

His expression softened, but he still looked doubtful. I couldn't do that trick he had of modulating his voice to push more emotion into it, so I hauled out some honesty. "I enjoyed talking to you at my house and I was looking forward to meeting you again, but not as an indentured driver." I paused and shoved my cold hands in my pockets. His brooding profile suggested he wasn't buying my stumbling offer to apologize or to make friends. I breathed in some cool air and tried again. "I'd like to know you better and possibly work together on this or another project. This business can be tough to maneuver especially for indies. I don't know about you, but I could use all the friends and support I can get."

He shifted uncomfortably, shaking his head. "You're offering charity," his face said we were still in I-don't-believe-you territory, "the truth is that you don't know the other..."

It was clear that my attempts to reach out weren't working. I needed to change it up. I leaned toward him, invading his space, his words halting abruptly. I looked deep into the endless darkness of his eyes and snatched one of his fries. "Get over yourself, Mr. Santoro, your back doesn't matter to me. I promise if I ever see it again, I won't scream in horror. By the way, I like freaks; I'm one too." My body wasn't damaged physically, but the grief, pain, and depression of the last three years had left me feeling like I was deeply flawed, not normal, so maybe we were members of the same club.

Disbelief flooded his face, morphing into indignation. "I asked you at the food truck if you wanted fries and you said no."

I rolled my eyes to heaven. "Obviously, I didn't want them then, duh." I took a bite. "This is good stuff," I waved the stubby end of the fry at him. "Like they've been seasoned. I think I taste paprika." I spied the tempting container of fried potato wedges. "Are you telling me you don't want to share?"

His half-eaten meal abandoned; he pushed the fries closer to me. "Help yourself. No need to steal them."

I had him distracted. I'd given him something to think about, and that was good. "You could talk about it. Talk about what happened after the accident."

He watched me pluck another fry. "What and end up as a character in one of your stories? I think I've said enough."

"Too late, I've already met you, and now you're fair game."

A chuckle almost escaped him. "Where is he from?"

"Who?"

"Cooper Flynn… you gave me a lot of material, but there isn't much on his early days in the file. Where is he from east, west?"

"He's from the Midwest. I like that hard flint attitude. I think it fits him."

"The file on Cooper was extensive, but there was nothing on the other characters."

I almost did a face palm. I was so concentrated on Cooper, I'd forgotten about all the other characters. My phone zipped. I dug into my bag and pulled out my cell. "Betty just left a text. It seems my car will be ready in an hour." I glanced up from the screen. "Looks like I'm not going to be your problem for much longer."

Austin turned the truck into the dealership parking lot and killed the engine. We had spoken little during the ride back. It was fine with me. I was lost in my own thoughts.

"Thank you for the ride," placing my hand on the door handle.

He swung his gaze toward me as if my goodbye caught him by surprise.

I smiled hoping to get one in return. "I think you've had enough of me for one afternoon. We can make another appointment for a real meeting."

He removed his sunglasses, taking his time to rub the tiredness from his face. "I wanted to say, that you didn't need to apologize for what happened at Georgia's… that was my fault."

It was my turn to be surprised.

"As you said, you were unprepared for what you…" he shook his head. "It doesn't matter, I reacted badly."

The unexpected admission from this fierce, kind man touched me. I didn't know how to respond. I was the cause of his humiliation and he apologized to me? I reached out, finding his warm hand pulsing with energy. "I'll accept your apology, but there's no need. I'm not a therapist, but if you ever need someone to talk with, I'll listen." I gave his hand a squeeze.

He gave a slight nod, but did not move to end our connection. I was staring at him, but this time he was returning my gaze. Fog rose up the windows from our heat as the moments stretched out. Austin twisted his hand palm up, still resting it under mine. A rough finger moved with slow long strokes at my wrist. I never realized that area was sensitive, but my body knew and reacted to his touch. Images appeared in my mind's eye of us in the back seat in a hot frenzy, desperate to be free of our clothing. I pushed the thought away that I was reading his mind, although I could see seduction in his eyes.

Austin leaned in; the move not unexpected. I slipped my hand away to brush some imaginary fluff from my coat, embarrassed that he stirred something in me and that I was holding the hand of a man that could be working for me soon.

It didn't appear to bother him that I retreated. He resettled himself unaffected by our moment. "Alright, as you wish, no more discussion about Georgia's. I'll think about your offer, but I do reserve the right to discuss why you're a freak."

I shot out a laugh. "Agreed, now I've got to find my car," turning away to place my hand on the door handle.

"Tell me about Molly?" his voice deep with longing.

It didn't quite sound like Austin. The accent was different. Was this Cooper? The voice he was creating for the series?

I was still facing away from him. "There's one thing you should know about her…" smiling to myself, "Sexually, she's insatiable."

A chuckle rumbled from his chest. "I've noticed."

I slumped back into my seat, looking over at Austin. He was leaning back, his head against the rest, his big body more relaxed than before. This time his attention was on me, his lips curved in a ghost of a grin. It was hard not to stop and stare at him or notice how we were still too close in the cab of his truck.

I pulled my coat tighter around me and searched for a way to explain the core of this character. "Kidding aside, Molly is a survivor. A hard early life left her with trust issues. That's why she doesn't love easily. There are no half measures where she's concerned. In her mind everything is all or nothing. For Molly there's only Cooper. She will fight for him because she's in it for the forever."

Austin was looking at me, but his thoughts were somewhere else. "Cooper is a lucky man to be loved by an extraordinary woman like Molly."

This was too good to be true. I clapped my hands. "I'd say you're a fan."

"Of Molly? Who wouldn't be? She's got brains, beauty, and would hurt you if you crossed her. I'd say she's perfect."

"It helps when the man is amazing too," It wasn't fair to leave out how strong Cooper's commitment was to Molly. "You know he loved her long before she realized what she had in him. So many times, she tried to push him away. He fought for them in his own way."

"That's true. I liked that he was patient with her. He waited until she could trust that he wouldn't leave."

"Exactly, fear of loss makes us do all sorts of crazy things." I wanted to scream hallelujah. He got it; he understood my work. I needed a narrator that felt as strongly about my characters as I did.

Someone was tapping on the glass next to me. Betty was smiling at us. I lowered the window.

"Hi, Austin," she was almost breathless.

He lifted his hand in a half wave. "Hey, Betty."

She beamed back at him while talking to me. "I noticed you were out here and thought I would save you some time. Here is your key and receipt. You didn't need new brakes after all. That's why we didn't need it for the entire day."

I opened the door. Betty moved to the side but didn't leave. I looked back at Austin. "Thank you for your help today."

"You're welcome. Remember, you're still coming to my house for lunch and to tour my studio."

We watched the truck pull out into traffic. I began walking to the back lot for my car, Betty keeping pace with me.

"Did I mention that I still hate you?" she said, "What was it like spending the day with him? What did you do? God, he's sexy. I know what I would have done…"

I'd known Betty for years. We'd even had coffee a couple of times, but this was too much. I'd had enough. I stopped in mid-stride and turned to her. "Girl, you need to give it a rest."

CHAPTER 7

Come Away with Me

There was finally a chill in the morning air, my covers felt too cozy to leave. Before I climbed into bed the previous night, I set my electric blanket to three, the perfect temperature for warm bliss.

I turned over onto my back, contemplating the ceiling and organizing the day's to-do list in my head, but my thoughts continued to stray to Austin. What I thought was brooding coldness was his way of hiding a secret. Austin thinking that his body was ugly was heartbreaking. The hurt burning in his eyes at my unkind reaction must have reinforced his fears. We managed to reach an understanding, but I think he would have left if he had lost the chance to be the voice of Cooper.

Parker didn't arrive at dinnertime, so I ate alone and watched TV until I began to yawn uncontrollably. I was probably already asleep when he came in. If he had used the side door, I wouldn't have known.

Daisy was content on a pillow in a corner chair of my bedroom. Her golden eyes observed me as I sat up.

After talking to Austin yesterday, I decided to table reviewing the bios of the other two readers for now.

I needed to write. With the search for an MN and a studio, I wanted to accomplish something today. I wasn't behind schedule; I just felt like I had to put words on paper, or, what passed for paper in my writing program.

My coffee maker was already on brew, the aroma filling the air. I'd shower and get dressed before breakfast. I pulled off my skimpy T-shirt and panties, dropping them on the ground, and headed toward the bathroom.

Footsteps were advancing down the hall. It must be Parker. I hadn't heard a sound until now. I thought I was alone in the house. My sweats were across the room. Making a dash for the clothing, I ripped them from the back of the chair. Daisy leaped off as if she were under attack. I was balancing on one foot, trying to get the other in the opening.

"Em, you up?" came Parker's voice. I heard a knock.

I yanked my top on and started pushing my head through the opening. "Yes, just a minute," my voice muffled by the fabric over my head. The door swung open as I pulled the hem of the shirt down over my breasts, but not fast enough.

"Sorry," he said, retreating into the hall.

I took a step toward the door. He was in the hallway, his back to me. I'm sure he didn't see anything.

"It's safe to come in," I called, adrenaline pumping from my hurried dressing.

Parker appeared with a grin on his face, staring at my shirt. I shifted on my feet, looking up at him. Daisy slipped out, knowing there would probably be some tension.

"You didn't have to dress on my account," said the poster boy for innocence.

I yanked the hem of my T-shirt firmly down over my hips. "Okay, house rules," looking at an almost repentant face, "Make sure

I clearly say, 'come in,' 'please come in,' or 'Hey, Parker, come in' before you enter. 'Come in' must be in the invitation."

He was still grinning. "Sure, for the record, I thought you said it was alright to enter. I didn't come here to catch you in your sexy peek-a-boob nightie, although that would have been a treat." His gaze wandered over my sweatshirt and pants. "If that's what you sleep in, I could give you some advice."

I crossed my arms.

"I guess that's a conversation for another time," he said and gestured toward the door. "I come bearing gifts and an invitation."

I couldn't imagine what he was talking about until he stepped out into the hall, then returned carrying a tray covered with a napkin. He removed the cloth with the flair of a magician, then lowered the platter to reveal coffee and bagels from the local coffee shop about a mile away. "I hope you will accept this humble token with my sincere apologies."

I inspected the offering. "I'll think about it," I grumbled.

"That's all I ask. May I?" he nodded at the tray.

I watched him wait for my answer. He was cute when he was contrite. It made it hard to hold a grudge looking at that face. I waved an imperious hand. "You may."

I sat crossed-legged on my bed while Parker settled the feast between us and took up considerable real estate on his side.

"What's the invitation?" I said, pulling apart a warm bagel.

He lifted the coffee from the tray and leaned back to the headboard. "I want to invite you to Santa Cruz to explore the boardwalk like we did when we were in high school. It looks a lot like Belmont Park in San Diego. I thought we could eat on the beach and watch the sunset." He rolled onto his side, the coffee resting on the bed. "The weather is still good, and we would have the place to ourselves, except for the locals."

My fork was poised over the smoked salmon that I'd just discovered on the tray. Parker was smiling, trying to inflict undue

51

influence on me. He was right about the boardwalk at Santa Cruz; I had been there a few times, and it did remind me of Belmont Park.

I popped the pink morsel into my mouth. My writing was ahead of schedule. Holly, my editor, hadn't finished with the last pages I'd sent her. My dominatrix editor was pushing me to turn up the heat in a couple of scenes between Cooper and Molly. She'd be frowning if she knew I wasn't hard at work on the revisions. She graduated from the 'hit me, beat me, make me write good copy' school of editors, but I loved her.

He was tapping the side of his cup, waiting for an answer. Why not? With Parker, it was always an adventure. "Okay, sounds fun. Give me an hour, and I'll be ready."

"Don't rush. I have a few things to do before we go. I'll pick you up around 2:00 if that's alright."

"It's fine. I need to return some calls."

He hesitated. Something was on his mind. "I have some time before I start my errands. We could talk about your wardrobe."

My head thumped against the headboard. Was he serious? Yup, he had an expectant look on his face. I glanced down at my clothes. I hadn't bought anything new for almost three years. What was wrong with my sweats… they were Lululemon? I huffed, hoping to convey my disbelief, but nothing penetrated his brain when he decided something. He looked back unaffected. "Thanks for the offer, but I'm good. Now get out of here so I can dress."

The bed shook when he pushed off and landed on his feet. He headed for the door, his stride unhurried, giving me a nice view of his backside. But he stopped in mid-stride and turned as if he had forgotten something. "You know, I still think we--"

The pillow I threw struck his jaw. He caught it as it grazed off his face. Parker studied the green silk puff, shrugged, then tossed it on the chair. He continued through the door without a backward glance.

The rented red sports car hugged the curves of Highway 17 until we cruised into the city limits under a cloudless autumn sky. The fog was beginning to burn off, but the beach town still looked like a black and white photograph.

Excitement pushed me forward as we jogged across the street just ahead of the oncoming traffic toward the casino arcade. It felt like the world was reversing and we were moving back in time.

He reached out to push the door but instead hesitated. The muffled sounds of the arcade filtered out to us. I stepped in front of him to enter. I turned around when he didn't follow. His eyes were soft, mood wistful, like he was trying to keep the moment. "Come on," holding my hand out, "This isn't an altered universe. "We're not going to see our younger selves in there; besides, this isn't Belmont Park."

He chuckled. "It might be fun to hang out with young Parker; at least I could warn him about a couple of things."

"And what would be the fun in that?"

A couple hurried past us, disappearing through the door. I grabbed his arm and pulled him through.

We stepped into an explosion of noise and flashing lights from the video games and vintage pinball machines.

Kettle corn and cotton candy saturated the air, along with the faint hint of decay from the old building. We didn't stop but continued through the heart of the arcade to a tunnel that led onto the boardwalk. I slipped past Parker, anxious to see more familiar sights, when he caught my hand to pull me back to him; his hands rested on my shoulders, turning me away from him. His citrus musk scent against the sweet sticky aromas made me aware of how close he stood behind me.

"Look," he said, his breath warm against my ear.

We were standing in front of the fortune teller's booth.

"I remember you would drag us to one like this, so you could have your fortune read."

An old white-haired mechanical woman dressed in a 19th-century lace cap and ruffled blouse sat in a glass box. Madame Rafaela's hand was poised over a fanned arc of tarot cards with a cup of tea at her elbow. The robot was life-size, and her all-knowing blue eyes stared at me.

"I remember," I mumbled, mesmerized by the old fortune teller.

Parker fished in his pocket for change. Finding the right amount, he placed the coins into my open palm. I pushed the quarters through the opening. The coins rolled and clinked through the machine, stirring the old woman to life. She blinked at me, then lowered her head, scanning the tarot cards before her. I moved forward and placed my hand on the glass, waiting for my future. A small card fell through a chute, coming to rest in a metal bowl in the machine. I retrieved the note. Parker was at my back reading the message with me. Madame Rafaela's prediction: *You will know love is real when you see the metal of their true self.* Lucky numbers, 10, 13, 23, 5, 4.

"Let me see that."

I handed it over my shoulder to him.

"Hmmm, this isn't as strange as some of the others you've had. You know they're a group of vending machine employees who make this stuff up." I snatched the card from him. Love was nowhere on my to do list. My life was fine right now, I didn't need to change anything. At least that was the big fat lie I kept telling myself.

After a long stroll through the sparse crowds on the boardwalk and enjoying a few rounds on the carousel ride to the sound of pump organ music, we returned to the car for our picnic and blankets. The day had been perfect, but twilight was near, and we needed to find our way to the beach.

Our neatly stacked supplies waited on the sidewalk while Parker made his last checks of the vehicle. I danced on the balls of my feet, fueled by nervous anticipation. I wanted him to hurry so we wouldn't miss a second of nightfall. "Come on," I pleaded, "we need to leave now."

Parker looked over at me, amused. "Some things never change. You need to chill. I'm almost done."

I shrugged. What could I say? This was me. I glanced up to the sky. "Hurry," I urged again.

He finally hoisted our stuff under one arm and took my palm with his free hand, "Come on, Nyx, we don't want to be late." He took a few steps until I pulled on his hand and he stopped. He looked down at me, then back at the car. "Did you forget something?"

"No." I shook my head. It felt too familiar. "You haven't called me that since forever. I didn't think you remembered."

"What?" He inclined his head. "That I called you the Greek goddess of the night?" His arm caught me around the shoulders. The squeeze he gave me felt nice. "You'd be surprised how much I remember," he said to the top of my head. "Now let's go before you blame me for making us late."

CHAPTER 8

Goddess of the Night

I stood at the top of the wooden stairs as Parker shifted our picnic basket, a shopping bag, and blankets to the bottom. I joined him, and we removed our shoes, but he asked me to wait while he transported our things to a spot he discovered earlier. I sat on a step a few rungs up from the sand and watched him walk out, disappearing around an outcropping of rock.

When Parker returned, he took my shoes and offered his arm. But I found his hand instead, and we balanced on shifting sand to our picnic. To my surprise, the blanket was spread out, our meal looked ready to consume, and music drifted softly from a portable speaker.

I turned to him. He was beaming like he had just constructed a house with only a hammer. "I don't ever remember you treating me like a princess."

Parker's chin jutted forward; the corners of his mouth turned down. Apparently, he took mock offense at my remark. I started to throw out another keen observation when something, in the way he held his head, and the angle of his body triggered a heightened awareness.

Maybe because I'm a writer this happens, but some people I observe will transform in front of me. In those moments I see another self, or it might be their pure self that existed in a past life. The impressions, when they've come, are vivid if only for a few seconds.

I gazed more intently at him, struck by the fading light that played on the gold in the soft waves of his burnished hair. Physically he hadn't changed. He was well over six feet, his body taut with lean muscle. But the trendy bad-boy looks had taken on a complexity. He had a dangerous confidence that kept his body in check. The emerald eyes that appraised me seemed quick to laugh or to fight.

In an effort to sustain the image, I tried not to stir, but it had reached its zenith. It would be gone soon, and I'd be left with a strong sense of the man from the past.

I strained to hold the vision a little longer because only a few feet away was a true Scottish rebel, a Jacobite ready to fight for his clan.

He stood with shoulders squared, feet wide apart, looking back through time. His white shirt torn open, revealing the broad, well-defined chest. His clan's green and red kilt was fastened about his hips and a blade was ready in his hand.

There was a flutter around my quiet heart. It was somehow too real. I wanted to be with him in that place. I wanted this Parker. Maybe this time I could cross into the apparition. I stepped forward to...

"I will admit my behavior has been lax in the past," he said, jolting me back to the man he was today, "but I have mended my ways, and I'm prepared to treat you in the style I think you deserve."

I shook my head to break the spell. I was daydreaming at night. It took me a few seconds to register where I was and what he said. I blinked. "You think I deserve?" This was too much. I tried to say it with a straight face. "Okay, where is Parker and what have you done with him?" And, more importantly, where was the dangerous Jacobite?

He reached for me. The move caught me off balance, and we tumbled to the sand. We dissolved into laughter like two old friends with a lot of shared history.

We sat on the beach, remembering the past through a rosy haze of memory until a painter's canvas emerged above us. We watched as midnight blues chased the streaks of yellows, reds, and pinks across the sky back-lit by the fading sun.

We shivered as the wind whipped the salted seaweed air and seagulls called to the rise of the night.

A blanket touched my shoulders. "You'll need this. It's getting chilly."

I looked up into his shadowed face. "You're cold too; share it with me."

He slid next to me, his heat and scent made me feel safe. It was strange that it wasn't Luke, but it still felt familiar and right. I lay my head on his shoulder as he tightened the surrounding blanket. I relaxed in his arms for a long time, content in our night beach world.

"Em."

"Hmmm?"

"I wasn't entirely honest about why I came back. There's something you need to know about my move to Mascot."

I stirred, registering what he said. Alarm bells were going off in my head sounding like large reverberating gongs. The tightness around my heart told me he'd finally found someone and wouldn't be leaving alone.

"Have you found someone who's made you reconsider your wicked ways?"

Soft laughter bubbled from his chest. "You could say that."

My intuition was right. "Did you meet her at work?" Throwing out the question casually. "Is she one of the flight crew?"

"No, it's someone I've known for a long time. You know her too. She's coming with me to Mascot."

It could be any one of a gaggle of women that had been after him for years. I was already a little jealous of the person who would be the center of his life. I turned to face him, my part of the blanket falling away.

"Who is she?" It was too late to hide how I felt. I know I shouldn't be so concerned, but he was family. Parker was my husband's brother.

He pulled the blanket off his shoulders and placed it on mine, wrapping me up like a child. "There are things I couldn't say at the house," he gave the blanket a final tuck. "Maybe that's why I brought you here, so we could talk like we did in the old days."

He seemed content, happy that he'd found someone. This would be okay. I wouldn't lose him. Parker was easy to love; he should be happy.

He squeezed my hand, sending a spark through me. "It's you. I've been waiting ten years to tell you I still love you, and I want us to be together."

The world went silent as I slipped my hand away. Concern creased his face as I withdrew. Wasn't this wrong? He was my brother-in-law, or does that stop after your husband dies?

He tugged at the corner of my blanket. "I tried to tell you before, all those years ago, but you didn't believe me."

"That's not true, you never said..."

Then I remembered that Luke had asked him to drive me to Santa Ana to pick up my wedding gown. He helped me with the massive toile and lace dress to my apartment. We ordered pizza and drank two bottles of cheap red wine. We ended up tonguing and groping on the couch. We were staggering towards my bedroom when I came to my senses and said no.

He was desperate to change my mind. He told me I was the love of his life and that I should marry him. I thought it was the wine talking, and he just wanted to get me in bed and have something to hold over me.

I'd blocked it all out until now. Parker was Luke's best man at our wedding. He watched my father walk me down the aisle, and then he witnessed Luke and I exchanging our vows.

He'd convinced Amy, one of my bridesmaids, to leave with him shortly after he had fulfilled his obligations as the best man. She later told me it was the best and wildest sex she'd ever had.

"You could have stayed after Luke was... I was alone." I said. "It came out like an accusation.

"It was painful after my brother was gone. That part was true," his emotions breaking through his words, "I knew if I stayed, I would have pushed you to be with me. I had to let you grieve. I hoped you wouldn't find someone in the meantime."

Few people knew how difficult Luke's death was for me to endure. Bex had a front row seat to the worst of my grief, worrying when I'd slip into the altered reality of my books. My writing sessions lasted days, weeks if I was honest. I'd spend my time wielding a sword at an attacker or making love to the hot hero; anything to avoid the numbing pain that never stopped. I still continue to struggle and will retreat to those marathon writing sessions if I'm overwhelmed. But if it weren't for Bex, I might have joined my husband.

Parker stood and pulled me to my feet. "Come on. I need to get you home. We're not dressed for a night on the beach."

I was missing something. "But you said 'she,' like someone else was going with you to Australia?"

His grin turned sheepish. "I admit that was a crappy thing to say. I needed to know if you'd even care if I was with someone. A new country could be the place for us to begin again. I'm going to use the time I have left to convince you to catch a midnight flight out of Oakland for Australia. We can leave after you've finished your book launch."

I was shell-shocked. I didn't know what I felt. When I received his phone call, I couldn't figure out why he wanted to see me. No, maybe I did think in the back of my head he wanted to reconcile, but as my brother-in-law. Not as my... what exactly did he want? "Parker," I began, not having any notion what I was going to say.

He was studying me. "Maybe this wasn't the best way to spring this on you. Let me make this clear. I want to build a life together. I want to love you and show you the world."

CHAPTER 9

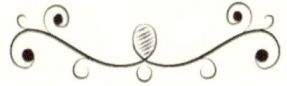

Dreamlandia

We were silent on the ride back home. Maybe the revelations were too big to talk about. When we got back to the house, Parker looked hopeful as we mumbled our goodnights before leaving for our rooms. I showered, changed, and sat on my bed.

My cell was sitting on the nightstand. I'd been unplugged for the whole day. I decided to see if there was anything urgent before I turned off the light. My mom had called, Bex left two voicemails, and there were two calls from Austin, but no messages from him. He must have had a question about Cooper. I stifled a yawn, then switched off the light. Sleep claimed me quickly.

I dreamed I was with my husband, cradled in soft white down covers, bathed in the light of dawn.

"Morning sunshine," he breathed in my ear. *I laughed and caught his gaze, bright with longing, a playful grin on his handsome stubble face. He gathered me to him and kissed me sweet and slow as happiness flooded through me.*

"Make love to me," I whispered.

Luke brushed an errant curl away from my face.

"*Please,*" I said.

He sighed and returned his mouth to mine to taste my lips more urgently than before. His strong body moved against me, alive with rising heat, eager to love me.

He trailed soft kisses from my lips to my breast, his tongue teasing my nipple. My fingers entwined in his silky chestnut locks. He was taking his time to build my desire, to bring me to that perfect release. But I was already smoldering, aching for more of him to touch me. If he didn't understand my need, I had to make that clear.

I slid a hand down, my fingers closing around his stiffening cock. I began to tease him into a harder desire so we could move together. He approved of my attention with a deep rumble of pleasure. "*Make love to me,*" I whispered again.

His palms fell to my sides, and his strong hands pulled me under him. He lifted his head, chin tilted up, his green eyes shining.

My heart stopped. "*No,*" I murmured, "*You're not--*" The breath I drew in hurt, like a knot over my heart. I wasn't gazing at Luke's loving face, but into Parker's wicked eyes. His hair tousled and face flushed, he looked like we had been making love most of the night. My fingers uncurled to release the cock I was holding.

"*Em, you're mine now,*" his insistent member pushing against my thigh. He slid his hand down to cup my bottom, but I rolled away to the opposite side of the bed.

Austin was there, stretched out on his side, chest bare, the other half hidden by a thin gray blanket. His face was dark and sensual, his tats prominent down his arm like markings on an exotic animal.

The covering irritated me. It needed to be gone. I grabbed the fabric and yanked the blanket from his lower half, the cloth disappearing as soon as it left my hand. I smiled to myself. What waited for me was his rigid cock, a pearl of pre-cum glistening at the tip.

Austin stirred; my attention drawn to his mouth that should be kissed. "*I can fix that for you,*" he said caressing my face with the back of his hand. "*Let me…*"

A tremor of desire rushed through me like a sparked current. I thrust my hand out to him, needing to pull him to me. But something new moved at the far corner of my vision.

I panned to my left to find Cooper strolling towards the bed, casually pulling off his shirt. He pitched the garment. It landed in a condensed pile near the bed.

Cooper was at Austin's back. The languishing Austin remained on his side, waiting for my answer. He didn't seem to be aware of another man in the room.

A boot scraped the floor, sending my gaze back to Cooper. I was lying naked next to one man and captivated by the other's broad shoulders and flat stomach. Cooper's gaze racked my body, making it plain that he liked what he saw, and he was about to do something about it. He grabbed his brown leather belt and jerked it from his waist. It clanked when it hit the floor.

He took a step closer, unbuttoning the top of his jeans. "Isn't it my turn yet?" he said with a lazy grin. "If anyone knows what she likes--"

The buzz of my phone forced my eyes open, but there was nothing to see in the darkness. I grabbed for the cell.

"Hell--"

"Molly," an unfamiliar voice said, cutting me off, *"I don't like how we left it in your shop yesterday. There's another reason I need you."*

I was half asleep, but I recognized the line. It was from the first book of the Cooper series, *Danger Rides*. Austin was speaking to me as the hero Cooper Flynn. I sat up and switched on the light, trying to get my mind clear enough to understand what was happening. This was crazy. Why was he saying lines from the book?

"Don't stand there like you're ready to kill me. Say something!" he demanded.

Okay, I guess he wanted me to respond as Molly. I took a deep breath. *"My answer is no."* I shouted in character as Molly. *"When are you going to get it through your thick, bounty-hunter head that I won't do this for you?"*

"Even if it means we might find your sister? This is the only lead you've had in, what? In five years?"

I couldn't believe he was feeding me lines from the book. What was this, a live demo?

"No," I said as Molly, *"because it's a cocksure lug like you who will get us both killed with that ridiculous plan you proposed."*

The phone went dead.

I stared at the cell. I still couldn't fathom what this was supposed to be. My character Molly was a thief and a con, but she was also a time-walker. She made her money taking lonely souls to other times to find their love matches while she stole from the locals.

To do what Cooper proposed, she would have to be a registered time guide with the government. Which she was not.

The government tested children in grade two, when the ability begins to show itself. Anyone with the rare gift is sent to an academy for the next thirteen years. At the end of their education, they're placed into classifications.

The most brilliant walkers work for the bureau in Washington. Everyone else did what they could to survive within the strict laws for time-walkers. As far as the authorities knew, Molly had only enough time-walking juice to run that small matchmaking enterprise. Somehow Cooper found out about the real extent of her abilities and that the man he was hunting stole her sister five years ago.

I placed the phone back on the nightstand. That was a hell of a performance. It still needed more nuance, but he almost had it. I thought of calling him back, but after the day I had, I decided to pull the covers over my head and wait for morning.

CHAPTER 10

Crossfire

I thought I'd slept through my alarm when I realized it was full morning. I checked my phone and discovered I'd just conked out the night before and forgot to set the wake-up feature.

I strained my hearing to detect human sounds. I knew every creak this house made, but I couldn't tell if Parker was anywhere around. He could still be in the guest room face-down in his pillow, sleeping. I knew it was the coward's way out, but I decided to sneak out of the house before he had a chance to start another awkward conversation.

I'd fed Daisy from an emergency stash in my room and packed my gym bag. The hallway was clear. I needed to pick up my keys by the kitchen door. Then I could slip outside, get into my car, and roll down the road. I advanced down the hall and around the corner. My silent, stealthy footfalls would have made a wolf proud. I stepped inside the kitchen and there was Parker, showered, shaved, and achingly handsome, reading something on his iPad with a mug of coffee at his elbow. My shoulders slumped.

"Good morning, beautiful," he said like he had just caught me. "You didn't think it would be that easy to get rid of me?"

I shook my head. "A girl's gotta try. Is there any more coffee?" I moved to the table.

"I only made a cup, because I'm taking you to Stacks for breakfast." He produced my keys, jiggling them.

I snatched at the keys. He pulled them out of my reach. "No, I'll drive. You drive like a maniac." He slipped them into his jeans pocket.

"Where's your red sports car?"

"They just picked it up. I only rented it for the day."

I folded my arms. "I can't hang out all day. I have a meeting with Bex and Holly will be calling to ask me about the new pages I promised to finish."

"Too late," leaning back in his chair. "I've been in your office answering calls. I thought I'd try to help out while I'm here. I've already talked to Bex."

"How did you convince Bex to talk to you?"

"She didn't seem to have a problem during our chat. You must have told her that I was visiting."

I'd forgotten about that conversation. It was said in passing like, I've got to get Daisy food before I run out and by the way Parker is staying for a while. I slipped into the chair next to him.

He shifted his body toward me, draping an arm on the back of his chair. "Bex says there's no progress on finding a new studio. She'll let you know when there's something to report. She also wanted to know how your meeting went with Austin. Is he a narrator you're considering?"

I nodded. "But Holly is waiting."

A shadow of a smile drifted across his lips. "And I also talked to editor Holly." He held up a hand before I could launch into my next objection. "I told her I was your new PA." His mouth quirked at the side. "You know, she's damn sexy on the phone. I know you call her the dominatrix behind her back, but with that voice, she can tie me up anytime."

I gazed up at heaven. "You're not her type."

"Why?"

"Because the woman has taste."

He ignored me.

"I want you to promise me. If it doesn't work out between us, I want her number. I bet she's kinky wild in bed." He growled.

I elbowed him with a sharp jab.

"Ouch," he wailed, managing to look hurt. "Okay, I deserved that," rubbing his arm, "I forgot how you can punch like a linebacker, but I like it when you care."

I shook my head. We were reverting to our teenage selves. "Why me?" I muttered.

"I guess you're lucky. We can talk about the benefits of me in your life over breakfast." He took out my keys again and jiggled them. I lunged at the shiny objects, and this time I snatched them back.

"Yes," I shouted, jingling my keys in front of his grinning face, "the maniac is going to drive."

There was a line for Stacks even in the middle of the week. We dutifully joined the queue. Less than a few minutes later ten more people showed up behind us.

Parker rummaged in his jacket pocket and pulled out his phone. He held it up, tapping on the surface.

"What are you doing?"

"I'm going to preserve this event for prosperity."

"Again?" looking around at the growing crowd and feeling self-conscious. He'd been pulling out his phone and taking a lot of pictures. He must have a ton of us by the red sports car, arcade, at the beach, and even at home.

He frowned. "I haven't seen you in three years... why can't I take a picture of the beautiful Emma? You'll thank me later." He assured me as his arm slipped around my shoulders pulling me close. The phone hovered slightly above us. The glare from the cell was glinting into my eyes. "Say sex," in a voice loud enough to be heard at the front of the line. Three girls in back of us started to giggle. My face felt hot. He had his arm around me too tightly for me to jab him again.

It took us twenty minutes to see the entrance of the restaurant when I noticed a man two doors down, pushing a stroller. He stopped at a candy store, peered inside, then a woman joined him. She stood next to him as they looked inside the shop. The man looked up, and I was a second too late to turn away. He caught my eye and headed toward us with the stroller and woman in tow. Parker saw me watching them. He plastered a grin on his face. "Who are they?" he asked without moving his lips. Before I could answer, Austin was standing in front of me. The woman stood watching us by the stroller.

"Hi," I said. He caught me by surprise. I'm a writer. If I'd had more time, I might have said something thought-provoking.

"Hi," he responded.

I waited for more information, but he just stood there. "Are you taking a walk in Campbell?" trying to feel less uncomfortable, although I didn't know why.

"We were headed to Psycho Donuts," Austin stepped closer. His gaze locked on me, then he spoke as though we were alone. "Something must be going on at the center across the street because the lot is full and there's a line."

Among this small group and with people passing by, it felt like our conversation was intimate. His brooding stare searched mine, triggering a memory. I flashed on my dream of him, and a tremor threatened to run through my body. I thought of his big muscled form lying on my bed and what I spied under the blanket. I leaned away from him to hide the flush I knew was claiming my face. I couldn't see the shop from here, but I looked down the street anyway. "Psycho Donuts is probably full," I said, trying to sound unaffected by him.

Parker slipped a possessive arm around my shoulder and pulled me to him as he leaned forward, extending his hand to Austin.

"Parker."

Austin clasped his hand and shook. "Austin, and this is my sister Magda." A pretty, dark-hair, dark-eyed woman came forward to greet us.

"I'm Izzy," a small voice squeaked from the stroller. A little girl, dressed in a gray wool cap, jacket, pink skirt, tights, and sneakers was intently looking at her doll. But what had me smiling were the sunglasses.

"This is my daughter, Elisabetta Marie. We call her Izzy for short," Magda said.

The Stacks line moved, and we were standing at the threshold. "It looks like they will be calling us soon," announced Parker.

Magda regarded me. "My brother says you're coming over for lunch. Have you set a date?"

"No, not yet," glancing at Austin, who managed to look stoic.

"He's a good brother, but bad at planning social occasions. Do you have any time this week? I know he wants to talk to you about the Cooper series, and he has been working on a demo."

Before I could respond, Parker chimed in, "We're free next Friday."

Magda glanced at Austin. He nodded. "That's settled. My brother will text you the time and address."

I get amnesia when I walk into this restaurant because I always order the Triple Berry waffles. I only remember it's a bad idea at the end of breakfast, when I'm stuffed, groaning and wondering if I can undo my jeans button without anyone noticing.

Parker was mostly quiet while we ate. It was at the end of the meal when I was almost comatose that he began a conversation. "Have you known Austin long?" he said. Pushing his plate forward.

I picked up my orange juice, then set it down. Adding more to my stomach's contents wasn't going to help. "I met him the day you arrived out of the blue."

His phone buzzed. He pulled it out of his pocket, frowned at it, stopped the call, then left it on the table.

I resisted the urge to ask who it was; more than likely it was work. Last-minute things to do when you leave a company.

"You know I'd like to help with your launch."

I looked up from staring at his phone.

"I'm serious. I want to help with the Bloody Moon launch."

"Passion Moon." I corrected, trying to stifle a laughing groan. It was hurting my stomach.

"I remember now, it was Luke's crazy idea. Anyway, It's the least I can do while I'm here. I know I'm taking you out of your routine. It can't be easy with me around the house providing distractions. I could free up your time to concentrate on your writing or anything else you might want to do." He emphasized that last item with an I'd-like-to-be-that-distraction smirk.

Besides the obvious come-on, I was mentally ticking the advantages off in my head. I did need extra help. He did make me laugh, and I wasn't opposed to looking at eye candy.

"Em?" I swerved my attention back to him. My jeans were threatening to burst. Damn them for making those irresistible waffles.

"You could bounce off ideas about Cooper if that would help." He was trying to sell this idea. "I don't think I've told you that I like the series. I've never read an action romance until I read your books. I bet you've got a lot of male fans too."

I shook my head at his apparent sucking up. I think he was mistaking my upset tummy for lack of enthusiasm. "You know, your author site needs updating," he leaned forward, lowering his voice to a stage whisper. "I could be your very personal assistant, and I'd gladly be your dogsbody."

I winced. I was picturing his head on a Great Dane's body. "What's a dog's body?" forgetting we were in public. The couple next to us turned around.

Parker gave the couple an I-can't-take-her-anywhere shrug and turned back to me. "I've spent too much time in England, and their slang is creeping into my speech," he chuckled, "Don't let me start swearing; I've picked up too many interesting phrases. It means to do the dirty work." He slid his hand across the table, grabbing my fingers. "I'd like to prove to you we should be together," he punctuated his sentence with a pleading smile.

I gave him a soft halfhearted sigh. How could a mortal woman say no to that face? "Okay, you can be my PA if you promise not to say that word again, but you do know there's no money in the position."

He faked astonishment. "We can barter for services--right?"

The waitress swooped in to pick up the small black folder containing his credit card. "I'll be right back."

Parker glanced at his phone again before returning it to his pocket. "I hope you don't mind. I'd like to leave soon. I've got to jump on a conference call for work." He hesitated then said, "I'm going to a jazz club tonight, and I was hoping you'd come. It's a hole in the wall, but the reviews for the place are excellent."

Parker left after his conference call and was gone most of the day doing God knows what, but it gave me time to write uninterrupted. I knew the suggestion to be my personal assistant was a way for me to spend time with him. I was afraid he expected some of that would be in my bed, and I didn't know if I was ready for that yet.

There were too many feelings to sort out on top of getting this launch done. I had to decide in less than two weeks on the narrator.

Kaulder had sent me a demo tape that was good, but I wondered what Austin's final demo would be.

My cell rang. I checked the name. Austin's name flashed as the caller. He probably wanted to give me the information on our lunch meeting, or maybe he wanted to ask if I had gluten issues.

"Molly," Cooper's voice was urgent, *"what happened in the fortress?"*

Austin had just dropped me in the middle of the book again. He was reading from the novel, but to respond, I had to use my memory to speak as Molly. Luckily, he'd chosen pivotal scenes, so it allowed me to respond with a close approximation of the dialog. I wrote the book through Cooper's point of view, so Austin would narrate as Cooper. I glanced at the ceiling, trying to decide if I should stop this drama. The first demo had promise, but then again, talking to Cooper was exciting. I jumped when he repeated the question again as Cooper.

"What happened in the fortress? The servant we bribed to keep an eye on you is too frightened to talk," I said, *but it was difficult to see her in the dim light.*

The gardener's shack was the only place I could talk to her without someone seeing us from the main house. Molly rested on my narrow wooden cot, her back against the wall. She drew her knees to her chest and turned away from me. She had me worried.

This wasn't like her; usually those flashing gray eyes were accusing me of something. Now, she wouldn't even meet my gaze. I took a quick inventory of the woman who had been brought here a month ago as a bodyguard. They cut her hair too short. One side was shaved to stubble. That was new. Maybe that's what made her skittish, but her uniform didn't look right. I crouched down next to her, trying to make her look at me. "We don't have much time. What happened? I've got to know what we're up against."

She didn't respond.

"Molly! Answer me!"

I took a shaky breath then launched into my part.

"It doesn't matter. I knew what I was getting into when I agreed to this plan. The important thing is that I located Lily. I saw her, Cooper. My sister, she's five years older, but it was Lily."

"You're bleeding," reaching out to touch her side. "Let me look at it. I've got something here to clean the wound until we can get you treated. I saw you practicing drills in the yard with the other guards; did a blade nick you?"

She shook her head.

"I just need to remove part of your shirt. Stop moving! I won't gaze at those luscious breasts of yours. I'm only doing this to help you."

"Afraid you might be mesmerized if you see me topless?"

That was a good sign. She sounded more like herself. "Something like that." I gave a low chuckle. "Hold still. I'll pull the fabric here."

"Aww...that hurt, goddamn it!"

I grabbed her arm before she could squirm away.

"You're awful quiet." she said studying me while I tried to examine her. "Is my side that interesting, or have you been stunned into silence by my beauty?"

"I can't see that well," I said, "it's too dark in here; I'll pull the lantern over."

"It's nothing. It's just a scratch," she protested.

"Molly, what happened? This isn't a defensive wound. You told me this happened during swordplay." I yanked more of the shirt away. "A branding iron made this wound. Armstrong's marked you. He's marked you as his property."

CHAPTER 11

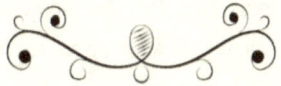

Heels over Head

W e were pressed tight inside Benni's jazz club with just enough room for the waitress to maneuver between the tables. We found seats near the back of the old store-turned-nightclub listening to a sultry singer belt out her blues set. She must have been a local favorite, by the size of the enthusiastic crowd.

We'd missed the first half of her set when the crowded restaurant we chose for dinner couldn't seat us on time. Rushing through our meal and arriving late to the club didn't give us much time to talk, other than Parker shouting comments in my ear to be heard over the music.

The music was sweet and soulful but ended too soon. Parker wanted to continue the party, but it was a weekday, and I had to keep to my writing schedule. I watched the band sit down to dinner, still keyed up from their performance, as I punched in the number in my cell to summon our ride back home.

I walked my unsteady guest to his bedroom, just to make sure he understood that was still the arrangement. I was leaning against the door frame, watching him linger inside his room. He glanced at his unmade bed then back at me, calculating. I guess I won in his estimation because he attempted a less-than-sober goodnight kiss. It was sweet, but long ago I made it a practice not to accept the intoxicated attentions of men. Even in the car ride back, I worried about the state of him. Through the night I watched him down a few beers and a scotch chaser, but he did stop towards the end of the night. Looking at him now, I was sure he was still entertaining a sizable buzz.

I'd suggested he take my sure-fire hangover cure, but he refused my remedy. I shrugged it off as his irrational male pride.

He did use the remainder of his charm offensive to offer his bed one last time. He leaned in close, and I could still smell the club on him and the truffle cheese fries we'd ordered to soak up our alcohol.

His hand feathered up my arm, and the effect was not lost on my happy limb. His hand continued the journey past my shoulder and up the wall until his arm came to rest above my head. His green eyes stared a hole into me, pinning me where I stood. I enjoyed his company tonight. It had been a long while since a man like Parker had given me his attention. I'd always been attracted to him and, of course, he knew it.

But this was my rodeo, I shook off the influence of those green tractor beams to gently and firmly convinced him it was futile to offer himself and his bed for the night in his state. He winked at me, then brought his finger up to touch the tip of my nose. "I see, we're playing hard to get. I can do that, because, you're worth it." He touched two fingers to his brow in a sloppy salute, turned and weaved a path toward his bathroom. I shut the door and headed to my bedroom.

This was not like Parker; despite his light tone, something was bothering him. I stopped my progress down the hall and looked back at his door. Or maybe he'd never had this much resistance from a woman.

Dating, or whatever this was, was new to me. I knew him as a teenager and later as my visiting funny, sexy brother-in-law. But this was completely different. Something appeared to be off, so what was I missing? I was feeling the effects of the evening. I wasn't going to solve this mystery tonight standing in this hall. I needed sleep and time to think.

I tied my hair into a ponytail and slipped under the covers. My big bed was a cold and lonely place to end my day. I punched my fist into the pillow to make an indentation and rested my head in the soft valley. Only a few steps down the hall was a warm bed with a hot man waiting for me to say yes to him. I turned over on my stomach and remembered my cat wasn't here either.

With Parker in the house, Daisy had stopped sleeping with me at night. I missed my warm, furry companion at the foot of my bed, but she was an independent soul and, no matter how much I tried to convince her with treats or toys to come back to my bedroom, I couldn't persuade her. I think she made it her sworn appointed duty to protect me, or the more likely scenario was that she had fallen under Parker's spell.

Whether she adored Parker, or she didn't trust him, Daisy was spending most nights near his bedroom. I'm not sure if he knew this, because by the morning she would be back in my room, meowing loudly at me for her morning meal.

I tossed myself around the bed, having a sleepless night. It was the kind of night where your mind jumps from one problem to another and, in the end, mashes everything together. The weird dream I had last night was on the top of my muddled list of things to ponder. Sigmund would have been over the moon with all the symbolism that dream threw around. That was a lot of men for one dream. Men that were all demanding my attention. I was surprised William Kaulder wasn't there trying to keep me for himself.

It had to be after 3 a.m. Too wound up to sleep, my gaze glued to the ceiling wondering if I should pull out my tablet to read a book or maybe do some writing. I decided to turn on the light when something crashed down the hall. Pushing out of bed, I rushed toward the sound. Flipping on the hall light, I found Parker on the floor in his T-shirt and shorts. He was a few feet from his door, holding his ankle and shooting daggers at my cat.

I bit my lip to stop the laugh that was trying to escape. If my body began to shake, it would be a full-on belly laugh. I blinked to make sure I wasn't sleepwalking.

Parker looked like he had robbed a hotel convenience store. The type of store that sells aspirin at 3 a.m. to its hotel guests and was souvenir central for every gaudy piece of clothing and useless branded item a tourist might buy. He sported a bright blue T-shirt that said 'I can't keep calm I'm Scottish' and neon shorts that must have been a revival of 80s fashion. Maybe we should have a discussion about his nighttime attire; he sorely needed some pointers.

Daisy appeared out of a dark corner and bounded toward me. I scooped up my cat and began stroking her tense body. "What happened?"

Parker must have known how absurd he looked. He had trouble making eye contact. "Nothing," he grumbled, "I was going to the kitchen for water. I didn't turn on the light and tripped over Daisy."

I gave him another quick check. He did look like he might be in pain. "Is it your ankle?" regretting my first reaction.

He grimaced and waved me away. "Go back to bed. I'm fine."

Ignoring him, I knelt and peered more closely at the ankle, "If you're fine, then why is your ankle twice the normal size?"

"It's nothing."

I poked it gently.

He yelped and gave me the evil eye.

"Please," unaffected by his stink-eye, "You'll have to do better than that if you want to scare me away." I got up with Daisy still tucked under my arm. Her antsy little body was tired of being cradled. "Where do you keep your sweats?"

He chucked his chin toward the room. "In the bottom drawer, why?"

"You can't go to the emergency with shorts and a top. It's cold outside." I stepped over him into the room and released Daisy.

"Why don't you stand guard girl, and make sure Uncle Parker doesn't escape."

He craned his neck to watch me while I moved to the dresser. "Very funny, I heard that."

"You were supposed to," I quipped back. I rummaged around until I found clothing that was a normal color and didn't have a crazy message on it.

I knelt beside him again. "I'm not going," he said, studying his ankle.

"Look, I can see you're in pain. You're going to need more than a couple of aspirins to get through the night. Can you wiggle your toes? Can you walk on it?"

He obliged, but the tiny movement of his toes seemed to distress him. He tried to put pressure on the ankle, attempting to get up, but fell back. "No, I can't right now," he groaned, frustrated from the effort.

"That's a good start," I encouraged, "Could you--"

"Bark, and roll over for you?"

This being helpless was getting to him. He wasn't going to make this easy. "I guess you'll have to roll over if I'm going to get these clothes on you. But you can bark if it helps the pain."

He did a slow grin and looked up from his ankle. "So, you're going to undress me?"

A short 'ha' exploded from me. Only Parker would turn an ankle injury into an opportunity to have sex.

It took longer for Parker to hop to the car with me holding him up than his time in the emergency room. The ER doctor pronounced his affliction as a left ankle sprain, prescribed something for the pain, warned him to stay off the ankle and keep it elevated and iced until his symptoms subsided. We picked up his pain meds and the crutches he insisted on at the hospital pharmacy.

The city was waking up with the sunrise when we arrived back from our adventure. Parker adapted quickly to his crutches, rushing ahead of me when we entered the house, heading straight for his bedroom.

It took me about twenty minutes to get him settled in his bed, iced, elevated, and medicated. All that time he was quiet, following my requests without a teasing word. I closed the bedroom curtains to darken the room and was about to turn off his lamp to let him rest when he caught my hand. "I know you're tired," looking as though he didn't want to be alone. "Would you sit with me for a few minutes?"

I sat on the bed next to his big, stretched-out body, a blanket draped over him and his head on the pillow. I took his hand. He studied our entwined fingers and gently squeezed. "Thanks. I'm sorry I gave you a hard time. I'm always on my own. I'm not used to someone taking care of me."

That declaration was shy, sweet, and unlike him. "You're welcome, Mr. Parker. I hope you will enjoy your stay at our humble establishment."

"I was hoping to take you dancing soon. I wanted to find a place where we could sway to the music on a crowded floor."

I considered his quirky suggestion. "Do places like that exist?" There were probably clubs like that in San Francisco. You could find anything there if you wanted it bad enough.

Parker released my hand, and I rose, edging away from the bed. He was probably tired and wanted a nap. He groaned and used the strength of his arms to pull his body up to rest against the headboard.

He extended his hand out in an invitation. "Come on," he said, his fingers giving a come-here motion, "I need to hold you."

I waited, trying to guess his real agenda. He needed rest. Heck, I needed to sleep myself. I knew I looked blurry-eyed, and my hair must have looked like a riot.

"Please." He glanced down at his body; ankle propped on a pillow. "There's no way I can have my wicked way with you; I'm harmless."

Parker Cameron couldn't be harmless even on his deathbed. I moved closer, making a show to straighten the cover. I was tired, and all I had to look forward to was crawling back into my cold bed to catch up on my sleep. Finding comfort in his strong arms might be what I needed. It had been a long time since anyone offered to hold me. He really looked more tired than lecherous.

I lay against his body, careful not to jostle his injured ankle on the opposite side. He draped his arm softly about me, and I burrowed into his closeness. He smelled of laundry soap, Parker, and summer days at the beach, his warm chest comforting.

"Did you ever think when we were kids in San Diego, this is how we'd end up?" I said, listening to the steady beat of his heart.

"I'll admit I envisioned a different future. I thought in some insane reversal of fate that I would be the guy you'd be growing old with, and by now there might be a little girl that looked like you."

I pushed away to look at him. "You never talked about kids, only the wild adventures you wanted us to have."

He absently stroked my arm. "I'm really the guy that holds his wife's purse while she tries on clothes in the fitting room; I just look dangerous."

I gave him a yeah-right look.

Grinning, he pulled me back into place. "Okay, maybe I do have more balls than that. But if I'd talked about reproducing back then it might have freaked you out, not to mention tarnishing my hot rep."

What he didn't know was that I was so fascinated with him when we first met that he could have begun speaking in tongues and

I wouldn't have thought anything of it. He continued without the on-edge vibe of the early evening.

"Luke had been talking for days about you coming over for dinner. He went on and on about you, like he does when he's obsessed about something. I was hoping to avoid the dinner, but my folks insisted I be there to pretend we were normal or something. I came through the kitchen, ready to tell my parents some obvious lie why I was late, when I hear you and Luke talking to my parents in the living room. I walked in, expecting another one of his plastic-looking girlfriends when I see you. Long, dark hair to your waist, in a yellow sun dress that set off your tawny skin flecked with gold. What can I say, Ms. Emma Benson, you knocked me out."

I stifled a giggle; of course, I'd remembered it differently. "Your mother was apologizing for you, just before you arrived, but she stopped in mid-sentence when you appeared in tight jeans, a shirt halfway out of its waistband, and your hair disheveled liked you'd been doing something disreputable."

He chuckled. "I probably was."

"You stood there staring at us, while your mouth opened and closed like a surprised goldfish until you turned back into cool Parker, the guy the girls at school talked about. I think you were the only junior in high school that had his own fan club that was listed as a sanctioned activity by the school."

"So, you knew who I was before that night. How the heck did I ever miss you strolling the halls?"

"There were a lot of plastic girls swarming around you."

He gave a real laugh. "What one has to do to please their fan girl base." He looked over to the side table. "I can't reach my phone from here; could you hand it to me?"

"Why, do you need to make a call now?"

"I don't. I want to listen to my playlist. I thought since we're talking about the past, might as well listen to something from back then." I dislodged myself and handed him the phone. Right now, I wasn't in favor of bouncing around to Pink or Linkin Park. I watched him swipe through his list and grimace. He handed the cell back to me. "You choose."

I did some swiping myself. I found a list titled Saratoga and punched that. He had synced his phone to the speaker in the room. The seductive sounds of Coltrane's *In a Sentimental Mood* wafted around us.

He closed his eyes. "I'd almost forgotten about that list." I nestled into his side again. "I'd add songs to that playlist after every visit with you and my brother. The music helped me remember our times together. This was one of Luke's favorites; it was playing on an evening we were waiting for you to finish dressing, to leave for dinner. God, he loved jazz and turned me on to it too; that's why I'm addicted." His chest fell in a deep sigh, his thumb softly flicking my arm. "I never thought Luke wouldn't be in our lives. Even when we'd argued, I knew he'd still be there when I needed him." He drew his arms around me tightly, like a child holds a beloved teddy bear, and I relaxed, feeling safe in his arms. "I was wrong leaving you alone. I was too numb to think about anyone else after his death, but I should have stepped up and been here for you."

He was right to stay away. It would have been complicated. Because of my husband, I was known in this valley where technology and venture capitalists ruled. Speculation about me living with my brother-in-law after his death would have been too much fodder for the press.

"One day we need to have a long talk." He fell silent. The hesitation was long enough that I thought he had fallen asleep. Then his voice came back, straining for calm. "It's been three years. Three years of not hearing his voice, of not meeting up for our long disjointed discussions." He took a breath. "After all this time you wouldn't think his not being here could still hurt like hell, but it does. Maybe that's why I never asked before. I keep breaking down our last talk over the phone the day before he died. He was a little more wistful, more remembering than usual, but nothing out of character. His last words were take care of yourself, then he added, I love you. I can't get the why out of my head. I need to know what happened Em. What happened the day he died?"

Tiny tendrils of dread crept over my heart. Talking about Luke would be like jumping into a ring to square off with a fighter that out classed me. I would be standing there getting a beating, not able to fight back. I couldn't give Parker what he wanted. I couldn't give him absolution, for whatever he thought he did wrong. "I understand," came my thick, whispered promise, "I will one day." That's all I had to offer.

We fell silent, losing ourselves in the music, the muffled outside noises, and our breathing. We lay together for a long while in a warm cocoon, drifting.

He stirred. His hand brushed my hair. I looked up. "You make me happy Em," Breaking the quiet with his hoarse whisper. "I've always been happy when you're around." He urged my hand to the opposite side of his hip. The move pulled me partially onto his chest, our lips close.

I felt for his other hand and slowly drew both to the headboard, holding him there. He allowed himself to be vulnerable to me without protest, waiting for what was next. It was curious this other side of him. I released his hands. We had been close at one time, long ago, but we never did intimacy. Tonguing on the couch, just before my wedding to his brother, didn't qualify. He wanted us to be together, but I needed to understand who he was in these moments to know if it was right.

His hands settled at his sides. His chin angled up. I leaned forward, looking into his hopeful face. My kiss brushed his warm, slightly parted mouth.

His lips were still, not giving the slightest encouragement to the soft, tentative touches I gave them. But the ragged exhale of breath signaled that I had his attention. I pushed further, tasting more of his sensual mouth.

I claimed only his lower lip, giving it my full attention. I ran my tongue along my prize, catching a wisp of stubble with my tongue while enjoying the sweet taste of him. He gave another exhale, but he remained still, not reacting to my exploration. His lack of activity drove me to tempt him more. I couldn't wait longer. I cradled his face in my hands, kissing him full on the mouth. My attempt was slow and languorous, my body moving to the rhythm of my lips until he opened a little wider, but not to return my kiss. I pulled back. How could I have read the moment wrong? Embarrassed, I pushed away from the bed. Parker caught my arm pulling me back on to his chest.

He grinned, tugging at my hair. "Do that again."

I did, and this time he responded with restrained passion, taking his time to discover me. Our lips and tongues probed and tasted until it seemed we had sucked all the air out of our bodies. I was on the edge of arousal. Soon I would want what his kisses promised. I hesitated to give us a moment. Parker caught my signal and drew back. "I'll have a second injury if you keep this up," he said, running his hands down my arms.

I sat up and reached for his hand. He was affected by our snogging session too. "That was nice, but why didn't you respond when I first kissed you?"

His mouth formed a lopsided grin. "You noticed that?"

"It was hard not to notice you doing a sleeping princess imitation."

He shifted, remembered his ankle, and frowned. "I'd never been kissed like that. It was too artful and sexy to stop you. I liked that you took the lead, not that you should do it all the time--"

"Oh no, God forbid," I teased.

He tugged at my hand. "Okay, you need to leave. Cuddling time is over before you have your wicked way with me. I need sleep."

"I'll let you rest." I slipped off the bed and made my way out into the hall. I pulled the door halfway closed, then popped my head back into the room. "Rest, Princess Parker, I'll see you later." I heard him groan as I closed the door.

He'd be sleeping soon, best to do the same. I walked by the kitchen and heard my cat's loud protests. I can't prove it, but I know she must be part Siamese. Her meows could bring the house down. I stepped inside. "Okay, Daisy, stop your complaining, breakfast is coming up now." I cleaned her food and water bowls while she watched me move around the kitchen like a zombie. I refilled them with water and her favorite grub. I leaned against the counter, watching her delicately take bites of her meal. I'm glad Parker and I stopped when we did. I was tingling all over like the night we kissed on the couch before my wedding. I was lucky he couldn't go any further. I'm certain his invitation to live with him was genuine, but I needed to be certain that I wanted to spend my life with him. Three years was a long time without a man in your bed, and he wasn't just any man.

CHAPTER 12

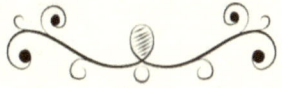

We Who Lunch

During the days after Parker tripped over my cat, he turned out to be an invaluable assistant. He returned calls for me, kept my social media up to date, even updated my website and Facebook. He also became a wiz on crutches.

We didn't revisit our kissing session, but it left us with residual sexual tension. On his part, he probably didn't make a move because he wasn't over the ankle injury. And I wasn't sure if I wanted to take the next step into his bed. I had to admit I'd been thinking about it a lot. I'd watch him when he worked with me in the office and I'd start thinking about his kiss and what it would be like to live with him. Maybe what it would be like to feel normal again.

The day of my luncheon with Austin, Parker had recovered enough to return to work on standby status. I tried to convince him it wasn't necessary to come with me and that I was capable of attending this meeting without him, but he insisted.

Monte Sereno boasts of thickly wooded sections only blocks away from the city. We stopped at a two-story structure of glass and wood that looked like a Frank Lloyd Wright design. Magda was sitting outside on the porch, looking like Gaia, the earth mother.

"Austin had to help a friend," she called out as we walked up the path to the house. "He will be here shortly, but in the meantime, he asked me to offer refreshments and entertain you until he arrives."

Magda gave us a brief tour of the downstairs, ending in the great room. A sparsely decorated space with couches, a few chairs, paintings, and art pieces. It looked more like the idea of a great room, not a place that someone used often.

Parker was quiet as he observed his surroundings, fascinated by the imposing fireplace. He ran a reverent hand along the polished stones of the hearth. "Who built this house?" he asked.

She turned toward him. "My father," remarked Magda. "He was the architect and builder. He built two houses on this property. My husband, Izzy, and I live in a similar style home about a five-minute walk farther down the road."

Then it dawned on me that Austin's last name was Santoro. It was Santoro Architects and Construction that had done most of the prominent buildings and homes in the valley. I seemed to remember; they even worked on the East Coast and Europe.

"I'm sorry I'm late. Couldn't be helped."

We turned to see Austin in the doorway, covered with dust. "I'll shower and change and be right back. I ordered our lunch; it will be here soon."

He returned twenty minutes later in a dark dress shirt and jeans. His wet hair was brushed back from his forehead. He took quick, long strides across the great room, heading for the kitchen.

"Would anyone like something to drink?" he called over his shoulder.

"I would," I said to his retreating form.

"Water would be fine," Parker said. "I'm actually on standby."

Austin returned with a glass filled with water and a beer with a frosted glass sitting over the top. Parker accepted the water, and Austin offered the beer to me. "I found this Portland IPA I thought you might like."

I stared at the beer.

"If you want to impress Emma," Parker chuckled, "never hand her a beer. Wine or spirits yes, but never a beer."

"Sorry, he's right," trying not to offend him, "It makes me gag."

Austin looked at the beer puzzled. "I have a selection of wine and spirits. What would you like?"

"Any white wine would be fine."

We sat in the great room, all of us uncomfortable while trying to maintain some conversation.

"I think we should eat," Magda said. "They've just finished laying out the meal. I hope you don't mind buffet style."

We proceeded into the dining area. Austin was trying to stand near me, but Parker managed to step between us. Austin moved away and I finally side-stepped Parker and walked to the head of the table. Austin looked relieved and handed me a plate.

"The food is from Kentaro, a new Japanese fusion restaurant in Old Town," Austin said as he reached for a pair of serving tongs. "They've been voted the best sushi restaurant in the valley. I know you like sushi. Let me know what you think."

Parker squeezed in between us again under the pretense of piling salad on his plate. I stepped back to give him room.

"Yeah," Parker smirked, "the other food Emma hates more than beer is sushi. If you have lima beans around here, then I'd say you're three for three."

If Parker didn't shut up, I was going to punch him, hard. Austin's lips drew into a thin line as he watched my brother-in-law toss a couple more items on his plate. He might take a punch at him before I could manage it.

I walked around Parker to stand next to Austin. I touched his arm to prevent my brother-in-law from moving between us again. "I think everything looks lovely, and I can't wait to try the other dishes you've ordered." He glanced down at me, looking pleased.

More awkward conversation followed as we ate until Parker decided to be charming and talked about his travels as an airline pilot. That lasted about two stories. Then there was a lull.

Magda rose, picking up Austin's empty plate. "Emma," Magda smiled, "would you help me clear the dishes? Someone is coming to clean, but I want to put some of this away."

"I can help," chimed Parker and Austin, getting to their feet. They looked at each other, annoyed. The air was so thick with caveman testosterone I thought they would start a shoving match.

Magda waved a hand at them. "No, that was wonderful of you to offer, but I want to talk with Emma. You two relax and get acquainted. I'm sure you can find something else in common, besides Emma." Both men shifted nervously, looking embarrassed. I had to turn away before I started laughing.

Magda just wrapped two dishes and shoved them into the refrigerator as she grilled me about my relationship with Parker. We reappeared ten minutes later with me a little shell-shocked. I wondered if she had learned interrogation techniques from the military. Austin stood up as we entered, and Parker scrambled to his feet a heartbeat later.

"I think we should begin our meeting," Austin said to me.

"Where do we want to do this?" asked Parker.

Austin and I stared at him. I pulled out my cell from my pocket. "I want to go over my notes with Austin," I wiggled my phone. "I think the meeting will be more productive if we meet alone. I'll call you if I need a second opinion."

I thought I had said it as gently as possible, but I had warned him during the ride over that I intended to take this meeting alone. Parker's face was pleasant enough, but he wasn't happy.

"Don't go to the studio," suggested Magda, her voice rising over the tension, "You're working on something creative. Take a walk to the edge of the property and stop by the pond to see the ducks."

Austin kept a wary eye on Parker as he swept his hand toward the door. I walked by Austin on the way out but looked over my shoulder at Parker. His face was a mask of betrayal. I hesitated.

"Go. I'll keep him occupied while you're gone. Go," Magda urged.

Leaves crunched under our feet as the crisp smells of the fading autumn rose where we stepped. I was aware of Austin close behind me as we walked the narrow path. The trail fanned out to a large pond with an impressive display of ducks and other birds playing or flying above the water. We sat on a small, well-used bench, Austin's bulk taking up most of the space.

He studied the parade of ducks gliding on the small lake. "I come here most days during my walks. This is how I take breaks when I'm working." A duck began ambling toward the bench. "Sorry, buddy," said Austin. "I've forgotten the bread, I'll come back later with a bag." I wanted to laugh when the duck appeared to nod and walk back to the water joining his friends. Magda was right, it was the perfect place to talk, but I wasn't here to relax. I spoke to Austin's profile.

"Your demos were different. They let me really hear Cooper. I felt I was in the heat of the action when we did the scenes together."

He sat up straighter and a satisfied grin moved across his lips. "I had to do something to catch your attention. I've wanted to work on this series for a long time. I hoped experiencing the dialog live instead of hearing it on tape would help you make your decision in my favor." He turned his dark gaze on me. It was like he was pulling me into its depths. I started staring at him.

"You said you had notes?"

"Oh, right." I looked at my pocket. Jeez, my hand was already inside. I pulled out my cell and scrolled to my notes.

"I like what you've done so far. I need, well, more."

He turned his body toward me and cocked his head. "More? Like what more?"

"I see your point when you put it like that." I had to stop looking at him, or I'd be speaking complete nonsense instead of sentences.

I looked at the surface of the water for inspiration. "Cooper is the kind of man who will make a joke as he's about to face down certain death. He's cocksure, maybe a little arrogant, but not so much that he turns people off, and he doesn't take no for an answer." I was finally starting to roll with my theme. I rose to my feet to pace and think.

"Are there any actors or characters who would fit his persona, like Indiana Jones?"

"No, Cooper's personality is bigger. He's dead gorgeous. You know, men want to be him. Women want to be with him, that kind of--"

"You mean like Parker?"

I blinked. "No. I, ah... no." I shook my head. "That's not true." Then I thought, *cocksure, doesn't take no for an answer, dead gorgeous.*

"And you're Molly," Austin's voice certain. "I thought you had patterned Cooper after Parker when we saw you in Campbell. But after today, I'm convinced. You're not satisfied with the demos because I think you want me to sound like him."

I sat on the bench, clutching the armrest. I'd always heard Cooper's voice in my head. Could it have been Parker's? Writers put people they know or meet in their stories. They even write some of themselves into characters.

"I can get the attitude and depth right, but I won't mimic him. If that's what you want, you'll have to find another narrator."

I breathed out a short laugh. "One thing I'm sure of, I'm not Molly Dixon. We share the same body type, but that's where it ends. It's not that I created Cooper to be a fictional Parker. At least not consciously. I always had a vague notion about him when I worked on his profile. I never used an actor or model as a prototype. One day he appeared, his story begging to be written."

This was tearing at me. Did Luke know who I was writing about? Did Parker? Did I hurt my sweet husband creating a character who was so much like his brother?

"If that's what I've done, this is a disaster. Parker is my husband's brother."

He didn't hide the concern in his eyes. "So, Parker is your brother-in-law. Does he help you with your business?"

"Yes. No. It's complicated. Parker's staying with me for a short time until he leaves for Australia." I looked off into the distance. "Luke, my husband, died about three years ago."

"I'm sorry, I didn't know..."

I leaned my elbow on the armrest and cradled my face.

"You don't understand," the reality of what I'd done hitting me hard. "My husband was a wonderful man. If I hurt Luke writing those stupid books about Cooper Flynn, then I'm a horrible, horrible person."

I gave a ragged sigh and buried my face into my hand. I felt a tear hit my palm just before the rest came streaming out. A strong hand touched my shoulder, and I found myself crying into Austin's massive chest.

"Just let it out," he soothed, rocking me gently. "Don't keep it in, let it go."

I allowed myself to cry, drawing somewhere deep inside my core. My body shook as I released until I finished with a whimper and a few sniffs. I grimaced at the wet patch on his shirt. Austin let me go. I kept my head down and rummaged in my pocket to find a tissue. I'm not one of those women who cry pretty. I must have looked like a red swollen mess. I swiped at my eyes and wiped my nose. I forced myself to look at him, trying to manage a smile.

A curious look crossed Austin's face. The man who looked so fierce when I first met him smoothed back my hair with such tenderness it made me want to weep all over again. He leaned forward, his hand tilting up my chin, and pressed a tentative kiss on my lips. He stopped and moved back, looking unsure.

I touched my mouth and stared at him. It didn't seem real that this man had just kissed me. That he wanted to kiss me. There'd been a strong attraction to him at our first meeting when I imagined him as a warrior and later when we spent the day together.

He'd been watching me all this time, waiting for me to react. He didn't seem worried, only curious. I slid closer to him, leaned in, and gave him a gentle kiss. His lips responded to my lead as I took my time enjoying him. I thought we were just going to share a sweet moment until it began to build. He pulled me closer, my body pressed hard against him. His intensity swept over me. I was getting hot and heavy with him like he was my college boyfriend in his parents' basement. I sucked his bottom lip, but in my eagerness, I nicked his flesh. My tongue tasted something metallic, and we broke apart. He held his hand to his lip, trying to stop the bleeding.

"I'm sorry," embarrassed that I had injured him, "I'm out of practice."

He waved a hand. "No, it's okay," his voice was distorted as he kept pinched pressure on his lip. I was worried. There seemed to be a lot of blood. I searched in my pocket for a clean tissue and handed it to him.

I stood. "Maybe we should talk about Cooper?"

"Of course."

"To be clear, I don't want you to mimic Parker. I think what you've done needs tiny tweaks."

"Give me your suggestions, and I'll do another demo." Austin stopped talking, his gaze on the path.

Footsteps were coming toward us. "Oh great," I said, staring down the trail. A few seconds later Parker appeared in the clearing.

"Em," Parker shouted, coming to stand next to me. "I'm sorry, but we've got to go."

Austin had gotten to his feet. The bushes rustled again, and Magda appeared flushed. She must have jogged to keep up with Parker's long strides.

Everyone appeared agitated, but they were all focused on me. "Did something happen?" I asked.

"Yes, the airline called," Parker replied. "I've got to report to the airport."

Austin stepped closer to me.

"I'll take you home," Parker said, reaching for my hand. Then his gaze pivoted to Austin standing next to me. "And why the hell is your lip bleeding?"

I turned to Austin. Red had seeped through the white tissue he held to his mouth.

"I bit my lip," he scowled.

Parker lifted his chin and scowled back.

"I told Parker it wasn't necessary for you to go," Magda said as she came near. "I offered to drive you back after your meeting."

I searched Parker's pleading face. It wasn't about him flying off for work. Maybe he wanted me to leave with him, to prove that he hadn't lost me. We probably needed to talk before he left.

"I'm sorry," putting an end to the meeting. Parker was giving me no choice. "Thank you for the wonderful lunch." I caught Austin's gaze. "I'll text you to set up another day to meet."

He nodded.

Parker's hand reached the small of my back, urging me toward the path. "Thank you," Parker said. "I'm sorry that we had to cut this short."

I took a few steps but stole a glance back. Magda placed a consoling hand on her brother's arm. Parker's arm slipped around my shoulder, his body blocking my view as we continued to walk.

CHAPTER 13

Learn to Fly

e drove back to the house in a cold silence until we entered the house. Our unspoken truce lasted just long enough for us to walk across the threshold. Parker shoved the door closed with a furious bang.

Our voices raged at each other with hurt and accusations over the events at our lunch. But underneath it all, it didn't seem like we were fighting about the same thing. Our anger came from a different place. I was bitter because he wasn't Luke, and he was resentful that I didn't choose him all those years ago. We finally looked at each other, tired of fighting, or maybe we'd spent all our anger. I lapsed into an irritated silence, wishing he would leave.

Parker approached me tentatively. He touched my hand, then pulled me into his arms.

"I'm sorry," his chin resting on my head. "That guy looks at you like he wants to eat you for lunch. Thinking of him touching you makes me crazy."

Turning away, I leaned against the sink, looking out at the bright day. I still wasn't quite over how Parker had treated me today. He stood at my back, hovering. I could feel his hesitation, the calculations he was making.

His arms circled my waist. His lips and a tiny brush of stubble at my neck sent shivers deep inside. Was it his touch that made me feel this way, or had it been so long since I had male attention that I was like a live wire ready to spark?

I turned to protest when he found my lips. His kiss was urgent, like a man who needed to breathe. He kept me captive with his passion, daring me to meet his with mine. His hand fell to my bottom; his strength lifted me onto the counter. I slipped my arms around his neck. He shifted me to the edge. My legs parted, and he moved in between them. His bulge visible and my panties wet, I was too aware of how far and fast we were going.

His hands ran down my sides. "Being so near to you and not touching you..." His lips brushed my ear. "Being a gentleman while I waited for you to decide..." He kissed my neck. "It's good I'm leaving. I've had too many unsavory thoughts about what I wanted to do to you in the night." My breath caught as his kisses trailed to my cleavage. "I hope you've been bolting your door."

I had steamy thoughts of my own about him. Too scared to make a decision, after our kiss I had begun to wish him in my bed, but he'd never appeared. I glanced at his flight kit in the foyer.

"Don't start this," I moaned as his tongue teased between my breast. "I don't think we have time."

"If I start," he jerked me to him, "I'll finish. I don't care if a planeload of passengers is waiting. I have a gift for you that can't wait. But you must be properly undressed."

I pushed him away, needing to slow the escalation of feelings. A question crossed his face. I took a breath. Maybe it was more than time to do this, or maybe our fight was just foreplay for what we both wanted. I kicked off my shoes, my heels flying past him like a declaration of intent.

His hands reached for my waistband. In one anxious motion, he yanked my pants and panties off together. The cold granite chilled my bum while his hands blazed the length of my thighs. He watched me react to his touch, enjoying his affect. I closed my eyes, not wanting him to know how much I wanted his fingers to touch me everywhere all at once.

I drew deep breaths, anticipating the course of his hands. The strong digits kneaded into the flesh of my thighs, sending me into a frenzy, but it didn't last. He pulled back, slowing his frantic touch to play softly at my mound.

His fingers teased my slit, moving enticingly over the small sensitive area. In the whole world, there were only his fingers and my aching need to invite him inside. I pushed my hips forward, and he parted my lower lips, running a stealth finger through my moisture. I moaned, clutching the counter's edge, afraid I would orgasm on his finger. My eyes flew open.

"You're wet and too ready," he mused, removing his finger, holding it between us, inches from my nose. It glistened with my fluid, my musk spicing the air.

Parker placed the digit in his mouth, savoring it like a sweet. Heat flooded my cheeks. He grinned, stifling a chuckle. "I knew you would taste like exotic honey." He reached for me. His mouth grazed my lips, drawing me into a shameless, consuming kiss, my essence still on his lips, now glossing mine. A hand dropped to my breast, playing with me through the fabric.

"Is this old?" he asked pulling at my shirt. I couldn't think with his kissing me.

"Ancient," I stammered.

He took a breath. "The bra?"

"Ol... old too," I managed to reply.

His lips trailed kisses to my cleavage, taking his time to play above my breasts. He shifted, gathering the cloth, and yanked the shirt open.

A hand brushed over the lace of my bra. His face loomed above me, intent on his task. "Are you sure?" the material already bunching in his fists. I arched my back and tipped my chin up to him. A cold rush of air passed over me as he made quick work of the flimsy fabric.

Clothes in tatters, I was exposed. I tried to pull the rest of the abused shreds off, but Parker stopped me. "No," he said as his eyes glazed with desire, "I like you partially ravished. You look hot as hell."

He brushed my nipple with his thumb and took the other in his mouth. My hands flew to his shoulders. I was moving back to slow down the rush of sensation that threatened to overwhelm me, but the cabinet stopped me before I'd gone too far. My moist nipple popped from his mouth.

"Don't move away from me," he growled. He grabbed me by the waist and pulled me back, latching onto my nipple. He took his time, lips and tongue teasing. I calmed at the less frantic pace, the scent of arousal prickling my nose.

He gave me a lick and looked up, more mischief in his eyes. "I think it's time for your present."

He scooped me off the counter and onto his shoulder caveman-style. My partially clothed breasts were hitting his back, my ass in the air. I gave an alarmed cry as I bounced while he strode toward his bedroom. He gave me a playful slap on my behind.

"Quiet! You're going to enjoy this," he laughed.

He muscled the bedroom door open with his shoulder. Then he threw me at the bed, my body airborne until I bounced against the pillows. He pulled his shirt over his head, and the pants followed. He stood looking down at me with the devil's grin on his face.

God, he was sexy, looking like the dangerous Jacobite in my vision. Looking like a man who was taking what he wanted.

The shades were down, mimicking evening, the semi-darkness somehow sexier. I jumped when he kicked the door shut. "We don't want Daisy watching," he said, advancing to the bed.

I couldn't help it; his caveman play made me crazy mad for him. I reached for his cock, but his briefs were still on.

"No," he whispered, staying out of my reach. "I said I had a gift for you."

Why was he still dressed? I could see he was turned on. I rolled to my side, looking at his bulge. "I can see that."

He drew a light finger across my cheek. "On your back." I rolled and settled myself. He sat next to me.

"Open your legs wide for me, Emma." He watched as I slipped my feet onto the cover, knees up, parting my legs. He moved closer. "You're beautiful, Em," he breathed. "You're my beautiful, beautiful girl." I smiled at him, and he tossed his circuit-jamming grin at me.

Parker shifted the warmth of his body next to mine. He gave me a long, slow kiss, touching my face when our lips parted. His hand brushed my breast, trailing down to my belly, then rested on my hip.

I thought he would roll on top of me but, instead, he moved to the end of the bed.

A flush of heat rushed through me as he lowered himself between my legs. Gentle fingers massaged my thighs; he brought them to rest on my mound. Tenderly spreading my slit, his mouth was a few inches away from my sex. His hot, moist breath tickled and taunted me, making me agonize for his kiss. His lips touched me. The pleasure I craved shot through me, wild and immediate. I groaned, loudly.

I heard a satisfied chuckle bubble up from him. His tongue flattened out, covering me with long, lazy licks like I was a lollipop he needed to savor. My legs shook with the sweet sensation; he had to push my legs wider apart to stop me from smothering him.

His tongue was relentless as he worked me into a fever. I moved my body, guiding him to my sweet spot, but he ignored my signals. I cried out in frustration as he continued to build my climax. I thought I was going to faint if he didn't let me release.

"I need it now," I screamed. "Do it now!"

"Say my name when you come," he demanded.

"What--?"

He licked me again. Close, but not where I needed it.

"Say my name, or I won't finish." Another wave of pleasure rolled through me.

I was too far gone to care what the hell I said. "Yes, okay, I'll say it," I grunted through my teeth. "Just do it now." Parker found my sweet spot, his tongue darted and prodded as I began to catch the wave of pleasure rising. He sucked my clit; I moaned. His tongue flattened, washing over it. I moved my hips. His tongue hit that sweet, sweet spot.

I gasped, my back arched, my body exploding into surrender. Still in the arms of euphoria, my promise to him was on my lips. I took a breath.

"Parker!" I screamed at the top of my lungs. "You're a fucking asshole!"

I sucked in air. My senses sailed like a kite suspended in the wind. It veered toward earth, then hit bottom. I lay spent, my body tingling.

Parker's body began shaking with soft laughter. The evil sound vibrated, tickling my pussy. I couldn't help it. I started laughing too at the absurdity. It was a typical Parker move. Wild, crazy, and, damn it, it was fun. This was better than a hundred spa days. He rolled away, making his way to my side. He gathered me in his arms and kissed my hair.

"That's why I love you, Em girl," he continued to chuckle, "You don't let me get away with shit."

I shifted into his warmth and he held me tighter. "Thank you," I said.

"Believe me, that pleasure was mine. I'm just sorry I have to leave soon, or I'd give you the proper rogering that you need, as the Brits say. This will have to do until I get back." He winked and bounced off the bed. I threw a pillow at him. He dodged and headed for the bathroom.

I must have fallen asleep because the next thing I remembered was Parker sitting next to me dressed in his captain's uniform. He leaned forward, touching my cheek.

"The car is here," he whispered. "I'll see you in a week."

I sat up, leaning against the headboard. His goodbye kiss was sweet and gentle until I grabbed him by the lapels and gave him a kiss that he would remember when he fell into his bed tonight. I was pleased that he was as hungry as I was for round two.

He slowly, reluctantly pulled away from me, his eyes shining with emotion. "I love you; don't get distracted," the hoarse declaration rushed out. "We're going to have a great life together." He pushed off the bed. I looked up at him. It was true what they say about a hot guy in a uniform. He gave me his signature grin and said, "Remember me, Nyx." And then he was gone.

CHAPTER 14

Honey, Honey

Staying in Parker's bed for the rest of the day was not an option; besides, I had an overwhelming urge to write. I padded down the hallway and dumped what was left of my shirt and bra in the bin, threw on sweats, and headed for the office.

The hunch was spot on. My writing session was the stuff of legends. The words flowed onto the screen without effort. I did stop a few times when I'd have a sensory memory of Parker's expert tongue at play. I'd gasp at the shivers of pleasure that racked my body. Jeez, my body was doing it again. If this continued, I'd have to take a stress-relieving shower with the hand-held nozzle set to pulse massage.

I got up to look at a new photo I had pinned on the inspiration board a few days ago of Parker and me in front of the red sports car. I moved my finger over his face. He wasn't Luke, who made me feel safe. Parker made me feel like I was walking the cliff's edge.

I liked my play with him but I was still unsatisfied. I won't lie, I wanted him inside me. It was like I was a book, and he had just put a placeholder in until he could come back when he had more time. But he'd said as much.

So why was I also thinking of a kiss on a bench near a duck pond? Why did Austin kiss me? Did he just want to make a sad woman feel better? There had been too much passion to convince me of that. I touched my lips. Then what was my excuse for kissing him? Maybe I should put that on my things to ponder list and consider it later.

I glanced at my desk. My writing program was open, the curser blinking next to the last word I typed. I slipped into the chair. I'd been thinking about a new story. Of course, I wasn't going to leave the romance genre. I loved the idea of people struggling to heal themselves, change, and find love in the process too much to abandon it. I'd always liked writing something hopeful with a happily ever after or at least happy for now. I'd been thinking about a contemporary romance. Something that mixed light and dark elements. I must admit that I wanted to push some limits. Something that didn't involve magic, a bounty hunter, or walking in a different time. I wanted to write about someone like me, a modern woman who had been hurt, faced challenges, but found herself along the way and made her own unique HEA.

I don't know about other writers' processes, but my inspiration comes from a few sources. Flashes of scenes and characters introducing themselves. I know it sounds strange, but that's the way I work. And I need to know how it ends before I begin. I like to know where I'm going before I start the journey. I outline, but I'm flexible within the framework of a story.

In preparation, as if to tell the universe I was serious, I cleared most of the items off my inspiration board, including all the family photos. One exception was of Parker and me in the sports car. Even the picture of Luke and me in Aruba was placed in the family album. It would be hard not to see him every morning and touch that photo, but I thought I was strong enough to attempt a new start.

I did pin something new. The board had a few character names. Tessa, Ben, and Matt. My flashes for this story were wild when the idea came to me, but it was a start. I was also thinking of another pen name. Amelia Zaitlin sounded about right for this series. So much had to be done to launch a second series under a new pen name, it would be almost like starting over. It would be an exciting and scary new project. I glanced at the clock on my desk. It was time for a break.

I needed some tea and thought I'd drive down to the supermarket a few miles away when I decided to grab my tennis shoes instead. There was a mom and pop market at the bottom of the hill. A five-minute walk each way would give me the exercise and the break I needed.

I was halfway to my destination when a thought crossed my mind that the hill I was on had somehow gotten steeper than I remembered. The cell in my pocket pulsed. It was my mom. I owed her a phone call, so I'd better take this unless I wanted a call every twenty minutes from her until I picked up.

"Hi, Mom."

"Hello, Emmaline--"

I shook my head. She was the only one that called me Emmaline outside of anyone who went to grammar school with me. If she used my name instead of calling me honey, then something wasn't right. "Mom, could you give me a few seconds to put my headset in place?"

"Yes, of course. Where are you?"

I stopped to attach the plug into the cell and put the buds in place. "I'm walking on Westlake Drive going to Amato's."

"I remember that place. Your father loves their deli. You know, I remember another deli in Santa Barbara…"

If I didn't re-direct the conversation, I would have finished my shopping, returned to the house, and would be feeding my cat before she got to the point of her call. I loved my mom, but sometimes retired people forgot about time. "How is Dad?"

"Your father is fine. I assume that is your subtle way of asking your mother to get to the point."

Great, now I've hurt her feelings. "No, Mom. I was just wondering. You sound distracted, like something is bothering you. Is Rosie alright?"

"I suppose you are going to start asking about your cousins next. Yes, my cat is fine. How is her sister?"

"Daisy is great. Keeping me sane." There was a pause, like the line had gone dead. "Mom, are you still there?"

"Yes, I'm still here. I was just pulling up a podcast on my computer."

Okay, this was scaring me. My tech-challenged mom was listening to podcasts. "Whose podcast are you listening to?"

"Addison Finch."

I stumbled, but luckily, I caught myself before I kissed the pavement. To be fair, I shouldn't say that my mom was technically challenged. She wasn't that interested in the Internet until it came to me. She knew enough to type a word in a search box and click on links. She even learned how to cut and paste, which makes her dangerous, especially if she sees a cat video.

She acquired the skill because she was obsessed with all things Angela Stryker and surfs the net daily for any interesting information related to my pen name or my books. If she found something new, I would get an email with a link to the news. She found mostly articles where I'd be mentioned with other writers in my genre.

"Addison Finch? Is that his real name? Anyway, do you know him, because he seems to know you? He devoted almost a whole thirty minutes to Angela Stryker."

Addison Finch, or Addy Finch, was a self-proclaimed romance book critic. He did review books, but most of his podcast was tittle-tattle about the industry or author interviews... when he could get someone to agree to do his podcast. I'd heard, from a few writers, that his author interviews were on the rise. I'd also heard he was trying to build up a following to get a spot on a local TV station; his ultimate goal was syndication.

"Honey, are you still there?"

"Sorry, I was thinking. No, I don't know him. He's asked me to do interviews, but I always refused."

"You might want to reconsider. I didn't understand everything he said. I suppose it was romance industry jargon, but it didn't sound good. It was something about ghosts. I've sent you and Bex a link."

"Thanks."

"Are you coming down for Christmas?"

"Yes, Daisy and I are coming."

"Good, then we can make it up to you for not seeing you on your birthday. Honestly, this is the last time I let your father make the travel arrangements. Imagine getting the dates wrong."

"Don't worry about it; it's fine. I'm a big girl. I can be alone on my birthday." It would be tough, but I'd plan something special. Maybe Parker would be here and we could go out to dinner. Mom didn't know Parker was staying with me. I didn't want to open myself up to questions that I didn't have answers to at the moment.

"Honey, I think I would feel better if I gave you your birthday gift early."

"Really, Mom, I'll be fine."

"Please, I feel bad enough. We've gotten you a spa weekend at that big resort on the beach at Half Moon Bay. But you know I can't bear for you to be there by yourself, so I've asked your friend Bex to join you, and she agreed. Of course, we will pay for Bex's weekend as well. I've already checked, and they can accommodate you on your birthday weekend."

Actually, that would be more fun than anything I could come up with. "Mom, that's a great gift. Thank you."

"I'm glad. Your father was so devastated about his mistake, he has agreed to deluxe accommodations. You will both have a suite with a sea view. Oh, and I hear the spa package is lovely: Yoga, massage, hot stones, there's even Calistoga mud. It sounded so restful, I almost told your father to go to Puerto Vallarta alone and that I would join you instead. He just sat there looking like your basset hound Charlie. You remember, the one you picked out from the shelter when you were in third grade?

"But you know I can't bear for him to be alone. No telling what the man might find to get up to. Oh, my Lord, I didn't realize the time. I hate to cut this short; we're having such a pleasant chat. I must run, we're going out to meet friends for dinner. Love you."

I tossed my keys on the kitchen table and headed for my office. I punched in Bex's number and placed her on speaker phone.

"Hi, Emma. How did you know I just got off the phone with a studio in Eureka? It's cold up there, but really beautiful this time of year. I'll have more information in a few days. By the way, I just received a text from your mom. She said you agreed to the Half Moon Bay spa weekend... I can't wait!"

When did my mom learn to text? She was getting scarier than a mom trolling you on Facebook; could Skyping be far behind?

"Yes, I think it will be fun too--"

"Have you called to discuss how to get the most out of that weekend? I've just pulled their website up. I'm already studying the options. Your parents were very generous. Did you know we have the option of breakfast in our rooms?"

"If you don't mind, I'd like to talk about that later. I wanted to discuss the link Mom emailed you."

There were a few taps. "I see it here. I haven't opened it yet. No offense, but I thought it might be another cat video."

The title of the email read: Something interesting. There was no explanation in the body of the email only 'Mr. A. Finch.' "I would have thought that too, but she told me this is a link to a podcast Addy Finch did a couple of days ago. She said he devoted almost thirty minutes to Angela Stryker and her books. The curious thing is he mentions ghosts."

"Maybe he was suggesting a new storyline for your series; you know he does that. He fancies himself a writer although he's never published anything yet."

"Did he call you about this podcast?"

"No, just the request he emails me every other week asking for an interview. Those emails aren't even personal... he has them on automatic send."

"Alright, do you have some time to listen to the podcast with me? I've got you on speaker."

"I've got thirty minutes. My next client isn't due for another hour. Let's do this."

I clicked the link. Some chirpy intro music came up, then Addy's clipped English tones slid over the music as it faded away. "Today, we will continue the authors of the fantasy romance series. These are the very authors that you voted as your top five favorites in our online poll. Don't just think this will be a boring retrospective. I have new, interesting information on each of the authors, but you will have to wait until the end for your reward."

I paused the link. "Do you mind if I fast forward? What my mom was concerned about is probably at the end."

"Yes, I was thinking the same thing. Addy always leaves enough time so he can expostulate."

"Is that your word for the day?"

"Yes, how did you guess? It's from this new app I have. I need to incorporate it into conversation three more times. Then it will be a permanent part of my vocabulary."

That made sense. I wondered why she used the word vagility. I mean, she used the word correctly, it just didn't match her usual speech pattern. "Fine, then let's hear him expostulating." I clicked the link.

"I'm sure you enjoyed that interesting journey into the world of Angela Stryker. We all love her larger-than-life characters that can barely function under their overdeveloped libidos. I wouldn't be surprised, if we ever saw Cooper Flynn in the flesh, that he wouldn't have a permanent hard-on."

A 'ha' exploded out of Bex that was cut off abruptly. "Sorry," she mumbled.

I'd never heard Addy's podcast. I will admit that he was entertaining. I was Angela Stryker, and I was hoping he would get to the good stuff on her.

"Since I always keep my ear to the wind for interesting morsels for my addicts--"

I stopped the podcast again. "Don't tell me that's what he calls his fans."

"Yep, the show is called *Addictions to Love*. And of course, being the narcissist Addy is, he couldn't resist calling them addicts. I've even heard them called Addy's addicts. Yes, I know it is insensitive, but that's his karma, not mine."

I resumed the podcast. "It seems they are finally close to selecting a narrator for the Cooper Flynn series and it's rumored it might be the oh so sexy narrations of William Kaulder. You know, ladies, the one who could read prescription information and make it sound hot."

I swear I thought I heard him take a shaky breath after that statement. He was good, but that wasn't a stretch guessing that Kaulder might be considered for the voice of Cooper.

"But that leads me to something I have been pondering for a long time about the success and the speed in which the books have been published. I have no proof of this, and as your chief addict, I know you rely on me to provide you with the truth. I promise I will get to the bottom of these doubts.

I am venturing speculation, an opinion, but not to claim all of it as only in my imagination. I have heard rumblings about this from sources who are in a position to know, but I can't name.

I think there is no Angela Stryker, but a team of corporate ghostwriters who write this successful series. We do know Angela Stryker is a pen name. Her bio states that she is a real person with a husband, a couple of kids, and a dog living in California. We hear she is a recluse, but if you listen to the two phone interviews she has given, they sound like two different people. One last morsel for you to savor. Some chapters and books in the series feel like they were written by different authors.

This is entertainment, and we will buy the books and enjoy the stories no matter what, but this is an age where truth is sacred. If these books are produced by a group of ghostwriters, then admit it and let's all move on.

I invite Angela Stryker to join me on this podcast at any time to respond. Addy out." The intro music returned with a few announcements. I clicked off the link.

We were both silent. The creak of Bex's chair came through the speaker.

"I'm not going to sugarcoat it. If we ignore him, this could be a problem."

I sighed. "How many followers did you say he has?"

CHAPTER 15

I Roll and I Tumble

The calendar on the desk reminded me it had been over a week since Parker flew off after our lunch meeting at Austin's house. The decision of who would be the narrator of the Cooper series was still not resolved. Austin's revelations about Cooper and Molly bothered me, and I couldn't decide if his observations were valid. And as far as I knew, we still didn't have a recording studio.

I checked my phone. There was no call from Bex. I'd text her later about stopping by her office tomorrow to talk about the MN. I wanted to talk to Austin one last time before making my decision. One thing that was heavily in his favor was his state-of-the-art home recording studio. If I chose Austin, we could make a separate deal for the use of his studio. Jay, the book's audio director, and his crew were already signed on to do the project; we just needed a place to record. As far as I knew, William Kaulder didn't have his own recording facilities.

Daisy and I had just finished dinner. I was about to call up the last episode of The Real Housewives of... I never remembered which one, when the phone rang. I wondered if it could be Parker. Maybe he was on a layover and wanted to talk dirty. No, the screen flashed Austin's name. Maybe this was my chance to talk to him before tomorrow. I punched 'accept.'

"Just listen... Don't say anything, just listen," he said as Cooper.

All night we trekked through the forest, trying to lose ourselves in the dense wood until we found a refuge. The sounds of men and dogs were always in the distance, maybe a mile or two away. Armstrong was hunting us the old-fashioned way, out of boredom or maybe arrogance. He probably knew no matter what he did, or how long it took, he would find us.

If Armstrong finally managed to bring us back to the fortress, Molly would be sold, and I would be tortured and killed for daring to steal his property.

Molly looked at me, her smile weak. The wound on her side had opened and was oozing blood. I had managed to keep us hidden with the one piece of tech in my possession. Checking the gizmo again, we had maybe three more hours until the mouth of the cave we were in would be visible. The only silver lining was Lily. We had gotten her out and back to her own time.

"Got any more brilliant plans, hot shot?" She was still drowsy from sleep.

Good, she was awake, but her face was flushed, eyes a bit too bright. I was afraid fever was taking control of her body.

"I do," giving her a grin I didn't feel. "I'm just working out the details."

I needed her to keep fighting for her life and to somehow get strong enough to guide us back to our own time. Right now, she hated me for everything I'd put her through. I just hoped I'd gained some merit for getting her sister out.

"I'm the last person to criticize," she said, "but you need to work faster. I can get us back tonight, but we have to be at the time portal at Mizar in the Tellus wood before midnight." Her gaze moved around the room. It looked like she was going to say more, but her eyes rolled back and she slumped forward.

I got to her in two strides. I held her in my arms. "Molly," I called. She was unresponsive. "Wake up." I couldn't lose her now. "Come back... come back to me!"

I drove down the lonely road, guided by the reflectors along the center divider. I squinted at the headlights barreling down the opposite way. The vehicle was going too fast for this two-lane country road. I veered off to the side just in time, nearly avoiding a collision. Some crazy, determined blond in a gray SUV was flooring it. Our eyes met for an instant when she moved past me. I made a mental note not to cross that witch if I ever met her again.

Gravel crunched under my feet, letting me know this might be a bad idea. The house was dark except for one light on the second floor. It didn't look like the welcome I expected.

I shook off my doubts and pushed the ivory button next to the door. A chime rang. A blurred mass moved past the window to the door. Light flooded the porch as Austin filled the open doorway. He moved aside to let me enter.

"Why can't you just pick up the phone and ask me to come over like a normal human?" I asked.

His face almost cracked a smile. "How was the phone demo?"

I really hadn't thought of it until now. This time he narrated both characters. I'd been so focused on Cooper's voice, I had forgotten he would do everyone, including Molly. It worked. The nuances I thought were missing in Cooper's voice were there when he had done a complete narration. "Good, really good."

Then he really did smile. I thought he was handsome before; now he had godlike beauty. "I think we should celebrate. Do you drink champagne?"

I finally got to tour Austin's recording studio. I sipped champagne and covertly determined there would be enough room for Jay and his crew to work with Austin. I wanted to talk to Bex more about it when we met tomorrow. Then I'd give Austin the good news that he would narrate the Cooper series.

I set the glass down. "One is my limit if I'm going to drive," I announced to a surprised Austin. He must have known I would eventually leave. "Thank you for the unique demos and the champagne. We will let you know our decision tomorrow."

Austin stood, placing his glass down carefully. "Is Parker still off flying somewhere?"

"Yes, he's been gone since our lunch."

"Maybe you could stay longer and we could talk. I promise no sushi or beer."

Daisy was the only one back home waiting for me.

"It's a celebration," he coaxed. "We can have more champagne. Look, the bottle is practically full. I'll get a car to take you home after."

When was the last time a handsome man asked me to spend time with him? Oh, yeah, a week ago. I guess when it rains, it pours men. Once we started production, Austin wouldn't have time until he finished the project. Now would be the only time we'd have to talk.

"Sure, I'd like to stay," I lifted my glass for more champagne.

We sat in an alcove of his studio. It was probably the place where he or a crew would rest or just discuss ideas. Once I got Austin talking, he was much more relaxed than at any other time I had seen him. He seemed to like his life, which centered on his work and family, more now than before the accident. As far as I could tell, there didn't seem to be anyone special in his life other than his niece Izzy.

"Your home is beautiful. What else is on this floor?"

"Two bedrooms, mine and a guest room, two bathrooms, and a kitchenette with a sitting area and the studio. I wanted the studio close to my bedroom so I could work anytime I was inspired."

Austin nursed his glass of champagne. I noticed the tiny wound on his lip that I had inflicted on him. I watched it, mesmerized, and thought about our kiss. Don't know why, but I just wanted to sip my champagne and look at him. He stopped talking.

"You're staring again," he said, breaking through my fog.

"Sorry, I think my mind just wandered; it's been a long day."

He seemed unconvinced.

"If you're hungry, there's enough food in the kitchenette to feed a small horde."

"Exactly how large is a horde?"

"About one to two hundred. A small horde is about fifty people."

"And how do you know this?"

"I read a lot."

I stifled a laugh. "Makes sense."

Austin picked up the bottle and topped off my glass.

"I've always been a fan of audiobooks. How do you create a character?"

"Reading background material on the character is a start. But if it's a period piece, I research the history related to that time."

"Yes, but how do you create that uniqueness?"

He sipped his champagne, considering the question. "Experimenting based on the information I have. It's probably close to how you build characters in your novels."

"No, I'm sure there's more."

He placed his glass down on a side table. "Let's try something."

He got up and pulled a chair to the center of the room and motioned me to sit. I sat, watching him rummage in a drawer until he found a large kitchen towel.

"Do you have a problem with blindfolds?"

I glanced at the cloth. It made me uneasy and if I were honest, a little excited as well.

"I want you to experience only sound."

"Okay," curious to see where this would lead.

A rush of tingling anticipation traveled through my body as Austin took his time to fasten the towel snugly over my eyes, blocking out the light. He silently took a few steps away from my chair, not stirring for long moments until I thought he had changed his mind about the demonstration. Then he shifted and took in an intake of air.

"Hey man, what kind of stuff do you want on your burger? You know you gotta make up your mind, dude, there's about a zillion cars behind you waitin' to order."

I laughed at a teenager taking an order at a drive-through. Since I couldn't see, I could swear some high school kid had just wandered into the room.

"Dr. Moore, I do hope you have time to look at my little dog Precious. She has been feeling very poorly today."

"Yes, Lady Winslow, I'd be happy to. She doesn't bite, does she?"

I smiled to hear an English lady and vet discussing her dog. I didn't know Austin's range was so extensive.

I sat there waiting for another example, but Austin remained silent. I thought he was finished with his demonstration. I reached for the blindfold to pull it off.

"You came. You're a beautiful sight for swollen eyes," he said as Cooper.

I froze. We were in the book again. What was he doing? I already told him the voice was right. Why do another scene, and why this one? I thought for a few seconds where this line was located in the story.

This was a pivotal scene between Cooper and Molly. They were finally captured. Molly's unconscious form was taken away, and Cooper was beaten by Armstrong's men and thrown into a cell to wait for a public trial and hanging. Armstrong waited to begin the trial until Molly was strong enough to attend. He hadn't decided if she would hang with Cooper or if he would sell her to pay for the trouble she caused him. Armstrong visited Molly every day during her recovery. He told himself it was to check on his property. She charmed him a little more during each visit until she persuaded him to grant her an unsupervised hour with Cooper. In exchange, she would take her sister's place as his willing bed-warmer.

Austin was waiting for me to respond. He wasn't going to voice Molly, or he would have launched into her part. I think I wanted to know what it was like to have Cooper next to me. I jumped into my part.

"Why wouldn't I?" my voice sultry. *"Armstrong told me he was going to keep me for himself. He believes I had no part in my unfortunate abduction. He*

wants me to take Lily's place. It's the bargain I've struck with him, in exchange for an hour with you."

"Why are you here wasting your time? I should be visiting the hangman in a few hours."

"I still needed to thank you for getting my sister out. I didn't know if there would be another opportunity for me to be grateful."

"You're welcome."

My arm circled her waist, pulling her to me. I looked into those gray eyes that were daring me to do something.

Austin stopped talking. I heard him shift his feet. At this point in the story Cooper kissed Molly.

"Do it," I whispered. "I want you to kiss me," I said as me. But I didn't know if he understood that I was asking, not Molly.

He didn't hesitate and pulled me to my feet. The discarded chair crashed to the floor. His kiss was consuming, and I kissed him back wanting more. *"We don't have much time. Make love to me."* I said it as Molly, but I meant it as me. I was slipping out of character. I wanted the same thing as Molly, but from a different man.

Austin pulled the blindfold away. I blinked as my eyes adjusted to the light. He held the cloth in his hand, looking at it, uncertain.

"What are you saying?" he asked as Austin.

I stepped closer to him, looking up at this serious man, eyes so dark I could lose myself and not find my way back. I didn't plan for this to happen, but my need for him was raw and immediate.

"I want you to make love to me as Austin. This is not Molly speaking; I'm asking."

He looked beyond me. "It's okay if you want Cooper. I can maintain the character. Just close your eyes, and it will be him."

I stood on tip-toes and pulled him to me. "Cooper is a few lines scribbled on paper. He's not real, but you are. I want to make love to you, a man who's muscle, blood, and bone."

He gently pulled my arms from his neck. "I never thought that you would want me after..." He shook his head and reached for my hand. Half pulling me, we stumbled next-door to his bedroom. I was deposited on a blue-gray coverlet that stretched across his overlarge bed. The modern rustic room was cast in a warm glow from the one lamp on his bedside table. Austin considered me with the same expression he wore in my vision, the first time I saw him at the restaurant. Even up close, he looked like a warrior.

Closing his eyes, he took slow, deep breaths. His chest rose and fell as he appeared to calm and center. He re-opened his eyes and directed his attention to me. I moved to the edge of the mattress, wondering why we weren't enjoying his bed.

Instead, he pulled his T-shirt over his head, letting it fall to his side. His chest was broad, smooth skin tight over carved muscle, and his broad shoulders and arms rippled with restrained power. He reached to unbuckle his belt, continuing to hold me in his sight. He stepped out of his jeans, and his boxers followed. He stood in front of me, his chin tilted up in defiance. Feet slightly apart, arms were loose at his sides, ready.

At first, I couldn't understand why he would strip for me, but then I realized he was allowing me to really see him, to know that he was not Cooper. I couldn't believe he was offering himself. I stood and stepped forward. I touched his broad expanse of chest, ending at his flat stomach. I briefly eyed his large, semi-hard cock, then moved to stand in back of him.

My promise not to scream in horror at the sight of his back returned to me as I observed it in the soft light. This time I touched what had repelled me with gentle fingers. But his body stiffened as I traced the disfiguring damage. Unmoving, refusing to relax under my touch, he drew in a sharp breath when I rested my cheek against him. But it was when I placed soft kisses on the parts he thought ugly that a tremor rolled through him. I continued, making each kiss an affirmation, until he calmed.

Stepping in front of him, I kept myself a few feet away. Locking his gaze, I reached for the hem of my shirt, pulling it over my head. The garment dropped to my side. I reached around and released my bra hooks. The rush of coolness brought goosebumps to my arms, but I ignored the sensation. I unbuttoned my jeans, pulling them down with my panties, and stepped away. I held my chin up, daring him to see me.

He touched me with his gaze as it ran the length of my body. He walked behind me, pressing his chest to my back. He hooked his arm around my waist and pulled me in close. I saw our reflection in the mirror. His face was buried in my neck, my right hand stroking his hair.

"I want you, Austin," I said to our reflection.

He swept me into his arms, placing me gently on the bed. He lay on his side next to me.

His hand rested on the curve of my bottom, giving it a light squeeze. "Tell me what you want."

I moaned.

Sliding his hand down my thigh, he found my mound and slipped a finger, parting my slit. "Would you like me to taste you?"

I placed my hand over his and moved it away. "No, tell me what you want."

He hesitated. "I want to watch you. I don't want to take my eyes off you."

I smiled. "Then what?"

"I want you to ride me."

Austin pushed a couple of pillows together to prop himself up. He held out his hand to me and I came to him. I tucked my knees in, fitting myself between his legs. His thick, erect cock was as beautiful as the rest of him. I was about to take him into my mouth to lubricate him when he stopped me.

He caressed my face. "I've touched you. I know you're ready. Climb on me now."

I threw a half-grin at him, then bent and kissed his cock.

He shuddered. "Please. I'm ready."

I straddled him, my knees digging deep into the mattress, my form hovering above his powerful body. He sat bathed in half shadow, pleasure on his sensual face like a king waiting for his concubine to please him.

His gaze followed my hand as it softly drifted to his cock, my fingers caressing then curling around its head. I stroked it, running my hand up its length, his satisfaction dangerously in my control.

I raised up a little on my knees and guided him inside me. Austin's groan was low and guttural as my moist walls met his thick mass, filling me. I leaned forward; my breasts smashed against his hard chest. My forearms near his head, I looked into his eyes as I slowly moved my hips.

"I want to see you. Sit up and lean back, keep your breasts high, and rock me."

I sat up. Austin slipped his strong hands under my bottom. His fingers gripped into my flesh. I used the strength in my thighs and his hands, guiding me to ride.

I rode him, slow and seductive. His half-lidded eyes followed me as our bodies moved together. Each movement of my hips registered on his face as our energy flowed between us. Him inside me was so damn good, but I wanted more. I dropped my palm to brush lightly against my clit. He reached for my hand.

"Let me touch you there. Use my fingers instead."

I caught his palm and guided his warm, callous digit to my sweet spot. I sighed at the touch. The wave of emotions almost too much to endure. The sensation of him inside and his thumb brushing against me sparked the beginnings of my release.

Austin returned his hands under my bottom and urged me off. Slipping next to him, I burrowed in close to his side, watching. Waiting for him to lead me, my body humming with desire. Right now, I'd do anything for him just to have him fill me up again.

He kissed me long and slow. "On your back," he whispered.

I rolled over, and he shifted on top of me. The delicious weight of his big hard body pinned me to the mattress. I opened my legs, and he entered me, filling me with pleasure.

"Wrap your legs around my waist."

His first thrust was deep, and I cried out at the intensity.

He hesitated, his body still, his cock inside me. He kissed me, concern on his face.

"If this is too much--"

"Harder," I urged.

His eyes widened.

"Fuck me harder," came my strangled cry.

He waited for a heartbeat, then another thrust came, almost pushing me into the box spring.

I pushed my hips up, clenching his cock. He groaned. I wanted him to pound me into the mattress, beating down everything inside me until there was nothing left, no world, no room, no bed, just the feel of him bearing down on me.

His hips did a slow grind followed by a solid thrust until he was in his rhythm. We were consumed with satisfying our need, burning up like two super novae as we pushed to get every ounce of pleasure from our lust.

The sound of his hard grunts filled my ears. My release was coming. The smell of his spiced sweat on me made me feel alive and want him even more.

He was changing his pattern. He must be close to his climax too. I was letting go, ready to ride the wave. Austin kept his face close, watching as I moved under him. There it was, the pressure building inside me. He kissed me lightly on the lips.

"I've got you," he whispered. "Come with me."

He ground his hips, pushing me farther into the bed. I gasped. I wanted to wait for him, but I couldn't hold on to it any longer. He would have to catch me. I closed my eyes, breaking our contact. Turning my head to the side, I buried my face in the pillow, inhaling his spice from the cloth.

"Look at me, love." His voice was urgent. "Look at me when you come. I want to see your beautiful face. I'm waiting for you. Come with me now."

His hips did a slow grind. I held onto him as he moved. My nails dug into his broad back. It was there. I couldn't wait. It was taking me.

His heavy body jerked. My body exploded. I screamed. My soul tearing free, in that uncensored moment until I began to drift as my cry cooled to a whimper. Half in my body and half out, waiting to settle. He lay on top of me, snug inside me, our bodies slick. The air, thick and carnal, hung about us.

His forehead touched mine, his mouth set in a self-satisfied smirk about to kiss me. I was holding on to him, my fingers digging into his biceps while tiny tremors ran through me like the aftershocks of an earthquake. I was on overload. Our love making had mixed up too many emotions and I was paying the price.

He pulled back. "What's wrong? You're shaking, are you cold?"

My head bobbed, embarrassed by my reaction. He rubbed his warm hands down my arms a few times, his worried face assessing me. He moved off me, settling us at the headboard. Finding a tangled sheet, he pulled it up to cover us. Austin was careful to shift me in front of him, my back resting against his chest, his arms around me. "Take long breaths, concentrate on your breathing."

I nodded, knocking my head against his chest. "I'm fine, just give me a minute." I drew in a breath, the way I learned in my grief group.

"Can I get you something?" he reached for the coverlet.

I held out my hand to stop him. "I'm good, don't fuss, just talk to me."

He leaned back, silent, rubbing my arm. Maybe he thought quiet would be better?

"I need you to talk. It's really not as bad as it looks. I haven't had an anxiety attack for a long time. I thought I was past them. This one snuck up on me." I smiled, "Look, I'm good. We can talk about anything. Tell me about your dirty biking. I mean...never mind, let's talk about whatever you want."

"I'm trying to work out what happened. Did I do something that scared you?" I tried to squirm around to look back at him, but he held me in place. "Maybe, I pushed you too hard?" he said.

I was out of practice. My body blowing up after keeping my emotions in check after all these years wasn't his fault. I took another long breath and felt better. "Assuming will only get you into trouble," I said redirecting the discussion. He was being sweet, but overprotective. "I know what I wanted. I asked you to make love to me." Funny, If I had exploded in bed with him inside me, it would still have been worth it.

He gave me a squeeze. His lips grazed my hair. "I'll take you at your word. But I don't care what you say. If I think I'm hurting you, I'm stopping."

My little freak-out was done. I twisted around to kiss him, his arms around me. I pulled away to rest my head on his chest. "That's better," I signed, "I'm not done with you yet," I said.

"You need to be sure. I can't hold back if you want to continue. We can stay like this if that's what you want."

I slipped my hand down, finding his cock and squeezed, giving him my answer.

He blew out a breath. "If I have too, then let's see what else I can do to you."

Still dark, it had to be well after midnight. Reluctantly, I slipped out of bed. For a few moments I watched him sleep the sleep of angels. I was so wicked, I wanted to wake him up again just to have his body on top of me and his cock bearing down on me again.

I stepped outside the room to retrieve my bag from the studio, collected my clothes from where I discarded them, and headed into the master bathroom. The blue and gray tiled space was neat except for a bath towel, toiletries and a cell sitting on the far side of the double sink. I placed my things on a chair and turned on the shower.

I'd run a marathon with Austin chasing me. I hoped the hot water from a steamy shower would restore my aching body.

I dried off and put my clothes back on. I needed to leave and be in my own space to think. What we did changed everything. In some ways it made things clearer, in others more complicated.

I raked my fingers through my wet hair when a flash of light and buzzing caught my attention. I glanced at the opposite side of the double sink and saw Austin's phone coming to life. I was curious and picked it up. I focused on the message.

"Was it worth it? Everything you did to get Molly Dixon in your bed?" It was signed G.

I sat down hard on the closed toilet seat and reread the message. No, I shook my head. That couldn't be what this was about, was it? Who was G?

My mind began flipping through memories. My first meeting with Austin at the Waterline, he thought I was Bex. At our lunch at his house, he thought I liked sushi and beer; that was Molly's thing. The day he spent driving me around, he talked about her like a wistful lover. At the duck pond, he said I was Molly.

He didn't want me, he wanted her. He never once called me Emma. He probably would have loved it if I'd stayed in my Molly character while he fucked me senseless. I put the cell back on the sink counter.

"Shit, shit, shit," I mumbled under my breath. I unzipped my purse and found my lipstick. I scrambled onto the sink counter, kneeling to be level with the mirror that took up most of the wall. My shade of lipstick was deep pink. In gigantic letters that took up every square inch of mirror space I scrawled in shaky, serial-killer letters, 'I'm not Molly Dixon.' I slipped off the counter, grabbed my purse, his cell, and yanked open the door. Austin was standing just outside in all his naked splendor. I tossed him the cell and pushed past him, running down the stairs. I found my key fob on the move and hit the button for the car to open. I slipped inside, threw the car into reverse, backed out to the street, shifted into drive, and floored it like a crazy, determined brunette.

When I returned home, after that fiasco with Austin, my phone rang non-stop. I finally had to turn it off. I was in such a foul mood; my poor Daisy hid from me until I apologized and gave her a treat. I angrily went to bed and shut out the world.

CHAPTER 16

A Walk in San Francisco

*G*roggy from too little sleep when the gray dawn arrived, I moved through the morning in a fog. My appointment with Bex was today. I decided to drive to San Francisco for the final discussion about the MN. It would have been easier to do it over the phone, but I was still raw from last night. I needed time to sort out my feelings. The bustle of the city would be what I needed.

I sat in her office, still agonizing over the choice while Bex's impatience was growing thin. Austin's demo was much better than Kaulder's, but I couldn't leave it as a cold business decision.

Austin broke one of my cardinal rules. How could he think I was Molly Dixon? If I had to listen to Cooper's voice, knowing it was Austin narrating, I'd never leave that night behind. That sullen, talented man affected me, made me want him, then took a mallet and smashed my heart.

I picked up my tea from her desk. Luke and I decided we should find a fresh voice for Cooper, but he wasn't here, and it was my decision.

"Emma Antonia Benton Cameron!"

I looked up at the mention of my full name. Bex placed her hand on the phone.

"Why do I have to decide now? Can't I put this off? I'm sure a few more months won't make a difference."

"No, this is already in motion. I don't see why it's a hard decision, you've had more than enough time."

"True, but…"

"I can tell them we've moved the deadline. Maybe they'll wait for your decision a few more days. But if you want this project to be finished in time for the Passion Moon event, we've got to start recording no later than next Monday."

"Fine, I'll go with William Kaulder."

Bex raised an eyebrow. "I thought you liked Austin?"

I shifted in my seat. "I think if Kaulder's voice and reputation are attached to the project, it will take the series to new readers."

Bex watched me, elbow on her desk, her face resting against the back of her hand giving me a *I don't really believe you, but I'm going to nod like I do anyway* look.

"We've talked about attracting new readers, right?"

"Okay, I'll text his manager and give her the good news. She pulled out her cell, gave a few quick taps, and it was done. "I'll call Austin unless you want to tell him?"

I felt my lips pull back into a grimace. Bex's eyes widened. "Noo-problem," she said, stretching the words out. "I'll make the call." She looked like she was going to ask why, but thought better of it.

"Any progress on finding a studio?"

"Yes, but it's in Canada. You know, rugged-looking men, very polite."

"When did you start defining a place by its men?"

She smiled. "It's a new hobby. Anyway, that's the closest location I could find on short notice that was approaching a reasonable rate. The problem is that you'll need to hire a Canadian crew if you want to stay within budget."

I really did grimace this time. "What happened to the Eureka studio?"

Bex shrugged. "They backed out a few days ago," she said and swiveled her chair enough to see outside. The sun was trying to make an appearance. It was warmer than it looked for a gray day. "I've got an idea. Why don't we take a walk? The city is decorated for the holidays, and it's almost lunchtime. We can head down to the Ferry Building for a bite and on the way; we can flirt with the guys in suits or tight jeans hanging out in Justin Herman plaza. Your choice."

The cool breeze off the sea was in our faces as we trudged down the hill. I regretted not changing my heels for tennis shoes two blocks away from the office. My ankles were going to take a beating on this short jaunt. I didn't mind the chill as we walked among the crowd of sightseers. The office workers from the nearby buildings were trying to catch what passed for sun today. My stomach was doing a slow rumble, reacting to the smell of food in the air.

"I hope you don't mind me saying this, but you look frayed around the edges," Bex said, sidestepping a tourist that was looking more than walking.

I sighed. "I had difficulty sleeping last night. And there was the decision on a narrator, and the studio, anyway--"

"You know you can't con me. I've known you too long."

That was true. She knew me before I started writing.

"Not that I'm shutting you out, but I'd rather not talk about it, at least until I can process."

"Fair enough, I just want to point out that I have an excellent ear and anything except for bloody mayhem, nothing shocks me."

I laughed.

We were about a block away from the plaza passing a group of artist tents when something caught my eye in a jewelry stall. A woman was working in the back of the booth. She stopped, raised her head, and nodded. I took a step to the counter, and the heat from the desktop heater singed me.

The woman was in her early twenties, a throwback to the hippies on Haight-Ashbury. Her black hair streamed to her waist, competing with the billowing turquoise kaftan. An embroidered pattern of gold and dark blue threads swirled down the front of the garment. Her exposed arms and hands laced with bangles and rings jingled as she moved. I caught a whiff of patchouli as she came near.

She smiled a greeting. "May I help you?"

I smiled back. "Yes, your jewelry is beautiful."

"Thank you."

I pointed to a necklace in the case. "It's this piece I'm interested in."

She removed the long chain, placing it on a swatch of fabric on top of the display case. Three charms of the moon's phases rested at the base of the necklace. Bex came to stand next to me, squinting at the piece. "Sterling silver?" she asked.

"Yes, I am a silver and goldsmith." She looked at me. "Are you attracted to these charms because they caught your fancy or is the moon your personal symbol?"

It hadn't occurred to me before, but I did use the word moon in many of my book titles and even used it as part of passwords. Somehow, I felt a pull to this piece.

"Probably both."

Bex angled her head toward me. "I never knew that. You'd better keep that to yourself or else you'll get a slew of moon-related gifts from fans and friends." She shuddered. "Birthdays and Christmas would be a moon nightmare. Although, nightmare moon could be a good book title?"

"The moon is a good choice," offered the silversmith. "It is a woman's symbol full of strength and mystery. Charms are containers of personal power. You draw on their strength when touched. They are charged when you keep them close to your body. It is common to add other symbols of your life to balance the moon. Is there something else that is important to you? Perhaps a career or hobbies? I have other charms. She pushed the fabric aside."

"She's a writer."

"I have a typewriter, a pen, or a book?"

My gaze ran down the row of perfectly crafted metal. "Can I see that one? The last one in the last row."

She placed it on the cloth. I scooped it up, holding it by my fingertips. I had seen this symbol as part of a pattern among tribal tattoos on a right shoulder.

"Is that a phoenix?"

I nodded at Bex.

This must be Austin's personal totem. It would fit. Recovering from his injuries must have been like rising from the ashes.

"The Firebird would be a nice counterbalance to your moon. The heat of fire tempered by the cool moon. Would that represent someone significant in your life?" the woman asked.

Bex extended her hand for the charm. She held it up and studied it for a few seconds. "You know Austin has a phoenix on his arm."

I shrugged. "Does he?"

Bex peered at me. "It's kind of hard not to miss anything on those massive biceps."

"Oh, I hadn't noticed," I mumbled.

"Ah-huh," she said and placed the charm back on the cloth.

"If you buy the chain and four charms, I will give the firebird to you for free. Maybe there is another symbol that represents? You mentioned Austin?"

I cringed.

"Do you have a microphone or a Samson?" asked Bex.

"Samson?" I said.

"You know Samson and Delilah. Austin is like Samson, big, brawny with that black hair falling past his shoulders." She took in a shaky breath.

The silversmith and I both stared at her.

Bex looked down. Her already pink cheeks were blazing red. "Sorry."

"I do not have a Samson," the woman said, pulling her bemused gaze away from Bex, "but I can design a medallion piece showing this man's likeness. I would just need to see a photo."

"No, the necklace with the moons will be fine." I rummaged through my bag for my wallet. The silversmith pulled out natural tissue paper and a small brown bag. I was leaning over the counter. I opened my wallet, and a small, folded square of paper fell out onto the cloth. I placed the wallet back in my purse and opened the note.

Em,

I'm sitting at the foot of the bed writing to you. The same bed where I enjoyed you moments ago, my beautiful Emma. I'm watching you sleep and waiting for the car to arrive. But all I can think of as I gaze on your perfection is the feel of your silky chestnut hair, the scent of your skin, and the honey taste of your lips. And I have to stop myself from taking you again. What will I do? I haven't left, but I already miss you. Love, Parker

My heart dropped.

"Miss?"

I looked up into the silversmith's warm brown eyes, brows drawn together, questioning.

The woman had completed packing the jewelry. She had set the bag to one side on the counter. "Your Austin sounds like such a wonderful man; I have placed the phoenix charm in the bag. No charge."

I stared at the bag.

I shook my head. "I'm so sorry. I apologize. I've wasted your time. I've changed my mind." I turned and brushed past a stunned Bex and headed down the hill.

"Emma!" called Bex, her voice growing faint, drowned out by the noise of the crowd. "Wait."

I was just inside the entrance of the Ferry Building when Bex caught up with me.

She was panting from her brisk walk. "What's going on? Are you alright?"

"I'm fine. I just had a scare. No, that's not the right word, an unpleasant reminder."

She studied me. "Let's go have lunch, and you can tell me what has you so spooked."

After the waiter placed our entrees on the table, I told Bex the whole story.

"I had no idea. I thought Parker was just visiting."

I slipped her the note. She sighed dreamily, then frowned. "Getting this out of the blue, after a night with Austin. Are you sure there's no second chance with him? Austin, I mean, not Parker?"

I pushed the salmon around the plate with my fork. "He broke my rule. The man didn't want me. He wants that sexy, thrill-seeking Molly. Anyway, it was over before it began."

"Are you sure? It can't be as bad as those fans that wrote to you thinking you were Molly?"

"I thought they were sweet and confused until that one sent me a ring and marriage proposal and stalked me for months."

"I know some of those messages were pretty suggestive."

"No, some of them were pornographic. It still freaks me out when someone confuses me with my character. Anyone that thinks I'm bigger than life sexy Molly Dixon will be sorely disappointed."

"What are you going to do about Parker? He's going to expect to continue where the two of you left off. Will you tell him about Austin?"

My glance wandered to the bar where a couple, sitting close, seemed only to have eyes for each other. Why couldn't life be as simple as that? Why were there always complications when it came to, well, anything?

"I guess the question is who do you want? If you want to try with Parker, this is the real world. You don't need to tell him anything that will hurt him. Especially if it is truly over with Austin."

Since these men had come into my life, I was beginning to think I might have another shot at happiness. After last night, I thought that happiness was Austin. I wanted to believe that the message I saw on his phone wasn't true, that it was a mistake. Then I'd remember the phone demos and everything else that happened. At least Parker knows it's me he wants, but for me it wasn't that simple.

I looked over at the couple, then back at Bex. "I still don't know how I feel about Parker. This all happened too quickly. I haven't had enough time. I do know it's over with Austin. But when the silversmith gave me the phoenix charm as a gift, it freaked me out."

"Then what I'm about to tell you makes sense now. Austin's manager contacted me just before you arrived. He's offering the use of his studio. At the time I didn't think anything of it because you'd been leaning toward using him since he talked to you after that lunch fiasco.

"But this was the strange part, at least for me at the time. Austin said this was the least he could do. He's offering the studio for below market. He will also work around our crew's schedule."

I sat back.

"Right now, it's your best option. Handling the production is my job, so you wouldn't need to be there." She gave a self-satisfied smile, then crunched on an asparagus spear.

"Okay, but I want to meet Kaulder at the studio."

Bex began coughing. She grabbed her water and gulped a few mouthfuls. "Why?" she croaked.

"Because it would be rude not to. It just occurred to me that the first session will be next week if you haven't changed the tentative schedule."

She shook her head no.

"I'd like to come to that first session to meet him and say hello to Jay and his crew."

"Are you sure? What about your rules about actors and celebrities?"

"I'm willing to take a chance and meet Kaulder anyway. You know, professional courtesy; it's the least I could do."

She gave me a 'yeah, right' look.

I glared at her. "It's strictly professional. Besides, you know Jay is a time-is-money director. I can meet Kaulder quickly, give a quick pep talk to the crew, and be out of there in 15-20 minutes. I'll even bring donuts."

"What about Austin? It's his house."

I waved a fork at her. "It's your job to make sure he's nowhere around." I smiled.

"Gee, thanks."

CHAPTER 17

Jay and the Boys

Life was getting back to a new normal, or what I liked to refer to as LBPA, or Life Before Parker and Austin. I was using the time before Parker's return to try things I wouldn't have attempted a few months ago.

Luke had been an intricate part of my business. He was a constant sounding board for story ideas. But I'd been thinking about the new characters I pinned to my inspiration board. They were occupying more of my thoughts lately as ideas for scenes vied for my attention. I had to open a new section in my writing program for the new romance.

It was surprising that in the middle of writing a scene for the new story, *Dissected Love*, I decided to put aside the next book in the Cooper series to pursue the new project. It seemed like a giant slap in the face to Luke's legacy. The books had been outlined for quite some time; I just needed to write the novels. It was clear, while I worked on *Dissected Love*, that I needed to step away from an action romantic fantasy and work on something that was entirely my creation. It's not that I had fallen out of love with my series; I just needed a break.

When I drove onto the driveway of Austin's home, his enormous black truck was not in sight. I had called Bex on her cell a mile from the house to make sure he was nowhere around and that Kaulder and the crew were waiting.

After switching off the engine, I just stared at the house. It seemed like years had been packed into only a space of a few days. Maybe now the whirlwind would dissipate long enough for me to catch my breath before Parker's return. People were right when they said everything can change in a New York minute, only this was Monte Sereno.

"Hey, everyone, look sharp, boss lady is here," Jay called. I entered the house balancing a pink box filled with hot donuts to enthusiastic cheers and whoops. They crowded around me like I was the teacher on the first day of kindergarten. Someone relieved me of my burden, and I was free to greet the crew properly.

I'd worked with this all-male crew since my first book. Usually, Nancy Mueller, the narrator for the Molly Dixon series, worked with them. She didn't seem to mind being one of the boys, although I heard they treated her like a princess.

I knew their wives, children, and current girlfriends. I hugged everyone and then noticed Kaulder sitting Zen-like in the corner with his marked-up copy of the book next to him. He raised a glass of orange juice to me. I began to stroll over to him when Bex quickly stepped in front of me at the last minute.

"William Kaulder," Bex said with formality, "I would like you to meet Emma Benson, also known as Angela Stryker. Bex used my birth name for the few people who knew me as a writer.

He stood and gave me a slight bow. I extended my hand, and instead of shaking it, he raised it to his lips and bestowed a whisper of a kiss.

I smiled. "Nice to meet you."

His picture didn't do him justice. He was tall, dark, with roguish eyes that held your gaze. If I wasn't careful, I'd be following him home. He probably used all that charisma to create the mesmerizing characters that he made famous.

He elegantly swept his hand toward a seat. I was about to obediently move toward it when Bex tugged at my elbow.

"Remember, you don't have much time. You're on a tight schedule today," she said, keeping her back to him and screwing up her face as she spoke.

"I apologize. Bex is right; I do have another appointment."

"Lunch, perhaps--"

"Please excuse us, Emma needs to say a few words to the crew before she leaves." He looked taken aback but recovered quickly, resuming his charming manner. I admit I was surprised too. But this was planned as a brief encounter and nothing else.

Bex pushed me toward the corner. "I don't know how long you have until Austin returns."

Ice surged through my blood. I shot a glance at the door. "What? You've got to be kidding."

She leaned in to me. "I explained the situation to his manager, well, an edited version. But the only way I was able to get him out of here was to convince his manager to keep him away. She didn't tell him you were here; I'm afraid if he finds out he will come back to see you. The manager said that Austin mentioned to her that something had happened between the two of you, but he wouldn't give any details. Apparently, he's been trying to find a way to talk to you, short of stalking you."

"Then I should leave now?"

She pulled out her cell. "She'll call the minute they finish their meeting. Even if she calls as they are leaving, you still have another twenty minutes before he gets here. Talk to the crew. They're happy to see you, but Jay's already hinting we're burning up too much daylight."

I gave a half-smile to Kaulder, who returned a nod. I walked back toward the men, who were lounging in the reception pit a few feet from the studio.

Even addressing a few people was uncomfortable for me. I shifted my feet nervously while I looked at these supportive, grinning faces.

"Look sharp, men, our leader is about to speak," Jay said.

They chortled.

I grinned. I liked these guys.

Deciding to give some weight to the occasion, I stood straighter, lacing my hands behind my back as if I were Patton addressing the troops. "We embark today on a new project with a new talent. We are very fortunate that William Kaulder has consented to be the voice of Cooper Flynn." The crew clapped and hollered. Kaulder just raised his glass to acknowledge them. "Mr. Kaulder…" I continued.

"Call me Will."

I turned to see Kaulder taking a sip of his drink, his eyes sparkling with mischief. "Ah, yes, Will," distracted, then pulled my gaze back to the men. "You've all done some incredible work in the past. It's because of your totally awe-some skills (laughter), but more importantly, to your pursuit of quality that has made the Molly Dixon series successful. I have no doubt that you will make magic again with Cooper Flynn. If you need anything to support you on this creative journey, we…" I indicated Bex with a sweep of my hand, "would be happy--"

"Donuts every day would be great," the youngest crew member shouted.

"Whiskey, even better," someone near Jay offered. They shouted their agreement.

"Preferably non-alcohol would be more appropriate…" I grinned. "Just let us know."

The car eased down the endless driveway, then I turned onto a private road shared by the neighbors heading toward the highway. The properties on this stretch sat far back from the street. There were no fences. The homes were hidden by a thicket of trees, giving the effect of driving through a lush grove. My mood was lightening with each turn of my tires. I switched on the radio, feeling I had just dodged a bullet.

Some distance away, I spied a gray over-priced sedan barreling toward me in the opposite lane. It couldn't be that crazy blond that practically ran me off the road the last time I was here; that witch drove an SUV. But the driving style was the same. Oh Lord, maybe it was her in a different car. The vehicle was about five car lengths in front of me, closing the distance. I slowed down to prepare to pull off to the shoulder if the driver became erratic.

The screech of the sedan's wheels gave me a jolt. The gray vehicle made a hard left, fishtailing into a full arc in front of me. The car came to a stop some distance away, blocking my side of the road and part of the oncoming portion. There wasn't enough room to get around the stalled car even if I used the shoulder.

Instinctively I hit the door locks although that was automatically engaged a few minutes after my car was in motion. I plunged my hand into my purse and fished out my cell. I punched in nine before I saw him emerge from the sedan. He stood next to his vehicle for a moment, looking at me. "I don't freaking believe this," and hit the next button too hard. The phone flipped from my hand and bounced off the passenger seat onto the floor. He made a quick check for cars, then headed toward me. I released my seatbelt and made a dive for my phone. My fingers managed to brush the phone case, but it was just outside my reach.

A big hand rapped on the driver window.

"Emma..." tap, tap, tap.

I looked up, still prone across the seat. "Go away, Austin."

"Have you come to see me?" his voice sounded muffled through the glass.

"No!" Like it was the last thing I would ever do on this planet. I was irritated at his stupid antics.

He arched that damned eyebrow. "Then why are you here?"

He didn't give me enough time to reply. Instead, he threw his gaze down the road toward his house. "Has something happened?"

I understood the concern for his family as he looked down the street. His sister's home was only a few minutes' walk from his house. They were close, and he adored his niece Izzy. But that wouldn't explain why I was here. There wasn't a plausible lie I could tell, not while I was on a private road less than a mile from his house.

"I came to meet Kaulder and wish the audio crew luck at their first session." I had pushed myself upright and was now almost nose to nose with him, only there was a window between us. He looked tired. Good, I thought.

"Please lower the window; I'm not going to hurt you."

"Then why did you use your car as a roadblock?"

"I thought it was you. I figured it was easier to do that than to follow you and chase you down."

I frowned at his car.

"Come on. Unless you want to jog to the main road, you're not going anywhere."

The window moved down painfully slow, letting in a blast of cool air with the scent of his spice and a memory of me in his arms after we made love. "How are you?" he asked, the concern sounding genuine in his voice.

I pushed the memory away. If I'd let it run to its conclusion, I'd ram his car. "I'm fine." I continued to stare ahead.

"I've tried to call, email, text. You haven't answered."

"The message I left on your bathroom mirror was your answer."

"Can't you even look at me? I've missed you."

The pleading in his voice compelled me to turn toward him. His eyes were soulful. This was the same face he used when he came to my house to apologize for leaving me abruptly at our first lunch meeting.

"Emma, you've got to talk to me..."

My fairness gauge reluctantly kicked in. I'd made a judgment without giving him a chance to explain. The awful experience with my overzealous fan clouded my reason. I threw my hands up with equal parts frustration and resignation. "Fine. Then tell me the truth. Did you pursue the Cooper project because you thought I was Molly?"

Something unreadable skittered across his face. The muscles around his jaw tightened while a monumental battle raged behind his eyes. He was struggling to find the words, but all I wanted was a yes or no. That would tell me if my gut was right.

He leaned into the door. "Yes, that was the reason at first, but not now--"

Cradling the steering wheel, I touched my forehead to the smooth surface. I really wanted to bang my head bloody. Screw honesty; it didn't set you free, it hurt like hell. Didn't he know he meant something to me? It happened with each contact, until I wanted to be with him, asked to be with him. "When was this?" pressing harder for the truth. "When was this epiphany? While you had me on my back screwing me? Is that when you realized I couldn't possibly be her?"

"No," he shook his head. "It happened before that night. It was at the duck pond when everything changed."

"I don't believe you," I shot back, angry that his face was growing blurry, moisture threatening to escape from my eyes. I wasn't going to cry again in front of him. I looked away. "At least get the lie straight. That's where you told me I was Molly. It had to be later. Damn it, I saw the text after we were together... Was I an open secret with your buddies? Had you been bragging how you were going to get me to your bed?"

"When I said you were Molly, I meant that. But when you were--"

I stopped listening to him. I wanted to rage at him for the lie. Wasn't he supposed to be the misunderstood hero of my personal story, who just needed some understanding? No, I had gotten it wrong; he was really another stalker who wanted Molly to be his very own sex toy.

A horn blazed in the distance. As if it was a call to arms, the noise was joined by a cacophony of unrelenting blasts. Our attention snapped to the sedan.

"Hey, Austin. What the hell are you doing?" shouted a dark-suited man halfway out of a limo window. There were about eight cars queued up in back of the gray sedan, with more arriving behind them. It appeared that every neighbor was out here waiting to drive the private road to their homes. The way the line was forming, it wouldn't take long before the trail of cars extended back to the city street. Was anyone in those mansions I just past, or were they all out here giving Austin a hard time? The drivers continued to lean on their horns and added shouted obscenities, some in other languages.

Go around!" he yelled back, waving at them to drive around his car.

"Excuse me," the man shouted back, "but there's no room to get around. Come on, move the car. You can talk to your lady friend later."

The man looked like he might come over to discuss the point. Austin seemed uninterested, continuing to focus his attention on me. "Give me a minute," he yelled over his shoulder, "This is important."

"Don't worry, we're done," I said watching the cars. "You should probably..."

He interrupted me with a fierce expression. "No, I'm not letting you go again. Not until I've finished answering your question."

"Austin... You can't--"

"Look, I narrate books for a living, I don't write them. I'm not good at flowery speeches. I wish I was, then I could make you understand how I feel about you." He paused, shifting to settle an elbow at the window, trying to press closer. "You asked me to tell you when I realized you weren't Molly. It was at the duck pond. Not at the beginning, but when you surprised me with an un-Molly reaction and showed public emotion. When you were helpless with regret, crying for your husband, letting me see your deep sadness. I realized you weren't the perfect, fearless heroine I'd been desperate to meet. It was in that moment that I realized I wanted to protect you, to keep you safe, not Molly."

I slipped my gaze to our quiet, fascinated audience. My bet was that they wouldn't stay like that for long. "You're saying one gesture changed your mind?" Irritated, that this conversation was too public to allow me to think clearly.

"You're all I think about," he said, his confession thick in his throat. "I've never told anyone, but I read from the Molly series nearly every day. Before you think it's weird, it's no different from reading poetry or listening to songs that you have a connection with. Those words on paper were my touchstone. I felt a connection with Molly through your books. I'd see her face, or at least the model that's on your covers, and I'd feel I could breathe again. But after the duck pond it changed, and her face doesn't haunt me any longer. It's your pissed-off face I see--"

A horn blast brought us back to our surroundings. Austin swore an oath to himself, then threw an imperious wave at the impatient horde, his irritation growing as he watched them. "Molly..." he began. Another short beep sailed out in protest, this time from a driver further down the line. "Don't move. I want to continue this conversation," he said with a distinct note of do-what-I-say-woman.

Ignoring his audience, he made an easy jog to the car. They were enjoying this outing because the horns started up again even when they saw him enter the sedan.

Austin deliberately adjusted his rear-view mirror, then raked his fingers through his dark locks, which sent them into a new frenzy. I sat back, my arms folded, watching his obvious power play. He threw a glance at me before he put his car in gear to reinforce his earlier instructions, mouthing 'wait for me.' I had to look down so he wouldn't see my face.

Finally, he pulled his vehicle to the opposite side of the road. I turned the key in the ignition and put the car in drive. He scrambled out of his car, shouting across the road to me as the cars roared past, drowning out his plea to come to the house to talk. I placed my foot on the gas pedal and sped away. It almost worked. He nearly had me believing his feelings were real. He hadn't realized he'd called me Molly, but I did. Austin's reflection was watching me. He was imitating a pissed-off statue in my rear-view mirror.

CHAPTER 18

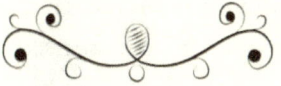

Trespasses

Parker's one week away was turning into two. Eos was making sure he'd work all his remaining hours in the sky. I was happy for the reprieve. It gave me time to prepare for his return. Then there was Austin to consider, who'd been successful at bringing my attention back to him just when I thought I was moving on. That meeting on the road was a reminder that I was still attracted to him, but there needs to be more than mind-blowing sex to make it work. I'd decided not to tell Parker about my night with Austin. We hired Kaulder to narrate the Cooper series. There would be no more contact with Austin.

I was rinsing a cup in the sink when I noticed Magda walking up my path, struggling with a big brown package. The phone rang. I wiped my hands on a dish towel and picked up the cell from the counter; it was Bex.

"Let me guess… you're calling to warn me Magda will be dropping by," I said, a bit annoyed.

"That's right. How--? Never mind. Magda was visiting me and said she was thinking of dropping by your house today."

"I didn't know you knew her?"

"For a while now. We happen to be in the same book club. I told you about them."

"I don't remember--"

"I thought it was a good opportunity to send you the Cooper series book cover art. I know you like to hang them in your office. She's saving me a trip. Don't thank me. Bye, bye."

I swung the door open to a surprised Magda. Her finger was already hovering inches away from the doorbell. She gave me a shy half-grin that echoed her brother's smile.

"I wasn't sure if you would be available this time of day. I hope I haven't disturbed your writing time."

"Don't tell anyone, but I'm taking a break. I was just about to have tea. Would you like to join me?"

She looked uncertain standing in the middle of my kitchen. No doubt Austin had sent her as an envoy, something she probably did out of love for her younger brother. I wondered how much of our unfortunate drama he had revealed to her.

"Please sit while I make the tea."

We engaged in light banter about her daughter Izzy while I banged cabinets and filled my electric red kettle. She was asking my opinion on the serious matter of play dates when I set a steaming cup in front of her.

"Thank you for the tea."

"I'm just guessing, but I don't think you came all this way to ask my advice about Izzy or to do Bex's deliveries. Thank you, by the way, for the posters," I said taking a seat.

"I was happy to do the delivery and to have the chance to see you again."

I doused my tea with cream. "What advice could a woman with no children have to offer?"

"Ah, now you would be surprised. Someone without children can give another perspective. I think you have good instincts, and doesn't everyone have an opinion? Do you like children?"

She was falling back into her not-too-subtle interrogation mode. It was unclear why. I thought she had extracted what she needed the afternoon we all met for lunch.

"I like them fine."

Her gaze traveled around the kitchen. "I like these mid-century Eichler homes. You've done some remodeling?"

"We did an extensive remodel when we bought the house." I took a sip. "I'll give you a tour if you like, but I'm curious, are you here to plead your brother's case?"

She set her cup down. "I'm enjoying the warmth of your cozy kitchen. Maybe we can tour the house later. As to pleading Austin's case, he is the only one that can do that."

I sat back and crossed my arms.

"Let me first say that my brother is very sorry about the impression you were given at your last meeting. Of course, his actions are up to him to explain. I'm fuzzy on the details of why he should make that assumption, but I have my suspicions. I did want to see you again. I enjoyed getting to know you at our lunch."

I looked down at my cup.

"Did he tell you about his fall from a scaffold and the surgeries?"

"I know about the injury, but not much else."

"Some men don't like to go into detail about such things. Austin is no different. He is very private. I'm an attorney. I have this need to lay out the facts."

"Wouldn't Austin be upset if you shared this information?"

She waved a hand. Again, a gesture that was reminiscent of her brother. "The newspapers reported much of this at the time of the accident. You know, the son of a prominent Silicon Valley architect injured on a company construction site. It was news for a few days until the president made a trip somewhere."

I smiled. I couldn't help it. I liked Magda and her straightforward-Mother-Earth vibe.

"I think it's important for you to know what happened after the accident. Perspective is important, don't you think?

I don't think it mattered what I thought. She'd already decided. "Yes, perspective would be helpful."

She gave a slight nod. "Austin did sustain trauma to the body, but during the fall he also suffered a head injury. He was diagnosed with a mild head trauma."

I didn't know that bit of information. I was too aware of the scarring on his back, but I never guessed there might be deeper problems he was battling. With the brain, it could be anything from motor skills to mental issues.

"A head injury, even a mild one, can impact personality. In my brother's case, significant parts of his temperament and nature changed."

"Are you sure you want to discuss this? I've only met Austin a handful of times, and since we've chosen William Kaulder to narrate the Cooper Flynn series, we won't have any more contact."

Magda sat back in her seat and studied me. "You forget I saw the two of you together. He is very interested in you, and I saw the way you looked when Parker escorted you from the duck pond. Austin was excited to meet you when he heard about the Cooper project; his interest grew after he met you."

I traced the rim of my cup. His excitement was limited to meeting who he thought was Molly.

"Please, Emma. I would feel better if you at least understood. I'd like to continue?"

She probably wouldn't leave until I heard the entire story. I nodded my agreement.

"About the head injury, it was a while before we realized something had changed. He tried to hide it from us at first, out of fear, or possibly he thought it would pass, but we eventually noticed. He was quick to anger, sullen at times, unsure. It was a considerable change from the Austin we knew. This concerned all of us, but especially my father."

It explained a lot about his behavior when we first met and the later encounters, but his personality was not the reason for my anger.

"He has been working on his recovery and is much better with his emotions. His response to a situation may be a little off, or even when he displays feelings. He tends to close down when processing information. With all this, it hasn't affected his intellect. Austin is an architect, but he chose to work construction. He likes the physical work of building more than designing."

I liked Magda, but I could see where this conversation was leading. "I have orange cranberry scones," I offered. "They go well with tea."

"Thank you, no, just the tea is fine." She picked up the thread of her story after a few seconds. "Going back to the impact on our family. It is important for you to understand that we are very close. My brother and I are first-generation Italian-Americans.

Austin is the only son, and he has been raised traditionally, groomed to take his place as the next head of the family.

Before his injury, he embraced these traditions and his place. But after the accident, he was not interested. My father believes that it is his duty to prepare whoever assumes the reigns from him. You see, the next head of the family will also manage the business."

My ears pricked up. "What do you mean by whoever? You're the oldest. Shouldn't you be groomed to take over?"

Magda shook her head. "My father, Marcus Santoro, is a traditionalist. He can be unconventional in some things. Well, as much as a man from his generation and background can achieve.

Adam Morel, my cousin, would be the next choice. He is the son of my father's sister, Juliet. We grew up together.

To finish this part of the story, it's important to know what occurred between my father and Austin. Long after the damage to my brother's body had healed, he continued to work on the effects of the head trauma. My father, seeing that his son was physically improved, tried to return Austin to his old life. It was a struggle, but eventually, Austin left the family to make his own life."

I looked down at my empty cup. "Would you like more tea?"

"Yes, thank you."

I moved to the counter and removed the kettle from its place. The time helped me to absorb the story, but of course, there would be more. I brought the kettle under the tap. "Please continue talking." She waited while I returned it to the base and flipped the switch. I leaned against the counter, waiting for the water to boil.

Magda watched me with narrowed eyes, trying to gauge what impact her story was having on me, but I was keeping my reactions to a polite minimum. "You said Austin was different. Did he change completely?"

She pushed a length of hair behind her ear, considering. "Not everything about the old Austin was lost. He still needed to be continuously engaged in some activity. Reading, jogging, it didn't matter. I know it was difficult for him facing days with limited mobility, but during his recovery, I gave him the Molly Dixon books in audio. It helped him. He became obsessed with the stories and fascinated by Molly. The series inspired him to become a professional narrator.

"When he discovered you were searching for someone to voice the Cooper series, he wanted very badly to do the project.

She paused and sat back. Her fingers twisting her wedding ring in a surprising display of nerves. "Austin wants to know if you'll meet with him? Of course, it is up to you where and when a meeting would take place."

This was the real reason for her visit. I'd already guessed as much. I had begun to feel something for Austin and I thought he felt the same. Magda had come all this way to help her brother, but her efforts wouldn't change my mind. "No, I'm sorry." Maybe this would finally put an end to this episode. "Please tell him I'm not interested."

Magda hesitated for a few moments, searching my face. She wanted to convince me to change my mind, and I thought she might try one last time. But when she rose, I knew she was done.

"I'm sad that you will not speak with him. What happened must have hurt you too deeply to consider forgiveness. Still, some of us wish we'd made a similar decision earlier in our own relationships. I admire you. You are a woman who knows her heart and how to protect it."

I pushed away from the counter. "Thank you for your visit, and I'm truly sorry that Austin struggled with his recovery. But I think my decision not to see him again is best for everyone."

"I will give him your answer. But I will leave you with this. On a professional level, and I say this not because he is my brother, but because he has an extraordinary skill as a narrator. No one in the world can voice Cooper Flynn better than Austin."

CHAPTER 19

Paris Moon

J was looking forward to my birthday weekend at the
beach. Half Moon Bay was a beautiful small coastal
community which attracted a lot of day trippers. People
who lived further inland could make a short drive to walk along the
beach, shop, or have their cravings satisfied for fresh seafood. It was
a different world from the valley, and I would be grateful for the
break.

Daisy wasn't too happy when she saw me talking to Mrs.
Swenson over the back fence. She just sat there with golden eyes
accusing me while I handed over her kitty bowl and food for a few
days to my life-saving neighbor. Mrs. Swenson ambled back to her
kitchen. I waited until she was safely inside before I had a heart to
heart with my furry BFF.

"Oh, you would do the same thing in my place," I said to my
unblinking cat. "Fine, we'll look for a nice feline hotel when I get
back, and you can have a few days off." She tilted her head slightly,
then in a burst of energy, she bounded off to parts unknown. I

couldn't tell if she was happy at the prospect of vacation time away from me or if something in the grass caught her eye.

I had closed the door on a very happy porter who was stuffing my tip into his back pocket. I walked deeper into the enormous suite. The absence of natural light in the room was noticeable. Finding the button, I activated the heavy drapes. Sunshine poured in as the two halves swept aside.

Stepping to the window, I inspected the expansive view. My nose almost touching the glass, I took in the beauty of the clear sky and the bottle-green sea. The movement of the ocean was eerily mesmerizing. Seagulls dipped close to the white-foamed caps as the waves, like liquid glass, ebbed against the rocks of the coastline.

Although the windows would not open, I could hear the crash of the waves below. It would be a sweet lullaby as I drifted off to sleep each night.

My parents were kind enough to arrange for our own suites. I'd have to visit Bex to compare the accommodations, but mine had two spacious bedrooms. Separate suites seemed wasteful since Bex and I would more than likely spend any time we had in the hotel in one room. Maybe they were thinking of privacy?

After a day at the beach, we drove into town for an impromptu shopping spree. After buying a number of things we didn't need, we ended our excursion with a relaxing hot drink.

We sat in the small courtyard of Luna Luna, an Italian bistro and bar. I was blissfully tired, the kind of tired you only get when you've spent the day on the beach. It was a late Friday afternoon. Only the tourist who had not worked today or left early to get a start on their weekend were here.

A cold beach-gray late afternoon, the lamps threw off enough heat for us to be surrounded in blanket-hugging warmth. The kitchen was preparing for dinner. The robust aroma of garlic mingled with other tantalizing flavors, which I couldn't identify, was torturing my taste buds. Eating right now was out of the question because in an hour I would be mewing like a contented kitten when a masseuse with big strong hands would be chasing my tension away.

Bex and I had met Nils, who was enthusiastically recommended by the hotel spa, briefly before booking an appointment. He was a big, strapping Viking with a shy smile and a strong back. It looked strong from the way it was straining his white cotton T-shirt. I was looking forward to a handsome man with fragrant warm oil on his hands touching almost every inch of my body. I hoped he was the silent type. I didn't like a chatty masseuse.

Bex took a sip of cider and sighed dreamily. "You've got to let me know if Nils is any good. While he's working on you in your suite, I'm scheduled for hair and a mani-pedi in the spa."

We were here to celebrate my birthday, but the launch was never far from my mind. I know Bex wouldn't approve, but I had to ask. "I'll give you my review, but how is the recording going? Are Kaulder and Jay churning out audio gold?"

She gave me a tight smile. "This is your birthday weekend; let's not talk shop."

"I'm in such a good mood a little shop won't hurt. They've been at it for a couple of weeks, and all you've reported is that it's going well. That's a big contrast when Nancy was working on her books. You'd give me updates along with amusing stories about the sessions."

She shifted in her seat. She was doing that thing with her mouth where it was bunched up on the side. That meant there was something she didn't want to talk about.

"Now I'm concerned. What happened?"

"Nothing really. It's just we're behind schedule again, and we might not make the deadline."

I refrained from pulling my hair out and calmed myself with a deep, cleansing breath and let it out slowly.

Bex pushed her glasses further up her nose and waited.

"Please, don't look like that," I said. "I just want to know what happened. And why they're behind schedule?"

She shrugged. "Kaulder is a wee bit of a perfectionist. At least that's what Jay says."

I'm sure she was sugarcoating it. That had to be code for Kaulder was a big fat pain in the... "How bad is it?"

"Jay seems to think Kaulder is more critical of his performance than he should be. He's insisting on continuing to work on passages that are very good. There was also a problem with the equipment that cost them a day and a half of recording."

"Did Austin drag his feet with the equipment repair?"

"No, when they discovered the issue, he addressed it immediately."

I took a gulp of hot cider and sat back. This project kept popping up with new problems every day. Maybe it was time I managed the recording myself.

"I just found out about the problem. Jay thinks he can make up the time, but he wanted to let me know. He has another job lined up after this, so he's motivated to finish on time. But--"

"Are you saying Mr. Rock Star Kaulder, aka Will, is on a different timetable? If that's true, then I think it's time I meet with him again and--"

She shook her head like a disapproving school teacher. I'm sure a tsk, tsk was coming next. "Don't do that," she said, using her 'you need to calm this shit down' voice. "I still have it under control. See, this is the reason I didn't want to talk shop. In all likelihood, it's been resolved or is on its way to being fixed. I don't want this to ruin your birthday weekend." Bex looked at the outdoor heater and rubbed her exposed arms. "The wind seems to be getting through this heat barrier. I'm going to the car for my sweater. Do you want me to grab yours?"

"Yes, thanks."

"In the meantime, order another cider for me. I'll be right back; then we can talk about dinner."

I sighed, "You're too good to me."

"I know, but we're friends. You've listened to me plenty of times. I know how important this launch is to you." She hugged herself. "Burr, I'm getting my sweater." She dodged a waiter as she walked to the parking lot.

Bex didn't need to know, but I wouldn't be satisfied until I had a chance to talk to Jay. If this didn't get straightened out soon, Kaulder was going to have a visit from me, Austin or no Austin.

I flagged down a waitress that was working across the room and pointed at my drinks. She made a beeline for the table and scooped up the glasses. "Another round, please." She nodded and disappeared.

My cell made a zip sound. I had a text. I smiled. It was Parker.

I'm sorry. I had to make an unscheduled Paris run to fill in for a sick pilot. I thought after my last flight I would be in Saratoga in plenty of time for your birthday. When I return, I'll make up for lost time. I'll bring you something back from the city of love, besides me.

Parker ☹

P.S. I'll call you tomorrow on your birthday.

I brushed my finger over the sad face emoji next to his name. I had hoped Parker would be back for my birthday. The longer he stayed away, the more I wanted, needed to see that wicked grin.

CHAPTER 20

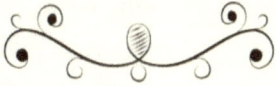

Lavender Blues

My hand slashed a path through the steam covering the bathroom mirror. I needed to clear enough to see myself in the extra fluffy hotel bathrobe. I took another swipe at my reflection to remove more of the mist. I had scrubbed everything during my hot, steamy shower, including the make-up from my face. Grabbing a length of my hair, I twisted it into a topknot. Not to appear immodest, because I was nude underneath, I adjusted the front of the terry-cloth robe and secured the sash around my waist just as a gentle tapping called me to my door.

I swung the door open to see Nils and a woman with short dark hair and large expressive eyes. She was almost as tall as him, dressed in the same white T-shirt and pants.

"Good afternoon," he said. The woman beside him giving me a supportive smile.

"Yes, good afternoon. Please come in."

"This is Elena," introduced Nils as he walked past me hefting a large carrying case. He placed the portable massage table against the wall. Elena followed, pulling a leather tote on rollers. They stood looking expectantly at me as though it was my turn to speak. I closed the door and leaned against it. I remembered booking time with Nils. Why would I need a second masseuse? Was this going to be some kind of kinky female-male-female-massage? I think my mouth was open. I looked at one, then the other, trying to decide what to say. I know I must have appeared puzzled or horrified because Nil's eyebrows crept up.

"Sorry," he said. "It looks like you didn't expect two of us. I guess no one told you at the booking desk that it's our policy to have a female staff member accompany a male when the massage is for a female client in her room. Elena will stay throughout the massage, but she'll only be an observer."

Relief flooded through me as I let out a breath. This woman was a chaperone.

"But, if you're comfortable with me alone in the room, she will help me set up then leave. We can call her back at any time or have her finish the massage if you like."

I'd enjoyed massages from males and females, separately of course, and never felt uneasy. "Thank you for thinking of my comfort, but I have no objection of being with you alone in the room."

His shy smile returned. "Then please relax while we set up." He glanced around the suite. "Where exactly would you like the table?" I was staring at the expansive window in the living room. I hesitated to suggest that location, but it would give me a spectacular view of the sunset. Nils came to stand next to me. "I wouldn't worry about having your session in front of an open window. You can't be seen from here. Believe it or not, we've checked. You will be draped at all times. If someone could see you, they couldn't see any more than what you would expose on the beach in your biki..." he coughed, "bathing suit." he smiled and cocked his head.

He needed to bottle that smile. They were going out of their way to make me feel comfortable enough to enjoy the experience, but seriously once he began, I would be halfway to dreamland. I usually fell asleep during parts of it; I would be that relaxed. "Sounds good." I was eager to start once I realized this wasn't going to be a kinky sex romp where at the end of the play, I would be presented with a commemorative two-disk video set of our adventures, in a lovely keepsake box.

Nils handed me a sheet and my attention came back to reality. "If you will wrap yourself in this." I relieved him of the cloth. "Elena will help you on the table when you're ready."

I left to change in the bedroom. Fastening the cool, thin sheet tight around my body, I was covered but felt more exposed.

When I returned to the living room, the table was in place, and Nils was looking out at the sea. Elena worked near the leather tote placing items on a small table. A strong scent of lavender filled the air, the familiar aroma already relaxing me.

He turned as I approached. "I'll be in the other room while you get comfortable. Elena will let me know when you're ready."

She moved around the table. "Please unwind your sheet, lay on your stomach and place the cover over you. I'll turn away until you're ready."

I strode past her. "Don't be silly." I yanked off the covering, hopped onto the table, swung my legs over and positioned my body face down.

"Good," she said, amusement in her voice, "I see you've done this before. This will make things very easy." She draped the discarded sheet over me, straightening the fabric, her hands moving lightly around my body. I felt my heart beat a little faster at her preparations. Not that I was turned on by her touch; it was the thought that she was preparing me for Nils' return.

"I will leave you now," she whispered. "I'll tell Nils you're ready. Enjoy your massage."

He didn't arrive immediately. I couldn't say how long I lay there, but I began to drift into that time just before sleep. A presence prevented me from my dreams. I turned my head to see him in the entryway. In my drowsy state and the soft lighting, I perceived the silhouette of a big man with broad shoulders standing with feet apart like a conquering hero waiting to take his spoils. Adrenaline rushed for a few heartbeats when my foggy brain thought or maybe wanted it to be Austin. He moved to the table, and I noticed his hair was fair, not dark.

"Elena said you've had massages before?"

"Yes, but I've never had a service from this hotel."

"Your comfort is my main concern. I'll do what I can to make this a satisfying experience. Would you like music during the session?"

"Yes, that would be nice." Rushing water and tingling bells with an overlay of chirping birds rose into the air.

"Emma, is there something else you'd like to listen to other than New Age?" he glanced at his phone. "I have jazz, classical, country... His face registered alarm. "Sorry, would you prefer I call you 'Miss'?"

I stifled a laugh when I realize he was serious. "Emma is fine, and New Age is perfect."

"Great, I'll begin on your back, but if there are any areas that you want me to pay close attention to, let me know now, or when I get to that section. Are there any parts you don't want me to massage like the feet? Some clients don't like their feet touched."

I gave him a flirty grin. "Touch anything you like," and placed my face in the cradle. He couldn't see me suppressing a laugh, but I heard him gulp. He gently lifted the sheet, moving it down the body to rest just below my lower back, revealing the top of my behind.

The first pass of his fragrant oiled hands on my back was heavenly. I couldn't help it, his touch made me mew and sigh as he worked. It was as though he was making love to me as his fingers played across my back and legs.

He tucked and draped quickly, careful to uncover only the parts he massaged. But a strange thing happens when you're touched so intimately: you begin to release inhibitions, especially when hands work close to the forbidden.

Women, for the most part, can hide arousal. I often wonder how men manage it. But this was the first time I had a strong attraction to a masseuse, and his touch was conjuring up all sorts of naughty scenarios. I needed to concentrate on releasing tension and less on wishing those expert hands would stray.

He was silent as a shadow while his hands danced across my body. The unworldly music and my cries and moans of pleasure were the only sounds that pierced the silence. I tried to quiet, but finally gave up. He was here to please me. If I wanted to scream my head off that should be alright.

My body was humming when the sheet was resettled, covering me completely. He bent close to my ear to ask if I'd like to lay on my back. I pulled away from the face cradle, settling onto my elbow, clutching the sheet to my breast. He handed me a small towel.

"When you lie on your back, place this over your breasts. You will be covered when I pull the cloth back to massage your front."

I arranged the cloth as instructed and signaled I was ready. He lifted the sheet and stared at me, red blooming across his face. I glanced down to see what was wrong. I still felt covered, and the material was in place, but it was way too small. It looked like I had placed a large Band-Aid over my breasts. I smiled. "You can get another cloth, but on second thought," my bad angel was getting the best of me, "I like this covering just fine, please continue."

He tore his eyes away from my chest and twisted away. His broad back bent as he busied himself at the small table. No doubt he was composing himself for the next round of work. When he turned to me again, he presented me with a face of professional composure. I smiled at him, but he was too far behind his mask to notice. He'd probably been in this situation before with an overzealous client who wanted a more enhanced service. I didn't blame him.

"I do have a request." He stiffened. Now I felt horrible about teasing him. I held the cloth at my breast with one hand and rolled to my side. I extended my other hand. He stepped back; his mouth opened. Maybe he thought I was trying to grab him. I huffed.

"Would you pay extra attention to these?" He looked at my hand as if an alien had just popped out of my belly. I wiggled my fingers. "I'm a writer. Sometimes my hands ache at the end of the day… please?" He nodded, but did not change expression.

I fell onto my back, looking at the ceiling. He probably thought I was some desperate woman who preyed on any cute male masseuse. Later, I would have to apologize and give him a huge tip. But for now, I would close my eyes and surrender to the decadent pleasure of his touch. This time I did fall asleep.

I woke to Nils' gentle voice. "I'm finished. Rest on the table until you feel you want to get up. Call the spa to have the table removed. I'm packing some items we brought. I'll move in and out as quietly as I can."

"Thank you," I whispered. I was still very drowsy.

I saw his shy grin through my fluttering eyelashes. He was close enough to kiss. "It was my pleasure," he said, straightening to his full height, his face above me. "Please ask for me again, even if you'd just like to have coffee."

I didn't respond to what I thought he said. It sounded like he had made coffee? "I'm going to take you up…" I was gone to dreamland.

I didn't know how long I'd been sleeping. Shadows filled the room, and the temperature was cooler. The table didn't feel as comfortable as it had been during my massage. I'd promised to meet Bex for dinner. I couldn't tell what time it was; for all I knew, I might have already slept past our dinner date.

As the fog cleared in my head, I was aware of Nils standing a couple of steps away from the table. It was a new moon with a few stars waiting in the dark blue sky, but not enough light filtered through the open window to help me see.

"Thank you for helping me out and giving me special treatment. I hope I wasn't too loud; I'm normally not a moaner—"

"Why would you be moaning?" came a hoarse whisper.

A slight tingle crept up my spine. I pushed myself up to squint into the gloom at a large male outline. "Nils?"

"Do you want it to be Nils?" He stepped out of the shadows.

"I don't believe it. Parker!" He was on the table and cradling me in his arms before I could ask him a million questions.

"God, I've missed you," he said, his hands entwined in my hair. He kissed me. His consuming passion shot through me like a rocket.

I broke our contact, gasping for breath. "Let me breathe," I laughed, "I've missed you too."

He brushed his thumb lightly over my lips. "Sorry, I've been waiting a long time."

I grabbed his hand and laced it with mine. "Me too, Mr. Parker. Me too."

He moved off the table. A second later a light was on. Parker turned to see me still sitting up, but the sheet had fallen to my waist. I reacted like a teenage virgin and snatched it back up, wrapping it tight. Parker gave me a savage grin. "What? I can't see what Nils has been playing with for the last hour?"

"That was a professional massage," aware that I had just spent an hour naked with another man.

"Didn't sound professional if moaning was involved?"

"The massage released a lot of tension."

He returned to the table. "I can help you release tension too." His lips brushed my shoulder. I shivered. He tugged at my messy top knot… most of it was already down, the rest cascaded to my shoulders. "That's much better." He nuzzled my neck. "Can't I at least peek behind the sheet?" He moved a finger over the edge of the fabric. I sighed and tried to catch his palm. But he avoided me, cradled my face in his hands and kissed me again, giving me the attention I needed.

I ran my tongue along his lower lip as his hand dropped to my waist. The sheet had fallen back to my lap. My breasts pressed hard against his chest, the soft cotton of his T-shirt rubbing seductively against my erect nipples.

My body was ruining his clothes. "I've got oil all over me. Let me go; I should shower." I began to push away, but he held me in place.

"No, don't. You look too sexy for me to wait. Come on, Nyx, let's do what you've been promising in your texts."

I blushed. "I haven't promised anything."

"I know. I need to teach you how to text dirty."

"We'll break the table."

"Believe me, this table can handle a couple of two-hundred-and-fifty-pound wrestlers. We won't hurt Nils' precious table."

I looked beyond him to the bedroom. "Why here? This suite has a huge bed."

He brushed a hand over my breast. "There's no oil. He must have cleaned away the evidence, or he didn't massage you in some of the best places." He tossed that heart-dropping smile at me that didn't reach his eyes. I wasn't sure, but there was something more behind those green orbs I couldn't read.

He was waiting for my yes. We were alone in this gorgeous place. I'd really missed him and it was a turn-on that he couldn't wait and wanted to have me right here, on the table. I touched his face. His excitement was contagious. I laughed. "I think it's time for a homecoming. Let's make a memory."

Parker left the table, pulling the sheet with him. A tiny breeze caressed my skin when the cloth snapped back, landing somewhere behind him.

I watched him strip off his oil-stained shirt and jeans. There was a noticeable bulge in his briefs, but it didn't take him long before that barrier was gone. He stood; a wicked lopsided grin aimed at me. Lord help me, he looked even better naked.

Parker rubbed his chin. "From what I can see, it looks like we have another less-than-satisfied customer. I'm afraid the hotel's reputation is on the line. But it's your lucky day; I'm in charge of customer satisfaction for the guests in this suite for the weekend."

"So, you're the fixer?"

"Something like that."

I found a towel Nils left behind, folded it without losing eye contact, and placed it just below the face cradle. I scooched down on the table and planted my head on the make shift pillow, looking up at him. This was definitely going to be good.

"Today is also customer appreciation day," he said. "It's your choice. Would you like your satisfaction to come through the front or the back door?"

"What do you recommend?"

"That's tricky. You're one of those rare women who looks good coming or going." He tapped his chin, trying to decide. "You've got my services all night, best to start with the fundamentals."

I scooted over to give him room. The table creaked from his weight when he landed. He inched my rear over to make space for his bulk. He wasn't brawny. He had long, lean muscles like an athlete in one of those sports that go for endurance.

I traced the light, burnished stubble on his face, his eyes shone, and he kissed me. His mouth was hungry like he needed to devour me quickly before I disappeared. His urgent moves aroused me as I worked to keep up.

His thumb made slow circles over my nipple. I closed my eyes and arched my back, wanting him to touch more of me.

"Tell me what he did to you?"

My eyes flew open.

He shifted, his warm hand roaming the length of my inner thigh. "Where did he touch you?" His voice was low.

I moved onto my elbow. I wasn't sure what he was asking. "There weren't any heated stones, no beating me with branches, or imps fanning me with huge palm leaves. It was a regular massage."

He rolled on top of me, settling me on my back. "I don't believe you."

My mouth went dry. What did he think we were doing? "It was just--"

"You've been a wanton little tart..." His damning face above me. "Haven't you? I know he fucked you. I saw it on your face."

"No, that's not true." Maybe he misunderstood when I thanked him for special attention. "Look, Parker, you thought I'd--"

"Don't lie to me." His cinnamon breath brushed my cheek. "You better tell me all of it because I'm going to keep you in this position until I get the truth."

I tried to squirm out from under him, but he was dead weight. Parker had officially gone insane. "If you don't get the fuck off of me, I swear I'll--"

"Come on, Nyx, play along," he winked, "Let's make this interesting."

I really looked at him. There was no anger. Damn it, he was playing. I searched his face again. Devilry was in those eyes. He wants to play. Okay baby, let's play.

He moved next to me, idly massaging my arm, waiting for me to begin my story.

"Oh yawn, is that all you've got? I think I'll sleep through this part of your foreplay," closing my eyes.

He playfully pinched my side.

I squeaked.

"Do I have your attention?" he breathed into my ear. "Make this good."

"Okay, alright. I'll tell you."

Parker nuzzled my neck and pulled my leg over his hip. Sliding his hand down, he took hold of his cock, using it to part my slit. My breath caught, hoping he would enter me. Instead, he moved the head of his cock through my moisture. "Go on, what else, and it better have every detail."

With our bodies inches apart, there was nowhere to look but into his emerald green lust. I breathed in his citrus musk that rolled off him like an aphrodisiac while the sexy little beast tortured me. He was enjoying this, watching me fight for control, teasing me relentlessly with his joystick. I wanted to forget story time, but then again, I really should get him back for that trick he played on me earlier and this exquisite torture.

I grabbed his shaft, my hand moving down its length. This time he moaned as I took control. "I really don't know where to begin," imitating an addle-brained heroine in a bad bodice ripper. "Nils massaged my back first, which was pretty standard. But when I turned onto my back, I closed my eyes while Nils got ready to do my front. When all of a sudden, he rips the sheet off my naked, quivering body. My eyes sprang open, and I looked up into his sardonic ice-blue eyes. It startled me so I gave a cute little cry. Like this," I demonstrated.

Parker was having trouble keeping a grin off his face.

My hold on him fell away. He took control again and he resumed teasing me. I shivered, having a problem multitasking, but I pushed on with the story. "I couldn't believe it," I continued, taking a shaky breath for effect, "He, he was naked and his big you know what was dangling." I paused and smiled my own brand of evil. "It was swinging, really."

"Get to the good part."

"Oh heavens," trying to look demure, "I don't know if I can say this part. I scrambled away from him, but that big Viking caught my ankle and jerked me back down. He kept his eyes on me as he walked to the head of the table. He was standing so close that his cock was practically in my face. I thought I was going to have to take that, you know, in my mouth. Instead he touched my hair and said something soothing in Swedish. An evil grin split his lips, and he switched to English. Nils said he wanted to do it old school and climbed on top of me. Before I had a chance to ask which school he was talking about, he shoved that enormous cock inside me. Jeez, that felt really good... oh, I mean, the nerve!"

Parker glanced away, his body beginning to shake, trying to suppress a laugh.

"He pumped me like a jackhammer while he muttered in Swedish. It was totally hot. The pumping, not so much the Swedish. I must have come at least fifteen times before I caught my breath, but he kept going at me for at least an hour until he finally came. I was stunned by what that big blond Adonis had done. I told him I was going to call the spa immediately about his behavior and to ask if he had any openings on his calendar for the next day. He just grinned and said he'd block out the whole week for me."

Parker slipped inside me, my body welcoming the pressure. His accusing face above me, still in our play. "You couldn't wait," his graveled voice a whisper.

"You're right, and he wasn't the first."

Face flushed, teeth clenched, he gripped the edge of the table above my shoulders. His wild thrusts pushed me into the padding, rocking the table with each lunge, the force of his drives threatening to collapse the table.

"You're a lying tease," he ranted in my ear. "I'm going to make you forget him, if I have to fuck him out of you."

"I've been bad, really bad. Make me pay for what I did." I wailed as the dumb heroine.

My encouragement spurred him on. He was raw passion playing the cheated, outraged lover. But my act was falling away into real arousal.

The intense ride was too hot and fast to sustain. My orgasm was coming on like a freight train heading for a concrete barrier. Parker was still trash-talking me, wandering heavily into slut territory, but his words were in the distance. The point of impact was just a few grinds of his hips away. I was ready. A thrust went deep, and I arched my back to meet him. My climax, pure and primal, surged through my body like a wave. I stilled to sustain the moment, but I came back too soon to a sharpened reality. Parker was in vivid focus, his uncensored face above me, pace measured, close to his release.

I was moving with him again, helping him to find his way. "You're mine," came the harsh refrain, "He can't have you. I don't care what you did with him, you're mine." He was still in his character, sustaining the outrage as he continued to bear down on me. I began to feel a whisper of another orgasm, but he was too near to his climax for me to find another release. His eyes shut, breath labored, he was ready to come. Parker's drive went hard and deep. My body accepted every inch of his mass, my sex clenched, holding him. "Emma," he gasped as his energy flowed into me, his weight pinning me to the rigid surface, the padding a memory.

He inhaled a few shaky breaths, then rose onto his elbows. A look crossed his face, then vanished. He gave me a quick kiss and rolled off. He gathered me in his arms.

"Parker."

"Hmmm?"

"That was a chapter for the history books."

"Oh shit." He bounced off the table.

"What's wrong?"

"Sorry, but we've got to get cleaned up. We have dinner reservations in less than an hour." He was already hopping into his jeans. The change from my hot lover to this crazy man was pretty funny.

"I'll go to my room to shower and change," he said as his head popped through his T-shirt. "Wear something nice; we'll be in the main dining room, and Bex will be joining us. I'll come back to walk you to the restaurant."

I stared at him.

"Come on," he pleaded, "Move that pretty ass of yours. I promise we can play again later. You can be a naughty writer and I'll be your reluctant PA?" He kissed me and touched my cheek. "Thanks, that was hot, by the way." He searched my face. "You're still mine, right?"

I gave a slow nod.

He tossed a grin at me. Then he was gone.

CHAPTER 21

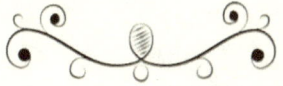

Surprise, Surprise

I wanted to talk to Bex before I met that crazy sexy Parker again. She had a lot of explaining to do. I put in a call to his room; he must have been in the shower. I left a message that I'd be downstairs waiting with Bex.

Parker takes longer to dress than any female I know. I had more than enough time to dress and be downstairs before he heard my message.

Listening to the hotel's music channel after my shower danced me into a party mood, ready to enjoy an evening out. I swept my hair up, applied my pink lipstick, and slipped into my little black dress. The deep slit in the front would give my date a peek of my breasts if I moved just right. If that didn't make his pulse beat faster, then the blue stilettos would.

I moved through a crowd that matched my own elegance. Californians love their jeans, and you might see them worn in the most formal occasions or at least a pair of sneakers. I was surprised to observe very little casual wear.

I found Bex standing near the entrance to the restaurant. She spotted me and did some energetic hops trying to flag me down. Her frock was a fifties-inspired Audrey Hepburn copper circle dress that cinched her tiny waist and flounced out at the skirt. The color brought out the highlights in her red hair. I always thought she was a throwback from that era. I moved to join her. She turned away to say something to a group, then she rushed forward, linking my arm.

"Don't be mad at me. Parker wanted to be here for your birthday to surprise you."

"There has to be more that you're not telling me." looking around for a place where we could sit and talk before Parker arrived. How did he--?"

"I'll tell you everything later. I've invited a few people to join us for dinner, then maybe after we can go to a club Nils knows about up the peninsula."

"What does Nils have to do--? Oh, hi, Nils," I said as he appeared from behind Bex.

"Hello, good to see you again," he grinned.

"Hi, I'm here too," said Elena from another direction.

Fantastic, two people who'd seen me naked a few hours ago. There's no awkwardness here. No wonder I didn't recognize them; they weren't wearing white hospital-like uniforms. Nils' muscular form was in dress shirt and slacks, the light grays accentuating his ice-blue eyes. Elena had an understated French style. She was wearing black heels, a black pencil skirt, and a white sleeveless shirt, the kind of outfit that looked like you just threw something together and still managed to look dead chic.

The crowd was growing thick around us. The press of people hummed with talk and subdued laughter.

The heat of a large body hovered close. A hand lightly touched the small of my back. It was the scent of citrus musk and the smile on Bex's face that let me know Parker had arrived. He lowered his lips to my ear. "I got your message, but I was hoping to escort you. I wanted everyone to see the beautiful woman on my arm." His arm circled my shoulder. I looked up at him, my insides fluttering; the killer grin was for me. Was it possible for someone to be extra handsome, or was it this moment?

"Parker," Bex said, "This is Elena."

She extended her hand. He clasped it and held her palm as he voiced a charming, "Hello." I even felt that greeting down to my toes.

She narrowed her eyes and inclined her head. "Have we met before?"

I searched his face. He didn't express uneasiness. Was this a conquest he had forgotten? I glanced at Elena, who was still holding Parker's gaze. The congenial air around us slipped into something thick with anticipation.

"Maybe you've taken an Eos flight?" Parker offered. "I fly a lot of runs to Europe. Your accent... are you French?"

"Belgian," she corrected.

"Aw, Belgium, the land of chocolate, beer and waffles."

She laughed. "Don't forget castles."

"You've seen him at the spa," Nils said. "I'll admit, he's a lot prettier right now. He's usually scruffy when he visits me. I've known this guy for a long time. How are you doing, man?" Nils put an arm around Parker, then punched him on the shoulder.

"I'd say I've known you for too long. I'm good. Glad you made it."

That's how Parker gained entrance to my room. They must be good friends to jeopardize his job with that stunt.

"Winston party?" came a voice from the hostess desk.

Bex interrupted the bromance reunion. "That's us. I put the reservations in my name."

The men were very attentive when we arrived at our table. They gave each other a guy signal only they could understand. It was a wink and a nod. Nils pulled the chair out for Elena while Parker did this interesting two-chair pull for Bex and me.

I had to admit we were a beautiful-looking group, which was confirmed by the stares from the other diners. The company and conversation sparkled like a sophisticated scene from a movie. Parker kept slipping his gaze to me and holding my hand when he wasn't making a gesture to prove his point.

Champagne arrived at the end of the appetizers. I was already a bit tipsy after the wine with the first course, but we were all staying in the hotel tonight. After the champagne was poured, Parker pulled me to my feet. He held up a glass, and I prepared for his toast, but for the first time since I've known him, he was tongue-tied.

He recovered and cleared his throat. "Emma, although your birthday is tomorrow, I wanted to toast you and wish you a happy birthday." The rest of the table stood up. "Happy birthday, Emma!" they cheered in unison.

The dining room dimmed. There was a commotion in the corner of the room. I turned to see a waiter pushing a cart with a small chocolate cake blazing with candles. Several other wait staff streamed behind them singing a chorus of "Happy Birthday." My eyes brimmed with tears at the wonderful gesture. Parker had arranged all of this just for me. I kissed him, careful not to spill champagne on his back.

"Happy, Em girl?" he whispered.

I kissed him again. "Yes, crazy happy."

The cake arrived at the table. "Make a wish... make a wish," the room chanted. I took a breath, made a quick wish and tried feebly to extinguish the candles. They must have placed all thirty-one of them in the icing. Parker, Bex, Elena, and Nils came to my aid and we managed to get them all out. The lights flashed on, and the staff moved away. My hand flew to my mouth as Mom and Dad walked forward, their arms outstretched to hug me.

"Don't cry, honey. Did you really think we would miss your birthday?" Mom said.

Dad flanked me. "We were never going to Puerto Vallarta... it was this one," Dad gestured to Parker. "He came to San Diego to convince us to have a surprise party for you. I have to say you looked surprised."

"Happy birthday, Emma," a clipped voice called.

"Caroline?" I said as a tall, elegant woman stepped forward. She offered her cheek to me. I dutifully kissed it. Caroline was never that warm, even when I was married to her son Luke. But she was a rock when he passed away. She couldn't be happy at the prospect of her golden son staying with me in Saratoga.

"Yes, happy birthday, Little Miss," said Dennis, Caroline's long-suffering husband. I hugged him; at least he thought I could do no wrong.

"I hope you finished those chapters before you came to the party..." a familiar voice warned behind me.

"Holly!" I left Dennis and threw my arms around her. "I'm so glad you came."

"I admit I was curious when Bex called me," she said, searching the room. "Of course, I wanted to help celebrate your birthday, but I also wanted to meet this mysterious Parker that has been your personal assistant for the past few weeks."

I caught Parker's eye and waved at him. Holly turned away from me to follow my gaze. Holly is what they call a Southern California surfer girl type, although I don't know if she can even swim. Long blond hair, blue eyes, a body that was made to be in a bikini. The kind of looks that sold lipstick and shampoo. She dressed in a winter white knit that clung to her petite frame. The choice of color made her look golden even in winter. She took a step forward as Parker joined us. "Parker, this is Holly, my editor.

She beamed and extended her hand. "I had hoped to meet you tonight."

He took her hand, and instead of shaking it, he kissed it. Looking up from her palm, he smiled. "It's my pleasure to meet you, Mistress Holly."

It was the duel of the circuit-jamming smiles. The whole room was in danger of a whiteout. I would have to avert my eyes soon, or I'd go snow blind. Wait a minute, he called her Mistress Holly.

"Don't look like that," Holly said. "During my first conversation with Parker, he told me you refer to me as the dominatrix. We actually had a laugh about it. Then he continued to tease me, calling me Mistress Holly." Her perfect brows drew together. "Am I really that hard on you?"

"Sweetheart, you're a regular ball buster, but I love you anyway. You're the only one that makes me look great on paper, give or take a comma."

"Did you really say I was from the editor's school of hit me, beat me, make me write good copy?" I swung my gaze to Parker. He just managed to look innocently handsome.

"Mr. Cameron?" a member of the hotel staff was standing next to him. "The room you reserved is ready if your party will follow me."

We entered a room filled with flowers and soft lights. It looked like we had stepped inside a botanical garden at night. This was an intimate space called the Potting Shed, perfect for our small party.

It was a long, narrow room with a starched white cloth on the table. Votive candles and apricot-colored rose petals were strewn down the center of the table with tiny vases of roses. Lights were woven through long-stem roses hung suspended above our party. The breathtaking display looked like it was raining flowers. The fragrance of roses and champagne roamed the space. At one end of the room sat a couch, and a table stacked with gifts. At the other, a three-piece jazz combo was playing soft rhythms.

I had to remember to close my mouth as I took in the sight of a dreamy landscape. A man dressed in black entered from the periphery of my vision and snapped our photo with a complicated-looking camera. The other guests streamed past us to inspect the location, not curious about the man in black adjusting a second camera hanging around his neck.

Parker took my hand. "Emma, this is Tony; he's our photographer. I saw his assistant somewhere, and she will be taking videos."

"Nice to meet you," said Tony, who looked like he was sizing up my bone structure. "We've been taking photos and filming you since your arrival tonight in the lobby. You'll be happy to know we got the cake reveal in the restaurant too."

I reached for Parker's hand.

"I wanted you to remember tonight and how you celebrated your birthday with the people you care about the most."

I looked around, still not believing this was true. "How did you do this?"

"Bex was my chief co-conspirator. She did all the legwork. She knew who to invite and what would make you happy. She has amazing connections in just about every hotel. This place and the decorations were her idea." He squeezed my hand. "I have a confession. I haven't been flying for the past week. I've been in San Diego convincing our very busy parents to attend."

"Were they reluctant?"

"No, but I hadn't been back home for quite a while, and it was my mom who had to rearrange her schedule. It's easier to persuade her in person, especially when she gets to dote over me for an extended period."

"Excuse me," Tony interrupted, "But this would be the best time to do formal pictures while the room is pristine. We'll continue to do candid shots throughout the evening."

We called everyone up to the front of the room. There was a small space for dancing in front of a dais. Tony positioned the group on two levels. He walked around, inspecting us through his camera lens from several angles but didn't seem to be satisfied with the arrangement.

Tony lowered his camera and shook his head. "You all look pretty chic up there, but the blond gentleman is not wearing a jacket." We all involuntarily glanced at Nils, who appeared worried. "I'd like to try taking a photo with all the men in shirts and ties."

We all murmured, trying to figure out how to comply. Parker, my dad, and Dennis shrugged out of their coats. I turned and collected all three jackets. I stepped forward with my hands full.

Tony gave a thumbs up at the reassembled group. "Looks good." He glanced at me. "There's an armoire at the other end of the room hidden near an arbor. Guests put their things in there. I'll use this time to take some shots without you."

The battered antique wardrobe was a mixture of old wood and pleasing floral scents. Anyone wearing their jacket after it was stored in here would remember where they had been for a few days.

I carefully hung the jackets, but the last one I placed on the hanger was Parker's. The feel of the suiting material was smooth silk under my fingers; it even retained the faint scent of his cologne. I ran my hand down the edge of the lapel and caught something sharp that almost cut through the skin of my finger. I pulled the jacket open. An over-sized lavender envelope peeked out from the inside pocket, with 'Emma' printed across the face.

Of course, I was curious. This had to be my card or maybe my birthday gift. Laughter and Tony's directions filtered in from the front of the room as the photographer continued to snap photos. I had a few more minutes before someone came looking for me. The envelope wasn't sealed. I told myself even if I did find out what he gave me I could still look suitably surprised.

I pulled open the flap and fished out the two sheets of paper. It was a copy of airline tickets with no dates; the destination was Greece. There was a picture of a gorgeous hotel on a white sand beach, and the second sheet was an itinerary that listed other locations, exotic and exciting places around the globe. It looked like he had planned a world tour for us. He told me that night in Santa Cruz he wanted to show me the world.

I folded the paper and returned it to the envelope. There was a card inside I somehow missed. Written on it in Parker's terrible handwriting: For my beautiful Emma. Let's start our adventure in Greece.

After dinner, I was able to walk around the room and spend time with everyone. Parker never left my side. He held my hand or kept me close to him as we spoke to guests.

He did leave me for a few minutes to speak with the band. When they started a lively set, we all danced, moving our hips to the music, laughing as we swayed and exchanged partners on a whim. Holly and I tried to perform a Zumba move, but we couldn't manage the steps and instead we stopped in a fit of giggles.

I think the only person happier than me was Nils. Tonight, he was channeling James Bond or Don Draper, having the time of his life dancing and entertaining three unattached females that vied for his attention. To his credit, the man knew how to work the room. He didn't forget the married women. Nils had my mom giggling like a love-struck teenager, and Caroline even gave him a reserved smile when he flirted with her outrageously.

I sipped my champagne and gazed at Parker. He sat next to me, absorbed in earnest conversation with my dad. He squeezed my hand, without missing the discussion, to let me know he was here with me.

I looked around at our guests. The mood of the party had changed. We had arrived at that time of all good parties when voices lowered, and the conversations turned wistful. We were in a happy, contented lull. It wouldn't be long before my guests would excuse themselves to depart for destinations elsewhere. Judging the crowd, some would be romantic. It was a magical evening.

Parker's chair scraped as it moved back. "I think it's time to open presents." He grabbed my hand, pulling me along to the couch up front. Somehow, he produced a microphone. "Could everyone gather around? Emma is about to open her presents. The trio who had just returned from a break, started up, and infused some life back into the crowd.

"Can I get a volunteer to help with these generous gifts?" Parker asked, his voice booming through the microphone. The only one not engaged in conversation was Holly. She tentatively raised her hand. Parker gallantly helped her onto the small stage, leading her to the couch next to me. The smiling faces looking at me were the people I wanted around me. Each man had retrieved his jacket from the old wardrobe. Everyone was in their original attire.

Holly read out the card while I tore into the box or gift bag that was attached. There were lots of oohs and ahs, along with some laughter as I revealed a gift. The laughter was especially loud when I opened Bex's present. In a beautifully wrapped box with girlie pink ribbon nestled in swishy tissue paper was a case of Post-it notes in vibrant colors of the Cape Town collection. And yes, any Post-it note aficionado knows they come in collections. It was funny and practical because it was my preferred method of keeping track of scenes in my books.

Holly handed me a card and whispered that it was the last. I had opened everyone's present, but Parker hadn't retrieved his gift from his pocket.

"Don't just stare at it, open it," called Nils. Some nervous titters followed.

It was a white envelope with a card inside. The typed message said 'watch the screen.' The room darkened and a screen lowered behind me and flashed on. A grainy video of a woman, young and pretty, smiling into the camera holding a baby. Tears brimmed in my eyes as I glanced at my mom, who had the same reaction. I must have been only a few weeks old when my dad took that film. The camera zoomed in on me as a not-too-happy red-faced baby. The video continued to chronicle my years as an adorable toddler, cute child, awkward and shy teenager, and young adult home from college. There was a painful photo of Luke, Parker, and me in someone's backyard. A shot of me on my wedding day. Then the screen went blank for a moment. The crowd complained with "Oh nos"... "Is it over?" someone remarked.

I thought the lights would finally come on. But no, the video resumed. There were recent pictures of me in my sweats, bleary-eyed. My hair was a riot as I had my first cup of coffee with Daisy at my feet. laughter came up in response.

Photos from Santa Cruz, Stacks in Campbell, and Benni's jazz club. It was a photo history of all the times Parker and I had been together over the past weeks. It ended with 'Happy Birthday, Emma.' They clapped and shouted.

The lights came on; the group quieted to a murmur. I stood looking at Parker, my tears threatening to spill.

"Can I help you?" My dad's clear voice rose from the back of the room. "You know, this is a private party."

"No," Bex said in a loud whisper, "it's fine."

I glanced toward the voice to see who had arrived so late. Everyone else focused in the same direction. Magda was in a long blue dress and shawl, clutching a box with an over-sized yellow bow. Austin, in a dark suit, dwarfed his sister while he managed to look hot as hell and menacing at the same time. His gaze found me. We locked stares. Something inside me told me to greet him and Magda. I took a step, but Parker caught my hand, stopping me. I turned to him. He was looking at Austin, his face flushed with anger.

"We're done, right?" I whispered. "I don't want to be rude. I want to greet our guests."

"Wait. There's another present; I haven't given you my gift." He pulled me to the middle of the dais. He flashed another look at Austin. There seemed to be a challenge in Parker's eyes. Austin stared back, unmoved. Parker turned back to me; the anger pushed just beneath the surface. "Em, you remember when we were kids, how we talked about traveling the world?"

I nodded. I had this uncontrollable urge to glance at Austin, but I forced myself to focus on Parker's serious face. Yes, we had talked about it, and going to Australia would be a new start. A world tour would be exciting.

He reached into his jacket, rummaging. He didn't pull out the envelope I had seen stuffed in the inside pocket. Something was in his hand, but I couldn't see what he was holding. Then he dropped to one knee. There were collective gasps from our rapt audience. Apparently, no one knew what was about to happen.

The ring he held in his fingers had a diamond so big it would have been visible from the International Space Station. A weight pressed my chest. I slowed my breathing, trying to avoid a heart attack. I inched back, but he clasped my left hand, urging me forward. "I want to marry you, let's explore the world together." The proposal was loud and resolute, enough to be heard into the hallway. "I want you to be my wife."

I finally understood why a director does a panning, slow motion shot of the crowd during a pivotal scene because participants' reactions tell more about an event than the action itself.

In the moment of the declaration, time slowed. It was astonishing how we can perceive several actions in seconds. I was aware of Holly first, her pretty features molded into a mask of disappointment. She turned away, her hair hiding her face. Bex's eyes widened, and her hand flew to her mouth. Caroline was rigid, her lips a disapproving straight line. My parents worried, Dad slipping his arm around Mom's shoulders. Everyone else was stunned into an unmoving silence, except for Austin, whose towering figured remained near the door, emotions clamped down. He stood alert like a sentinel watching.

This had gotten dangerously out of hand. I didn't want to get married. I was still trying to survive my last marriage.

Parker's eyes pleaded with me. Fear kept his body stiff. How could I embarrass him in front of our family and friends?

The ring was poised inches from my finger. "I love you, marry me. Say yes," he said, his voice an urgent, hoarse plea.

I closed my eyes. I couldn't hurt him. Not another man. "Yes," I breathed.

I opened my eyes, and the flash from Tony's camera nearly blinded me. The ring slid onto my finger, tight and final, like a cell door slamming into place.

The crowd sprang to life, rushing us with congratulations and slaps on the back for Parker and best wishes for me. I wasn't in my body. Parker had his arm around me like a vise. I had to stand on tiptoes to search for Austin. He and Magda were gone. A large box with a bright yellow ribbon sat on the table nestled among apricot rose petals near an empty, overturned champagne bottle.

CHAPTER 22

Aftermath

I finally excused my way out of Parker's arms and burst through the doors into the carpeted hallway. Luckily no one had asked to come with me. I was almost in a dead run as I flew down the deserted corridor in search of a place to be alone. The bathroom was the first refuge I found.

The water gushed out of the tap while I checked the eyeliner under my lower lashes. It was what I had suspected: the make-up was starting to make a run south. Pulling paper from the dispenser, I held the towel under the water, then lightly dabbed the excess black off. A toilet flushed. A door opened, and Caroline walked out of the stall.

The woman hadn't changed her hardline expression. Standing at the next sink, she tapped the soap dispenser and turned the water on. Her head was tilted down, scrubbing her hands too vigorously. I stood frozen, my mouth slightly open, watching her through the mirror.

Drying her hands on a towel, she addressed my reflection. "I want to talk to you. Wait for me in the hall near the paintings; I'll be there in about ten minutes." She strode past me toward the exit. The wet paper towel she tossed landed in the bin with a soft slop.

I waited on a bench near three abstract paintings. Caroline bustled in, dressed in a silver puffy coat with a female staff member following her. The woman's arms were filled with clothing, walking quickly, trying to keep up with my ex-mother-in-law.

"I was hoping to catch you before you returned to the party," Caroline said. "I thought we might take a walk. Renee was kind enough to help me carry Parker's coat and a few other items you'll need." She offered the jacket. "A hat and scarf are stuffed in the pocket. The coat is big, but it should keep you warm."

There was no excusing my way out of this meeting. I dutifully slipped into the parka, pulled the wool cap on, securing it over my ears, and arranged the soft scarf around my neck. Renee set a pair of sneakers down beside me. "I remembered we wear the same shoe size," Caroline said. "These are brand new; I haven't had a chance to wear them." Sitting down, I slipped off my stilettos and changed my shoes. Caroline, picked up my heels and handed them to Renee with a tip. "Please see that the shoes are taken to her suite. Thank you."

"Let's leave through here," she gestured to a side entrance. "There's a path that will take us to the beach."

We strolled out onto a long boardwalk that led some distance away from the hotel. Our silent hike in the salty wind, helped me to relax, then I remembered that this wasn't going to be a pleasant conversation.

I stole a glance at my sober companion. She moved ahead with purpose, setting the pace as if she were alone. Maybe she was too deep into her own thoughts to engage in frivolous chit-chat. That was alright; the music of the sea and the measured thump of our feet hitting the boards seemed better company than a strident voice. The path ended at an observation deck. It was here that we stopped briefly.

We were a long way out. The hotel was a blaze of lights in back of us. The view of the night sea was a dark outline of water and shore.

"Let's sit on the steps below," her voice startling me. "I'd like to be near the sand, and the stairs will give us shelter from the wind."

I followed her down a few flights until she settled on a step that allowed her to extend her long legs onto the beach. We were sheltered here. It was warm enough for us to remove our jackets. She pulled off her shoes and placed them next to her. She rolled up her midnight blue silk pant legs until the neat folds hit just above her calf. Caroline's tension drained away as she pushed her toes deep into the cool sand. I remained a couple of steps above her, my back against the rough, aged wood, my legs tucked against my body.

"Ah, that's better," she sighed. "I just needed sand between my toes. She swung her legs across the step, then rummaged in the pocket of her long tunic, her bangles tinkling.

She noticed me watching her. "Don't worry," she said, pulling out an open packet of cigarettes and a small box, "I popped back into the party and told Parker we were going to take a walk." She placed the items on the step between us and sat back. "I remember when I first met you. I couldn't understand how such a shy girl, that could barely string two words together, managed to capture the heart of my brilliant tech-savvy son. But you were stronger than I gave you credit for, and you didn't run at the first sign of trouble. I discovered you had many other good qualities over the years, but I think loyalty was the most admirable."

There was no use rushing Caroline. She was going to get to whatever was on her mind in her own time no matter how twisted the road. This was only an opening salvo. I leaned forward, elbows on knees, and waited. We had these same talks several times in the past. A 'let's get something clear' meeting.

She extracted a cigarette from the pack and found a lighter from the box. Her face blazed a bright orange when she touched the flame to the white paper and dried leaf. She took in a long drag and held it, turning away to the sea. A wave roared and crashed against the shore, then came a smooth exhale of breath. The unmistakable aroma of cannabis sativa curled into the air.

"I know it's legal, but you still can't smoke near the beach."

She turned back to me. "I'm not opposed to paying the fine; besides, I'm in favor of supporting the local government."

"But it's--"

"Please, save me the lecture on reefer madness... I grew up in the sixties. Well, at least some of it. You try raising two rambunctious boys and see what you reach for as a stress reliever." She tapped the ash in the box. "I know you think I was too hard on my boys. I had to be. Dennis is a fine man, but he didn't want to be the disciplinarian, so I took the job because I wanted our sons to be good men. Still, there were days." She flicked ash in the box, "Maybe one day you'll discover parenting never stops."

I hoped this wouldn't be a monologue on her failings as a mother or, worse, rehashing my past. She took a long pull, then her hand extended out to offer me the unlit end. It looked like an invitation to another bad decision.

She exhaled. "After the night you've had, I think you need it more than I do."

I couldn't argue. I accepted the smoking cylinder and placed the moist tip to my lips. I let the smoke into my lungs. I tried hard to keep it inside, but I was out of practice and coughed it out. I stared at the glowing joint between my fingers... who would have thought I would end the day getting high with my ex-mother-in-law? I shook my head and handed it back. "Here, you can have it; I'm useless."

She smiled for the first time and plucked it from my fingers. "Don't worry; you'll probably get a buzz from the second-hand smoke." She took one more hit, then rubbed the joint into the small box to extinguish the smolder and closed the lid. "That was a fascinating scene we all witnessed tonight," she said.

"It started out as a lovely night."

"I would imagine that last bit of drama was not expected?"

"No, I had no idea he was thinking of marriage."

"It isn't surprising, if you think about my son's history. I'm sure you've realized Parker has always competed with his brother. Really, from the first moment he discovered he had a brother, he has wanted whatever belonged to Luke."

She brushed one foot over the other to dislodge sand then wiggled her toes. "No two boys/men could be different. My oldest the quiet, steady rock knew exactly what he wanted from life. My youngest son knew what he wanted too, but it always involved chasing a skirt." She bent slightly to unfold her pant legs. "Unfortunately. Parker is at a crossroad. He is at the age where he needs to change his hedonistic ways or become a cliché."

I placed my head on my knees. She'd never shared these insights about Parker. I thought she was oblivious to her son's flaws. He did seem different during this visit. I'd never been the direct object of his affection, only a passing infatuation, so I assumed this was what it was like to feel the full-frontal assault of Parker's charm.

"The fact is that two brothers were in love with you. Even though Luke is gone, Parker is still competing. I think the marriage proposal tonight was a desperate attempt to win. He would never have made such a public play if he wasn't a hundred percent sure of the outcome. He told me he had asked you to live with him in Australia. He also confessed to me he wasn't sure if you would accept.

The ring he offered you was not in a box. He pays attention to aesthetics; details are very important. I think it was something he was holding in reserve. An extra incentive for you to say yes." She scooped the box off the step and replaced it in her pocket, then settled back. "I would bet all the sunshine on the beach that the proposal was meant to play out behind closed doors. It seems that plan changed when your mystery man appeared. It forced my son's hand. Like everyone in that room, we saw the determination in the man's eyes. The way he looked at you, it was clear he was coming to claim you, and it looked like you were going to let him."

I lifted my head. "Caroline, that's not true--"

She raised her hand. "I'm not making a judgment. I'm only telling you what I saw. When Parker offered the ring, you looked like he had pulled a rattlesnake out of his pocket, instead of a ring with a diamond as big as your head. It must have unsettled him, that his bet might fail spectacularly. Whoever that mystery man was, in Parker's mind it was Luke, and he still wants what his brother has. But that doesn't mean he doesn't care for you."

"Everything about this day has been a surprise. In fact, the last few weeks have felt like I've been living in a hurricane. I haven't been sleeping that well, and I still can't get back into my routine."

Caroline reached for her shoes. "Ah, two men fighting over you. Every woman's wet dream, or maybe not." She slipped on her sandals, careful to whisk away the last grains of sand. "Some women purposely court that kind of drama. Unfortunately, they don't realize the heartache it will cause." She gave a deep sigh. "Until polygamy becomes legal, you'll have to decide which one of those men has your heart."

I was trying to stifle a giggle. Did she suggest that having two men at the same time was okay? Was there a deep reservoir of feminist wisdom I had overlooked or was it the weed talking?

"My advice is this. Make your choice soon. Be respectful to whoever will hear your no. It's best to let them start their healing process as soon as possible. I'm sure you'd want to know if it was you who needed a decision."

"I thought you disapproved; at least that's what it looked like after Parker proposed. I was sure of it when we were in the bathroom. I thought you were going to challenge me to a fight for stealing your other son, or something equally scary when you said you wanted to see me outside. If there had been a window in that restroom, I would have crawled through it, rather than face you."

"Talk, Emma, I said talk. You do have an imagination. I didn't mean to give you that impression. I meant to give you an ear. What I disapproved of was Parker not giving you time to sort out your feelings. I know this is difficult for you even after three years. And for a brother-in-law to declare his love, it makes it even more complicated." She glanced at her arm, studying her bangles, then pushed the silver bands further up her wrist. "I wish I knew why he's in such a rush where you're concerned. He's had three years to say something, why now?"

I was miserable and a little spacey from the weed. The last thing I wanted was drama. But there's not much you can do when it finds you. I agreed to marry Parker in front of family, friends, and Austin. It seemed easier to run away. Where would I go? Back to San Diego? That would be going backwards. I wondered if there was any food left at the party? Maybe I could get room service. I glanced at Caroline. She had to be hungry too?

"There's something else I've always wanted to say. There was never a right time before. Maybe it will help with your decision. Or maybe I need to be clear with you, but I don't blame you for Luke's death. What happened was never your fault. I know you blame yourself, and that should stop."

My head shot up. Why did she have to open old wounds now?

I returned to the party alone and found Nils, Elena, Holly, and Parker sitting at a table in deep conversation. The hotel staff was breaking down the tables and sweeping up rose petals. Parker saw me and got to his feet, a question on his face. "I was getting worried. You've been gone a while," he threw a hand out toward his companions, "but I've been in good company while I waited." He looked a little unsteady. They were probably doing shots to keep him occupied.

"Glad you're back, Emma," Nils said, pushing to his feet, "I think it's our cue to leave. We'd planned to book a car ride to a club in Palo Alto. You're welcome to come."

He at least sounded like a sober citizen.

Parker put his arm around me. "Thanks, but I think we're fine."

Yes, he'd definitely had some scotch.

I had just given my last hug to Holly when Bex appeared in a swish of taffeta. "What did I miss?" she said, shooting a glance at Nils.

"Nothing," Nils said. "You're the last one to say goodbye, then we're off."

I hugged my friend. "Thank you. Have fun."

"Oh, I plan to," came the giggled whisper in my ear.

The hallway was nearly silent as Parker and I strolled towards my room. We could still hear TVs and occasional laughter from rooms we passed. He held my hand as we walked; something was obviously on his mind. For my part, he had put me in an awkward situation because of his fears. He couldn't just trust me to do the right thing.

We hadn't spent enough everyday time with each other to discover our feelings. Luke or Austin was always lurking in the background. We stopped at my door. I was rummaging in my purse for the key card.

"Nils let me know what a stupid move it was to ask you to marry me in front of everyone when we hadn't talked about marriage."

You mean in front of Austin.

I looked up. "Is that what you were all talking about when I arrived?"

"No, I wanted to go after you when you pushed out of my arms and ran away from me."

He'd noticed how desperate I was to get away. It must be the same for everyone that was in that room.

Parker sucked in some air and went on, "Nils convinced me to let you go so you could think."

Thank you, Nils.

"He's right. Living together and marriage are different commitments. You caught me by surprise. I did need time to think."

He moved in closer. I stepped back, the door frame halting my progress. He placed his arm above my head and leaned in, his lips inches away from mine. The smell of scotch heated my lips and tickled my nose.

"Let me come in and spend the night. I want to see what you look like when you wake up on your birthday." He took my hand, grazing his thumb over the engagement ring. "I've been thinking about marrying you for a long time. I bought your ring in Paris. If you don't like it, we can go back and choose another together. We'll need to find my ring anyway." His lips grazed my mouth. "I wanted to do this properly. I wanted our parents to be here when--"

The door swung open. Parker's posture went rigid, arms to his sides. My mom stood in the doorway, hands on hips, the corners of her mouth turned down. "Parker, it might be old-fashioned, but it's customary to ask her father for her hand. You had a week to say something. Your brother--"

Parker's eyes widened.

"Mom!"

Her fingers touched her mouth as if she was trying to prevent the rest of the words from escaping. Luke had gone to my father and asked for my hand before proposing.

She looked like a deflated balloon. "Excuse me. It must be today's excitement. You aren't children. You can sort these things out for yourselves."

I spied luggage just inside the door. "Mom, are you waiting for a room to open?"

"No, honey that's part of the surprise. We're staying in the second bedroom."

CHAPTER 23

Lie to Me

*P*arker, our parents, and I spent my awkward birthday together. Everyone struggled in the beginning to find a way not to feel uncomfortable. Thankfully no one mentioned the proposal. We were, after all, a family and had known each other for a long time. Eventually, we found a delicate balance and managed to salvage the day.

Parker asked that I continue to wear his ring until I decided to either return it to him or agree to a wedding band to complete the set.

I suggested we have alone time to talk and stressed the importance that it was just talking time. Not sexy fun time. He gave me a 'yeah sure' grin, which told me that he thought he'd won a small victory.

The things you see when you're looking out of the kitchen window while rinsing a coffee cup in the sink. I swear I was going to charge a toll with the traffic I'd been getting lately or maybe I should write a short story about the people that tread that path. That would serve them right.

Daisy was by my side when I opened the door. We were treated to Bex's astonished face. She recovered quickly and addressed my cat. "Hi, girl, is your mom around?" Daisy meowed and looked at me.

"Very funny. You're here early on a Monday morning. How was the drive?"

"The train and the ride from the station were fine. You know I love taking the train; they let you eat and drink on board, unlike Bart, who makes you feel like a criminal if you take a bite of an egg salad sandwich while you watch the landscape roll by."

I closed the door. "Spare me the debate on our transportation system. This visit must be serious if you've braved a trip here before noon."

"I thought it was important... Is Parker here?"

"No, he and his parents are still in Half Moon Bay for a few more days. Something about golf and San Francisco. In fact, when they leave, he won't be coming back here to stay with me."

Her brows drew together.

"Nothing has been decided," I said.

She grabbed my left hand. "Are you sure, because this industrial-size glass cutter makes it clear to the world that it's a done deal."

I pulled my hand back. "No, we decided to slow things down and spend time together. I've agreed to wear the ring until I make the decision. By the way, you have some explaining to do."

"Yes, Parker contacted me about your party. No, I didn't know about the marriage proposal. You know the rest."

"Oh no, you're not getting out of it that easy. Why were Magda and Austin there?"

She turned away from me. "Hey, is there any more coffee in that pot? I wouldn't say no to a scone too if you have one, or at least a cookie."

"No coffee until you spill."

She sighed and turned back to me. "I know Magda. I probably mentioned your surprise party. I might have invited her. I assume she told Austin. I'm surprised that she came; she's been a recluse since her child was born." Bex tilted her head. "If you're really over Austin, then it's not a big deal that he was there. Right?"

"Fine, tell me why you're here."

"First off I have something for you." She retrieved a box from her bag and held it out to me.

"What's this, another birthday present?"

"No, this isn't for your birthday. Open it."

I pulled off the top. The box contained a CD. "I don't have a CD player. Who has a CD player?"

"Read the card."

"Page 113, session 12." I looked at her. "What does this mean?"

She already had her phone out. "Where's your phone and portable speaker? I just sent you something."

I dug into the pocket of my jeans for my cell. Stepping to the table, I turned on the speaker. I found the text she sent. There was an audio file attached. I pushed the arrow.

Cooper's voice filled the room. It was a voice that was different from the last sample Kaulder sent me. This voice was deeper, sexier, and richer than any version. It gave me chills; it was like listening to an old forgotten lover. I stopped the audio clip.

She smiled. "Kaulder wanted to make this narration the best work he's ever done. This is why he delayed and continued to work on passages until he was satisfied. He's put everything he had into this character. The narration is amazing."

"Thanks, Bex. The CD is a wonderful gift. So, everything worked itself out in the end?"

"Let's get back to that. I want to talk about Addy. He refuses to go away, or give up the crazy notion that you are a group of corporate writers. He's just thrown out some new red meat to his listeners. Now he says that Angela Stryker contacted him and is anxious to reveal her side of the story."

"You have got to be kidd--"

"Just what I thought, you didn't consent to an interview."

"No. But that's good for us. Right? He'll find out she's a fraud and--"

"And we're right back where we started. He can twist that narrative any way he wants. The woman will either spew out lies or doesn't show up for the interview, which continues to support his theory."

"Can't we sue?"

"Addy will say the woman contacted him. Blah, blah, blah."

"Okay, you're the expert. What do we do?"

"I have an idea that might be a win-win for everyone. Why don't we set up an interview during the Cooper book launch? Or should I call it Passion Moon Madness."

I rolled my eyes.

"By the way I've forgotten to tell you that your little publicity stunt is snowballing into a big event. I've heard that some of the restaurants downtown are piggy backing off your idea of using the blood moon eclipse as a celebration. A few are creating Passion Moon menus; some bars are even offering special Passion Moon cocktails. I'll admit I thought it was a little hokey when Luke suggested the moon tie in, but he was right."

That was my brilliant husband. I was always surprised when his off-beat suggestions turned out to be gold. Then I remembered he wouldn't be here to see his idea in full bloom. I folded my arms to steady myself, hoping Bex wouldn't notice. But she continued to barrel through her story.

"We can do it in a hotel room and do a live feed. You can take questions from fans about the series. I'm thinking maybe a short segment at the end with Addy, but I haven't worked through the details."

"That's interesting, but--"

"I'll dangle the bait and see if his shark-like jaws will snap at it. I'll give you more information after I talk to him." She glanced at her watch. "I only have a few minutes before the driver comes back for me. I've got another meeting up the peninsula. Let's sit for a minute. I've got bad news about the Cooper recordings."

I slumped into a chair. "What is it? What happened?"

"First, I want you to know that stuff happens. But the equipment that Austin had installed failed again. Books one and three will be completed on time, but not book two."

"We can't release a set with one of the books missing."

"Yes, that's true, so I think we should concentrate on the ebook and paperback release, not the audio."

"Would the recording have been completed if Kaulder had kept to the schedule?

"Yes, but--"

"How many days did we miss from the schedule due to equipment failure?

"Four, maybe four and a half days."

"Do we still have time to finish the book?"

"Maybe, but it would be close... you don't want to publish a mediocre version."

"Is Austin going to replace the equipment?"

"Not right now. This is the last day the crew is working. Jay has a guy trying to repair it, but it doesn't look promising. Kaulder and the crew are at the studio in case there's a miracle and the problem is fixed--"

"I know you and Jay figure things like acts of God in the schedule. The way I see it, Kaulder's prima donna attitude and Austin's inferior equipment are costing me my audio launch."

"We can re-plan the audio launch. It will give us more time to make a bigger splash. Let's concentrate on the book."

"The fans already expect the audio release for the Passion Moon event."

Bex's phone buzzed. She checked it. "The driver is here, I've got to go, but I'll be back in my office in a few hours. I'll call you, and we can come up with some new strategies. It will be fine. Launches get pushed back all the time; they'll understand." She hugged me then disappeared through the front door. I stood there, my anger ready to explode, and I knew the perfect person that needed to feel my rage.

There were several vehicles in the lot when I arrived at Austin's house. That meant Jay, his crew, and Kaulder were all here and hopefully working. I marched to the porch and pressed the doorbell. When the chime ended, the only sound was the wind stirring the leaves and ducks complaining in the distance.

This wasn't happening fast enough for me. I had to sustain my rage. I pounded on the enormous wooden door. "Austin!" I shouted as if he could hear me. "I know you're in there. Get down here and open the door." I peered inside a window but saw nothing. Gravel crunched behind me.

"Emma?"

My heart jumped. I whirled around to see Austin standing on the path below the porch. He regarded me in a sweat-drenched tank and shorts. He pulled out his earbuds, dislodging a length from his bound hair. The surprise at seeing him defused some of my worked-up anger. I stared at him. Mind blank. "I came to see Kaulder, is he here?" I finally managed to say.

He took his time to trot the few steps. "The crew went to lunch. You might have passed them on the road." He reached the top and pushed the door open. "Jay said something about a restaurant in town. I don't expect them back for a couple of hours. They might return sooner if the repairs on the panel finish ahead of schedule. I'm waiting on another service person to show. Would you like to come inside to wait?"

I hesitated. I was ready for a showdown with Kaulder. I knew I would probably see Austin, but it was Kaulder I wanted to confront.

"I'm about to have lunch myself. I need to shower first. What did you want to talk to Kaulder about?"

"Book two."

"Ah, then you'd better come in."

I followed him upstairs to the reception pit outside the studio.

"If you'd like something before I come back, there's food and drinks in the frig, just push the beer aside."

"Thank you, I will." He left me and I enjoyed the view of his backside walking down the hall to his bedroom. He must have thought I was staring at him because he shot a glance over his shoulder and caught me ogling his nice posterior just before he turned into his bedroom.

When the water switched on in the shower, I walked the short distance into the studio. Part of the panel was dissembled and on the floor. The stand in the recording booth had Kaulder's marked-up copy of the book, bottled water, and a pair of reading glasses. That part checked out; he was working. I found myself in the frig, disengaging a can of cola from its plastic restraint.

I sat and picked up a fishing magazine from the table to flip through, finally settling on an article with stunning pictures about fishing in Ontario. I rotated in my chair when the smell of a clean body tickled my nose. Austin was standing near me in a black T-shirt, the cotton fibers working overtime to stay intact across his chest, and snug fitting jeans. His dark hair hung wet to his shoulders. His head inclined, intense gaze boring into me, deciding something.

"I still have a bottle of that wine you had at our lunch. It's chilling in the main kitchen."

I lifted my can of cola to him as a toast. "No thank you, I'm good."

"As you wish," he said and walked almost to the other side of the room, settling his large frame in an overstuffed chair. His face rested in his hand, looking like a king waiting to hear supplicants. I hadn't expected him to sit next to me, but he was giving me an awfully wide berth.

"I spoke to Bex this morning. She told about the book. Unfortunately, she sugarcoats everything because she's afraid I might react badly. I want to know what's going on."

"I think the character Cooper Flynn is some of the best work Kaulder has done."

"I agree, but the complete series must be ready for the Passion Moon event."

"It would be better if you waited for the finished product. Just because some sections had to be reworked, it shouldn't be rushed. I'll admit that the Passion Moon event you cooked up is a nice promotion for this genre, but there are other days. Better yet, why don't you declare a Cooper Flynn Day? I'm sure Bex can spin that."

"That day is meaningful to me--"

"Why, because that's when you and Parker fly off to the other side of the world?

I was making a mental note to kill Bex or at least maim her... what else had she told Magda?

"No, it has nothing to do with Parker. My husband chose the day. The promotion was his idea."

I studied the cola can in my hand for a few seconds, then placed it on the table. I was really getting tired of fighting for this day. This was just a book launch not scaling Mount Kilimanjaro.

"The latest Cooper release is the last book we worked on together. I'm honoring my husband, and the timetable we set for the book releases for this series. We always planned to have a Passion Moon celebration, and I will, but I want it to be a tribute to him."

He was silent for a time, absorbing this. "You're not just trying to wrap this up so you can leave?"

"I haven't decided about Parker or leaving."

That was an unexpected confession. I looked down, suddenly feeling exposed. My gaze fell on my ring. I was moving toward a life with Parker. He'd be a good choice, someone who would help start the next chapter of my life.

"Let me talk to Kaulder. I'll see what I can do before I leave." He got up. "It's best you're not here when they get back. He can be defensive about his work. I'll walk you out."

"You're leaving? For a few hours, days?"

"Initially, for a few weeks. A publishing company has asked me to do a narration of a new series. They want me to work out of their New York studios. I haven't been there for a while; I think a change will be good. I'm considering moving--"

"What about Izzy?" I blurted out just when my mouth decided to become a free agent. Why would that matter anyway, and why had my stomach turned when he said he was leaving?

"Magda is the one that encouraged me to go. She's pointed out several times that I can catch a flight any day of the week. There's nothing here to hold me. Like you, I can work anywhere."

We emerged from the house into a crisp bright day, the air saturated with rustic harmony. All of it barely registered through my dulled senses. My body moved with mechanical precision as I matched Austin's slow measured strides. He kept a proper distance from me, gazing ahead, features unreadable. My world had shifted again.

I leaned against the driver side of my car, ready to say my goodbye and thank him for intervening with Kaulder. Austin folded his arms. He was too close. He needed to work on his personal space issues.

"I wanted to say 'happy birthday'," he said, his gaze up and away.

"Thank you," I responded, trying to get him to look at me. "Why didn't you stay for the party? By the way, the set of coffee mugs was a wonderful gift."

"That was Magda's present. I had something else I wanted to give you."

That was awkward. What do you say to that? I'll take my present now, thank you very much? He studied me briefly, then found something more interesting to look at beyond me. Whatever his gift, and I was more than curious about what he had for me, it didn't appear to be forthcoming. "It was lovely to see you there. I meant you and Magda at the party."

"It wasn't a party," his irritation transparent, "because it wasn't about your birthday. Parker wanted to let me know that he had won."

I shook my head. "No, he didn't know you would be there. He planned a surprise party with Bex and our parents. He wouldn't do that."

He shifted and for an instant I thought he might walk away, but he set his jaw and slid his gaze to me. "I wasn't going to say this. I had convinced myself that I would stay out of it, but he's not right for you."

Wait a minute, he had no right. "Parker wants me."

"That was plain enough, but do you want him? I saw your face when he proposed. You should have looked like an audience member the day Oprah was giving out cars."

Again, with the proposal. Why does everyone think they know what I want? "I was surprised. The proposal was unexpected. But if you saw my face, then why did you leave?"

"Because I heard your answer," he said as he grabbed my left hand and jerked it up between us, the diamond glinting in the sun. "And you're still wearing his ring?"

I yanked my hand back. Jeez, he had nerve.

"Don't tell me that you haven't decided."

"I told you I haven't!"

"You've got to make a decision, or do you prefer to be led like a baying sheep? Oh, I've got it..." he said, as if the thought had just occurred to him, "...are the brothers interchangeable?"

That felt like a slap across the face. "At least he's not trying to charm a woman to fulfill his fantasies. Maybe I can help you out with that. I've been thinking about merchandising. Maybe I should produce a line of life-size, anatomically correct Molly dolls. That should take care of that big aching need you have."

"That's not what happened and don't be so sure about that ass Parker. He's got an agenda. Face reality and decide."

"What? I should choose you?"

"You know you want me."

Jesus Christ on a cheese snack, I was going to... I pushed away from the car and launched myself at him. I was standing toe to toe looking up. His face tilted down in grim interest. "Okay, here's a decision. I want you to stay away from me."

A self-satisfied grin curled his lips. "How can I? You keep coming here to see me."

Now I understood what it meant by seeing red. They should change it to seeing Austin.

My fingers bunched. That was it. If I could get my hands around that finely carved neck of his, I was going to strangle him. "You conceited ass--"

His hands made a swift transfer around my waist. My breath caught at the hasty advance. He pulled me forward, holding me tight, my breathing shallow. His face inches away, the almost black irises searching mine.

"Austin I--"

He pressed his hungry mouth to mine, and the sudden change jammed my thoughts, my senses whirling. Before I could protest, his massive body urged me back against the car, the cool surface of the window at my spine. My arms flung out to touch him, but he caught my wrists, stretching my arms over my head, pinning me. His tongue probed. I shivered and matched his need, wanting him to drown in me.

The night we spent together flashed in my mind like a sexy, crazy dream, his naked body defiant in front of me. The grind of his hard hips. The desperate whisper to come with him. It swirled around me until it seemed we were back in his bed moving together in a frantic rhythm.

He released my wrists, and I snaked my freed hands around his neck and held on to him. He was taking his time with his kiss and I was responding to the change. His big hands moved down my sides, searing through my clothes, stopping at my hips. My breath caught when they rested on the curve of my behind. I pushed my hips forward, but he pulled himself away, keeping a small distance between our bodies.

His forehead was inches from mine, his hands flat on the car above my shoulders. "I know you and Parker have history to build on and all I can offer is me, someone you don't know that stumbled into your life a few weeks ago. Emma, please, you've got to listen to what your heart tells you and what your body needs. I can't believe it's the same with him." He took a breath, searching my face, his words raw with emotion. "Think about this kiss and what we did that night we were together. Then decide." He brushed my lips one last time, then stepped back. I had to fight the urge to launch myself at him again, needing him to touch me that badly. I looked toward the house for a moment, not wanting to meet his gaze. When I brought my attention back, he turned to leave.

I watched him go. I leaned back against my car and ran the back of my hand across my sorely kissed mouth. His strides were slow and easy, taking his time to walk the path to the house. I never took my gaze from him until he disappeared inside and I was sure the door closed. Not once, in all that time, did he turn to steal a glance at me. I could still feel his body on me, his spice on my skin, but even that was fading.

In these last moments my heart ached so hard for him I thought it would combust, my need for him was that strong. But I pushed it aside.

Instead, I turned to what my mind had to offer, a stark dose of reality. Yes, what he and I had was off the charts attraction and it was great with Parker, but nowhere near the same level of intensity.

I had a long history with Parker, but knew almost nothing about this brooding man that affected me with his presence. I couldn't explain how everything about Austin seemed new and familiar at the same time. It was hard to reason, short of witchcraft, how he managed to gain a fast hold on my heart. But then there was Molly; it always came back to her. He'd wanted her for years. Even now I saw the yearning in his eyes for that perfect female I had created. I couldn't be that woman even if I was willing to try. Eventually, he'd realize his mistake. Disappointment would lead to him leaving me; then I'd be alone again.

I opened the car door, slipped inside, and turned the key in the ignition. A decision between these two men was way overdue. I glanced at the house again. Maybe I was hoping he'd come back one last time, but no, he made his feelings clear and there was nothing more to say; it all rested on me.

I gripped the steering wheel. "Austin," I whispered, "This was our last goodbye." I pulled the car out of the parking lot and onto the road. I'd chosen the man I knew almost everything about. I'd keep his ring and leave with him after the launch. It was time to begin a new life with Parker.

CHAPTER 24

Ice Rink

The best lazy days are in my backyard watching Daisy play with her pink feathered cat toy. I'm usually good at staying on my writing schedule, but today Molly and Cooper seemed to want a break from their adventures, so I declared a mental health day. That's why I was in a lounge chair under a tree with an ebook and an adult beverage. Only, I'd re-read the same steamy paragraph five times.

I closed my tablet and set it on the table in time to see the cat toy streak across the lawn. I was in a mood. It takes time to move beyond significant events, and I was trying hard to put Austin in my past where he belonged. So why did my visit with him, only a few days ago, still have me confused? Of course, everything he said about me was wrong.

Sure, we had off-the-charts heat between us, and I had to give it to him, he knew what switch to flip to make me lose my senses. But that, sadly, wasn't a basis for a lasting relationship. By now, he was probably gone to New York, working with a major publishing company.

I glanced at my phone on the table. Bex hadn't given me an update for a few days. I reached for my cell, then grabbed the drink instead. Now if the audio gods would smile on me and allow Kaulder to finish book two, one big headache would be gone.

Better not dwell on that and let Bex manage the recording. She still didn't tell me how or where Kaulder was completing the book. She said it was for my own good. That was code for 'so I wouldn't get impatient and storm the session.'

I'd only spoken to Parker a couple of times since my birthday. It was time to tell this man I wanted us to build a life together. Now that the decision was made, I didn't need to hold back. I set down my glass, picked up my phone, and punched speed dial. He picked up on the second ring.

"Parker, when are you coming home... I mean back?" I moaned into the phone. I couldn't deny it; I'd missed him. When I saw my wicked fiancée again, I would tell him the ban on non-sexy time was over and I was looking forward to more of our play.

"I miss you too. Hold on a minute." He muffled the mouthpiece. "I'll have a burger with everything on it. I'll be outside." The phone unmuffled. "I'm back. We just finished the front nine and now having a late lunch before we start the back nine."

"Where are you playing?"

"The Presidio; Dad got us the tee time. I'm playing with my parents and Nils."

"Tell them I said hi."

"I will. My parents are going back to San Diego tomorrow. I should be back by the afternoon. Let's do something." He sounded like the adventurous teenage Parker.

"What? Like dinner?"

"The ice rink is open downtown. I'll buy you a hot chocolate," he said, tossing in a strong incentive to a chocoholic.

"I heard Downtown Ice was open..." I laughed, liking the idea, "but I don't ice skate."

"I'm willing to give you a lesson. It will be fun. I'll have you skating like a champ in no time.

"When did you learn to ice skate?"

"During time spent in the Eos eastern hub. Look, I'll even throw in dinner at Joe's."

How many outdoor ice rinks have palm trees festooned with colorful, glittering lights that towered above an icy circle? It was the perfect cool, clear night to be outside enjoying the season. I was practically pulling Parker along as I weaved through the crowd to get to the rink. I dropped his hand and made it to the railing a few steps ahead of him. He reclaimed my hand. "Come on, let's get you some skates before you burst with anticipation."

Parker's patient instructions encouraged me to wobble around the rink with his strong arm guiding me. I held onto him for fear of doing a face plant in front of the small children whizzing by us. After clinging to him the entire time we skated, I finally attempted to skate unaided, which I managed for about twenty seconds before I took a spill. He pulled me up, and I melted into his arms when he gave me a sweet kiss. I was getting excited about sharing a life with this man. "I've got something I want to tell you," whispering into his collar. He tightened his hands around my waist. This was the perfect moment to tell him that I'd marry him and we'd be leaving together after the launch was done. Right now, I wanted him naked in my bed. I'd suggest ditching dinner at Joe's and celebrating breaking my no sexy-time rule with no games tonight, only the two of us fucking each other senseless.

"Tired already?" He released my waist and skated in front of me, pulling me along. "I think you've had enough for one lesson; we can come again next week if you're up to it. Why don't we return our skates, then we can talk?"

We found spots at the railing, watching skaters enjoy the rink. Parker looked handsome with wisps of auburn hair poking out of his wool cap and all I wanted to do his take him home and... "Parker, I--"

"Hold that thought. Everything is better with chocolate. Are you ready for the hot chocolate I promised?"

"Mmmm... sounds perfect."

A new group of skaters, mostly children, glided onto the ice.

"Why don't you stay here while I get in line for the drinks. Extra whipped cream, right?"

"You know me so well."

"Be right back."

I smiled, watching him head for the drinks cart.

Groups of warmly bundled skaters with varying skills continued to drift onto the groomed ice. The seasonal music pumped in from the overhead speakers helped to perpetuate the joy in the air.

A striking woman with a short bob dressed in black was shepherding three giggly girls about age ten. One of the girls appeared to be as accomplished on the ice as the woman. She had to be her daughter; they looked similar. The woman and her daughter were trying to tempt the two girls onto the ice.

The reluctant girls came out on unsteady legs, but to their credit, they picked up skating quickly and were moving slowly but confidently. The woman skated around the rink two times alone, giving a display of skill and grace. She stopped in a spray of ice close to me, watching the trio.

"You look like you were born on skates,"

The woman turned to me with cheery interest. "I grew up back east. In the winter my family practically lived at Frog Pond on Boston Common. Do you know Boston?"

"No, I'm a native Southern Californian; I'd probably shrivel up from the cold."

"You should visit. Boston is beautiful in the spring. Very historic," she said conspiratorially.

"Mom, did you see what I taught Ariel?"

The woman looked over. "No dear, show me again."

Ariel pushed out and made a slow turn. The girl beamed when she came to a stop.

"You're doing a great job, Sam," she said and gave a thumbs-up to her daughter.

"Do you live here now?"

"We live in the North Bay. We usually go to the rink in Union Square in San Francisco. We thought this would be a fun change. My name is Rachel, by the way."

"Emma."

"All right, it was a long haul," Parker said, "but good things happen to those that will stick it out in the cold. Here is your hot chocolate, my lady, with extra whipped cream. I even got them to add sprinkles..."

Parker stopped and blinked. One of the cups in his hands sloshed liquid onto his glove. He was staring at Rachel.

"This is Rachel."

"We've already met. How have you been, Parker?"

"Fine," he managed to say.

I pulled off my gloves and stuffed them in my pocket. He barely noticed when I took one of the cups from him. "How do you know each other?" I asked, taking a sip.

I watched them talk to each other silently. It appeared to be a heated conversation conducted with just facial expressions. It would be interesting to hear this exchange if they used their voices. Yes, these two had a history.

"She's a pilot at Eos," he croaked out.

"Mom," Sam called.

"Yes dear," she said, not taking her gaze off Parker.

"Ariel and Jasmine are hungry; can we go have pizza now?"

"Yes, I'll just be a minute. Take your skates back to the rental, and I'll meet you there."

Sam frowned.

"Go on," she encouraged. "I can see you from here. I'll be there in a few minutes."

The girl left and joined her companions. Laughter trailed behind them as they melted into the crowd.

Rachel's steel gaze came back to Parker. This woman had him spooked. He still retained that deer-in-the-headlights look.

"We're much more than co-workers; you should make him tell you the story." She swung her gaze to me. I was drinking my hot chocolate with both hands. Her eyes narrowed. "I see you got the diamond prize. Well done."

She pushed off the railing and gracefully weaved her way through the skaters after the girls.

For once in my life, I'd like to go out with Parker without some monumental life-changing crap going on.

We were in my backyard. Parker was slumped in a lawn chair, looking older and more tired than I'd ever seen him. I handed him a scotch, to loosen his tongue and to bolster his courage. I popped open a can of cola and draped myself on a lounge chair. I had already fired up the heat lamp and turned on the overhead string lighting. It softened the patio with enough light to feel relaxed.

"You're not going to join me?" he said, staring at the liquid in the glass.

"No, something tells me I should be stone cold sober for this conversation."

It was an impossibly long story, but the gist of it was that he fell in love with Rachel about two years ago when she joined Eos. She was married, but he didn't know that at the time they met. They had been discussing marriage. He was about to propose when he discovered that, not only was she married, but she also had a daughter.

"How did you not know she was married?"

"Her daughter, Sam, lives with her father in Boston. Rachel has a flat in San Francisco. We would be there or San Diego when we had time off. No one knew about our dating. She wanted to keep it quiet because we both worked at the same company."

"You mean you were forty-five miles from here, and you never came to visit?"

He placed his drink on the table and rubbed his face like he was working on a migraine.

"Why are you here?"

"To see you, Em..."

I stared at him and took a long drag on my soda.

"It was a pretty ugly break-up," he continued. "She accused me of being a cheat. I never did, not since we'd met. She said I was too selfish to make a real commitment and that I would never marry and die alone."

Now it started to make sense. "So, you came knocking on my door to prove her wrong? And moving to Australia? Did you quit your job at Eos to get away from her?"

"I don't love her." The declaration came out in a frustrated moan. "I've told her that. I told her I moved on with you, but she won't accept that it's over. She's been here trying to get us back together. I knew she was angry, but I never thought she would go into stalker mode, but then again, I had no idea she was abandoning a husband and a daughter to be with me.

Why I left Eos was the truth. I've needed a new start for a long time. My invitation for you to leave with me was real."

"Is that why you didn't show up for dinners?"

"Yes and no. I thought I could diffuse the situation if I talked to her; other times," he shrugged, "I'm sorry, but you know you're not the best cook."

I shook my head and prayed for guidance. How did we get here? "You said you don't love her; do you love me?"

"Yes."

"Love me, or in love with me?"

"I said I love you."

"No, I could be your sister, and you would love me."

"We could make this work," he pleaded. "I know I fucked this up, but I've forgiven you--"

"Forgiven me? For not marrying you years ago?"

"No, for hooking up with that ass Austin.

I know my mouth flew open.

"Don't start pretending innocence. It wouldn't be you."

Obviously, I didn't want him to know about that mistake where I temporarily lost good judgment. I sat back in my chair. "How long have you known?"

He raked frustrated fingers through his hair. "I found out the day of your party." I came back to the house to get my suit for your surprise dinner in Half Moon Bay. I walked into your office to make copies of our travel itinerary as part of your birthday present. I saw the blinking light on your phone and thought I could field a call for you like I've done as your PA. I knew you wouldn't get to it until Monday." His chair creaked as he reached for his glass. "Austin was on the voice mail droning on about the night you spent together. I almost packed up then and left. But I needed to see you; I wanted to know if you were still mine or planning to dump me for that narrator on steroids. You didn't help my fears when you ran out after my proposal."

"You were angry when we made love in my hotel room, and here I thought it was hot play." Did everyone have an agenda?

He swirled the scotch around in the glass, contemplating. "I could never be angry at you. I was hurt. I thought we had some kind of an understanding before I left that we would see where this would lead."

A wave of tiredness swept over me. I felt I had been fighting against a tide and had finally given up. I slipped the ring off my finger. The metal tapped the surface when it hit the table.

He stood, pain taking his features as he picked up the ring. "I was serious about making it work. It could be like the old days when we were kids running wild in San Diego."

"But I'm not that teenage girl."

He was standing close, looking like he wanted to touch me.

I sat straighter in the chair. "Too much has happened," the words clogging my throat. "You should want me for who I am now, and not to prove to your stalker girlfriend that you can get married or to win an imaginary contest."

"I do love you. I always have." The hoarse declaration was almost too much to hear. He reached out to me, but I shook my head no. I couldn't. "I know you wanted me, but were you in love with me?"

I didn't answer because the truth was too hard to admit out loud to Luke's brother that the young girl in San Diego was in love with both of them.

I was young and afraid I couldn't hold the love of this wild, beautiful boy. I chose the safe option instead. Not that Luke was second best; I loved him with all my heart. But I longed for his brother. Like a gift Parker returned for me and it seemed I was going to have a second chance at love. How long would it have taken to find out this wasn't real and that we were just trying to rekindle some magic from the past?

Parker rolled the ring between his fingers; the diamond caught the light even from here. "Would it have been different if there was no Austin?"

I was silent.

"I need to know, was it Austin?"

He was demanding the same honesty I'd asked of him. It was only fair to give him an answer. "No, he has nothing to do with this. I'm sorry, I'll always love you, but it's not the kind of love to build a life together."

He gave me a tight smile. "You know, the funny thing is my mother thinks that I always wanted what Luke had. That's not true. I always made a show of wanting his possessions to get his attention. He was my cool big brother, and I wanted to hang out and be like him. I guess I never grew out of it, but he loved you, and you were the only thing that he had that I truly wanted."

He walked into the darkness, then stopped. Without turning, he asked, "At the rink. Were you going to tell me that you accepted my proposal and we were going to leave together?"

It tore at me that he knew. "Yes." I choked out the word. Silence followed while I fought for composure.

"I think Luke would have wanted us together," came his hoarse whisper, "wanted me to take care of you."

I tried to say more, but his footsteps echoed on the pavement until the gate closed behind him.

I sat in the lounge chair for a long time, thinking. The night sky was clear enough to see the stars, and a pale-yellow moon crested in its waning. A neighbor somewhere in the court was enjoying a fire. The sweet wood smoke was a faint perfume in the air. Probably someone was seated in front of the flames enjoying a book, content with his world, while mine crashed and burned around me.

I pulled my knees to my chest and began to rock. The sadness was coming for me and I couldn't fight it. Big fat tears rolled down my cheeks that splashed onto my shoes. I thought it would be different this time, but the one thing I feared, always feared, happened. I was abandoned and alone again. I took in a ragged breath, rocked my body harder, and cried more stupid tears.

CHAPTER 25

Pastrami Therapy

*I*t took a few days to fight my way back to some kind of normalcy. I even attended a meeting of my loss and grief group and spoke to the group leader a few times. Then I dug into my work and tried to move forward. I called Bex to meet me at the Refuge for lunch to sort the last details of the launch and to indulge in pastrami therapy.

Bex confirmed that Austin was truly gone. Apparently, Magda casually mentioned a few days ago that she was interviewing potential renters for her brother's house while he worked in New York.

Bex watched me with interest after delivering the news. "I'm sorry to have to start a meeting off like this, but I thought it was best to get it out of the way. I noticed that you're not wearing Parker's ring. Does that mean you made a decision?"

The waiter finally caught my eye, and I pointed to my empty water glass.

"No worries. Thanks for the update, I had heard he might leave soon. As for Parker, we finally decided that we would be better apart. I think we have too much baggage between us that needed to be overcome to make it work. Australia would have been an exciting place to live, but it's about fifteen hours from California and I would have missed my life in the valley. Anyway, thanks for agreeing to meet me halfway for lunch." The waiter set down an iced water and whisked away the empty.

"Are you kidding?" she pulled out a notebook and pen. "When you mentioned pastrami sandwiches at the Refuge, I almost grabbed my keys and headed out in the middle of a client meeting… and they were sitting in my office."

I gave her a weak smile.

Her brows drew together. "I know you're stress eating. It's been pretty rough for you lately." She hesitated enough for me to know what was coming. "We haven't talked for a few days. You sounded distracted during our last chat, how are you coping? Is everything alright?"

Her concerns were valid. She wanted to know if I'd regressed back to my old coping mechanisms. Was I crawling back into my books for comfort? I was tempted, but no. Maybe somehow, I'd gotten stronger. "I guess finding out that the two men that were fighting over me a few weeks ago was all an illusion. Parker thought I was a naïve teenager and Austin hoped I was a time-walking sexpot. I'd say that being me wasn't what they wanted. I'm okay. They were just misguided souls."

"When did you become so Zen?"

"Since I've been concentrating on my writing, instead of what was passing for a love life. I think I have an idea for a new series."

Bex's face lit up. "Before I get too excited, are you at the stage to discuss this project?"

"Almost, but let's get the Cooper series put to bed first."

"I like your thinking." She glanced at her notebook. "Let's talk about the book launch.

Bex, through her multiple connections, had managed to snag a room for the party at the Lorelei, a posh hotel in downtown San Jose.

She placed a line through a notation in her book. "Okay, logistics are taken care of, so let's talk about the launch."

"Why are you using a notebook?"

She glanced down at her agenda as if it had just appeared on the table. "Because these outside cafe tables are too small to hold my laptop; besides, I don't mind getting mustard on a cheap spiral notebook."

I sat back, "Okay, it just looked strange."

"Now that we've settled my unusual note-taking method, I want to continue. I've arranged a cocktail party and dinner to celebrate the launch of the newest Cooper book. I've invited the crew and their significant others. It will be a small but lively celebration. About an hour into the party, I've scheduled a webcast. We'll set up in a penthouse suite.

I opened my mouth to protest, but Bex cut me off.

"Before you start with the lecture that you're just a poor struggling indie author," she chose that moment to perform an impressive eye roll, "my contact at the hotel was kind enough to throw in a few hours' access to the suite."

"Okay, maybe I'm not poor, but I do have a budget. But you're good."

"Yes, I am, but this will give you a chance to talk to your fans. We'll have open phone lines and an online chat to interact with them. The best part is that Kaulder has agreed to do the thirty-minute interview with you."

I grimaced. "What's the status on the audio? Can we include the audio versions of the Cooper series as part of the launch?"

Bex leaned back, tapping her pen on the table. "I don't know what you said to Kaulder, but he's working furiously to complete the re-recordings."

"I didn't talk to him. He wasn't there when I arrived. I had a conversation with Austin."

"I could have sworn Jay said you talked to Kaulder. Anyway, he's on a mission, but the good news is that he will finish on time."

I almost raised my hand for a high five, but she looked like there was more on her mind. I placed a finger on my water glass and traced some droplets of condensation instead.

"I want to discuss Addy." She looked down at her notes and frowned. "I suggest a short interview with him after the webcast with you and Kaulder."

"I'm not sure I want to agree to that--"

"I did some negotiating with him, but I told him that you have to approve it before we move forward. It will be for twenty minutes, and he has to submit questions first."

"How do we know he will stick to the questions?"

"Two things, you will tape a promo spot for his podcast that will run before the interview, and second, you'll agree to reveal something that no one knows about the books or Angela Stryker. We can work out that part together or at least run it by me before the big reveal."

"Are you sure this is a good idea? What if he decides to go rogue?"

"I also hinted that if this experiment is successful, we could partner with him on promoting future books. That should keep him in line. If we stick to our end of the bargain, it should be fine. Besides, he let it slip that he's excited to be a part of the Passion Moon Launch."

"So, we tape the interview?"

"No, it goes out live. He's going to add another podcast in his schedule to accommodate us. This will be a special exclusive. I'm sure his fans and yours will be in a frenzy when we announce the interviews."

The waiter set down two plates of pastrami sandwich heaven.

"Do I have your agreement?"

I inhaled the heady aroma of pastrami, sauerkraut, mustard and sighed. Addy would be better as an ally instead of an irritating rock in my pointy boots. The truth was, I needed to change his narrative quickly. If he continued repeating these rumors much longer, fans would think that I was a group of corporate ghost writers instead of an indie author and it would be more difficult to counter something that was already an urban myth.

I'd been thinking that this incident may not be the disaster that I originally thought. This issue might have come at the perfect time to give me another nudge in my career path. As the popularity of my books grew, I was feeling more acceptance for my stories. I was considering a way to become more accessible to my fans to let them know the real person behind Angela Stryker.

Addy's podcast, *Addictions to Love*, might become a safe bridge to help me open up to an interested audience. "Yes, I think the plan is reasonable. Could you outline all your suggestions for me to review, then I'll give you a final okay?"

"I'll send the outline to you today when I get back to the office," she said pinching off a morsel of pastrami from her sandwich. She sampled it, making an "Umm" sound while her eyes registered bliss. Finding her crisp white napkin, she touched her mouth then replaced it on her lap. I thought she was going to tear into her sandwich, but instead she picked up her pen to draw another line in her notebook. I, on the other hand, was going in.

"There's something else. I've wanted to talk about this for a long time."

I tore my concentration away from the plate. I should have known this meeting was going along too smoothly. On Bex's emotional scale, this appeared to rate a low priority, but necessary.

"Since the buzz about the new book and the audio series, I've noticed an uptick in your social media presence on all the platforms. You've always insisted on handling that portion of your business yourself, and you should because the fans want to connect with you. But you're also managing Luke's old duties as well.

I know the increased responsibilities are limiting your time to write and edit. I think you should consider hiring a personal assistant. Maybe part-time at first to see how it goes. Some writers share PAs."

She was right, of course, but I just went through the experience of selecting a narrator. I didn't know if I was up to finding a PA and then there was the training part and deciding what duties they would take over. "I don't think I'm ready to go through another interview process."

She beamed. "I think I have someone in mind."

After the Austin recommendation, I wasn't sure I wanted her to suggest any more potential employees. To be fair, Austin was an excellent narrator, so she was good at spotting talent, and he would have gotten the job on his own if... "Who is it?"

"I want to talk to him first?"

Oh my God, "It's a he?" I groaned. "I think I would rather a female."

"Don't you want someone who will be good no matter what gender?"

"Just don't suggest someone who is even faintly attractive."

"Do you have a prejudice against the beautiful?"

I gave her my best yeah-right look. "You know what I mean. I don't want any more drama."

"I don't even know if he will be interested. It's someone I've come across in my travels, so until I have an okay to move forward, I won't mention who it is. I could put an ad on Carmen's list. I'm sure we would get a huge response."

I cast my gaze to heaven and shook my head. Help me, sweet Jesus, we'd have every creep within a fifty-mile radius applying.

She laughed. "Got you. That was too easy. Anyway, if my candidate isn't interested, you do have other avenues to find suitable applicants. Remember, you belong to a few writers' groups. We can ask around there or place ads on their sites... deal?

"All right, deal."

My sandwich was whispering to me. It was a generous portion, and half would be coming home with me. I hefted it, then took a bite. "Hmmm..." Jeez, I said that out loud.

"Emma?"

She was tapping her pen again. I placed the sandwich back on my plate, chewed a bit more, then swallowed.

"This is the last item I want to discuss. I know you want to do a tribute to Luke--"

"I would like to do a dedication at the launch party and the webcast."

"I can see that would be appropriate for the party, but your fans think you're married with two kids and a dog."

"For Addy's podcast, you asked me to reveal something no one knows about me. I want to share my real background."

"That would mean exposing your real name, Luke, and all the rest of it."

"Some of this is already known to the public."

"But you'd be opening up old wounds. You'd be reliving it again."

"Maybe I could help someone else. I think Luke would want me to tell his story. The real story. I wasn't strong enough to do it earlier. I think I am now. Fans will be curious when they see the dedication I've written. Did you read it?"

"Yes, it just says: for Luke. I see what you're trying to do, but are you sure?"

No, I wasn't sure. No one is ever sure when they take a big life-altering step, but somehow this seemed to be the right time to begin. Addy would get a better deal than he anticipated.

"I need your support on this."

"You know you always have it. Let's go over what you're going to say. This will spark more requests for interviews and research into your past. If there is one saving grace, it would be that the engagement with Parker is off. I liked him, but if you had decided to marry, it would have brought a salacious, even sinister element to your story."

She was right about marrying my dead husband's brother. No matter how innocent, it would have made the stuff of novels, but if Parker and I were meant to be, it wouldn't have mattered who he was, just that I needed to be with him.

235

"Now that I've made the decision, let's pick another time to discuss my reveal. I just want to enjoy my sandwich and my friend's company."

She smiled and put her pen and notebook in her bag.

CHAPTER 26

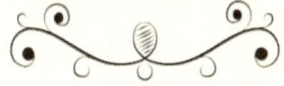

Bye, Bye, Bye

The day before the Cooper book launch, I was working in my office when the doorbell rang. I peeked out of the kitchen window to see Parker's handsome face smiling back at me. I opened the door, and he brushed past me to stand in the middle of my kitchen. I hoisted myself onto the granite counter, then I remembered what we had done on this surface the last time I sat here and slid off. Parker must have caught it too and grinned.

"I'm leaving early tomorrow for Australia. This is the only time I had to say goodbye."

I had hurt him, and still he wanted to see me before he left. "I'm sorry, Parker."

He folded his arms, his hip against the sink. "No need for regrets; I knew I had lost you in Campbell when I met Aston."

"Austin," I corrected.

He ignored me.

"I did a lot of thinking after our talk. I wanted to say I understand."

He seemed pretty upbeat after losing a woman he had waited ten years for... and wasn't I the love of his life? Maybe he was trying to show a brave face. We'd known each other too long to break ties completely after all this time. Even in the last three years, when he hadn't come to see me, he sent cards and notes. Now I realized it was the best he could do after Luke was gone.

"I've got some things to discuss with you before I leave," he said, extending his hand to me. "I'm sorry I can't stay longer. Will you walk with me to the car? I can give you my news there."

I shrugged and took his hand. "Sure."

It seemed awkward after all these weeks apart for Parker to walk by my side holding my hand. Our break-up was painful, but I'd missed him. I'd become accustomed to the scent of his aftershave in the morning. His clothes mingled with mine in the dryer, and our crazy sex play still made me blush. It all came back while we strolled. I did love him. We had history. Maybe I was too hasty. Could we have worked it out? "Parker, I'd like to--"

He released my hand as we approached a sedan parked in front, a driver waiting. A pretty, petite blond emerged from the back seat.

"Hi, Emma."

"Holly?" I turned to Parker and watched him take his place beside her.

"What's this about?" I asked, aware that two people were avoiding my gaze.

"You know we've been talking over the phone about you and your work," Parker said, confirming the statement to a nodding Holly.

Holly's cheeks flushed. I'd never seen my prickly friend so anxious. She squeezed Parker's hand.

"Parker suggested we talk to you."

I looked at him for a clue of where this was going, but his attention was on Holly.

He gave her a nod of encouragement. She stepped forward. "I didn't know he was your brother-in-law when I met him over the phone. I thought he was a PA you hired," she said in a rush.

"Yes, he was a big help during--"

"I invited him for coffee when we were working on the edits," she blurted.

"Right, maybe we should go inside and talk." I didn't think the driver needed to hear our discussion.

She continued, not responding to my suggestion. "He kept changing the subject when I'd bring up the coffee invitation during our meetings," she confessed. "It was at your birthday party when I realized you were together and that he was just being nice to me and didn't want to hurt my feelings."

I didn't want to hear this. "My kitchen--"

She bit her lip and looked over at Parker. He started to speak, his eyes mirroring her concern. "I think what she is trying to say is--"

"No, Parker," she interrupted. "This is my story to tell. You didn't do anything wrong." She turned to me. "When I heard the engagement was over, I called him..."

I stood there in blank confusion, trying to un-hear her.

Parker put his arm around Holly. She gazed up at him as if he was her whole world. Parker smiled at her but with a tired, haunted look. He wasn't in the same place as Holly, but that didn't mean it would never happen. His attention came back to me. "I've kept things from you and it's hurt you," Parker began, "We wanted to tell you..."

Why was Holly biting her lip to a bloody pulp while Parker fumbled around for the right words? It finally hit me. "I can't believe this shit! You're together? You've been together all this time behind my back."

Holly took a step back and glanced at Parker.

Finding her arm, he pulled her back beside him. "No, not in the way you mean. She's been an ear for me and a good friend, nothing more. I wanted you to know we've become friends. I didn't want someone telling you different."

I didn't believe them. How could I when it looked like she was in love with him. Parker stood there waiting for me to trust him. I was afraid of being hurt, but I was more frighten of losing him again. A relationship with Holly shouldn't matter, but it did. I knew I didn't have a right to be jealous, I'm the one that let him go.

"It's true," she said, touching my arm. "He never encouraged my blatant flirting when I thought he was your PA. Even after your break-up and he agreed to have coffee, he never offered more."

"Telling you about my friendship with Holly was only part of it. I'm going to Australia to find that new start I keep talking about and maybe find a way to change. You've done it," he gave me a half grin, "Changed, while I stayed stuck in the past."

Now that I wasn't looking at them through a cloud of jealousy, I could see the truth.

"You're my family," he said slipping an arm around my shoulders, "and despite everything that's happened between us, I don't want to lose that."

I couldn't lose Parker. It would have severed too many ties to my past. I exhaled relief, but still felt like an idiot for not trusting them.

Parker looked down at me. Something sparked in his eyes. "You know, I've been keeping Holly in stitches over your big-hair phase when you were a teenager. After my stories about you, I'm not sure she wants to continue your business relationship."

Holly inclined her head. "You know my views on big hair; this could seriously be a game changer for us. It would explain…"

Damn it, I was starting to smile. I reached for Holly and we hugged. "Thank you, for helping Parker," I whispered.

She released me, and I turned to my brother-in-law. "And Parker, stop defaming me. If you're the reason I lose the best editor I've ever had, I will hurt you."

Parker leaned toward Holly. "I've got to get my jacket from the guest room. I'll be right back."

He looked through the kitchen window. Maybe he was expecting Holly to come up the path.

"You know she's in love with you, right?" I said to his back.

He turned a tired face to me. "I like Holly, but I don't want to disappoint her. I've been honest about my feelings, and I've told her about you and Rachel, but I'm afraid she thinks my fondness for her will change."

"She's a big girl. As long as you're truthful, that's all you can do."

Something occurred to me. I know it was silly, but I had to ask. "Parker, you didn't tell her everything about us? I mean--"

He leaned against the counter next to me. "What, that you're kinky wild in bed? That's something between us, although I'll never look at a massage table the same way again."

"Thanks." I blew out a breath. I wasn't a prude, but I still had to work with her.

"Holly isn't naïve; she knows we lived together for a while. I even proposed to you in front of everyone. I'm sure she's already guessed what we were doing all those weeks?

He leaned closer to me, his hand covering mine. "I'm sorry I wasn't honest. I know it hurt you. I swear I'll be a better friend."

I gave him a long goodbye hug and tried to fight back the tears. He held me tight, my head on his shoulder. I wished this was the Parker who came to my door a few months ago. It might have been different, but no, I couldn't make this into something that it wasn't.

He kissed me on the forehead and stepped away. "Thanks for letting me stay here with you. It changed my life."

I watched him walk the path, knowing it would be a long time before I'd see him again. Midway down he stopped, turned, and gave me a sloppy salute. A sadness came over him and he stood there watching me. I felt our mutual regret that it hadn't worked out for us. Parker straightened, his devil's grin dazzling me from here. He lifted his fingers to his lips and released a kiss. I caught it and gently placed it over my heart.

CHAPTER 27

Little Mouse

*I*t was late, and past the time I should be considering crawling back into bed, pulling the covers over my head and giving the rest of this day a pass.

The Passion Moon event was tonight. I missed Luke and, instead of sitting at home remembering my past, I agreed to attend a launch party for the Cooper series. I wasn't a famous author, so this was not a splashy media reception. I had a loyal cult following that was respectable but growing. We would be celebrating the book and audio launch with a small cocktail party and dinner at a hotel downtown. It would be Bex, Kaulder, the recording crew with their significant others, and me.

I shimmied into a new red dress that clung shamelessly to my body. It was cut low, held up by thin adjustable straps. I'd bought it on a whim, years ago, but never wore it. After trying it on at home, I realized that it was too provocative, and the clasps needed to be fixed. I discovered if I moved too quickly the clasps opened, and the front fell lower. I was going to take it back when Luke saw me in it and convinced me to keep it. He always called it my hard-on dress.

Any man seeing me would immediately get an erection. Whenever we dressed up for an occasion, he'd ask me to wear it, but I just couldn't. I found a lace jacket that covered my assets enough to sit in anyone's company.

The car I ordered would be here soon. I twisted my hair into a chignon and slipped on my black heels and left.

The hotel was packed. There were always concerts, plays, and events going on in downtown San Jose. I searched the large sign board located in the hotel lobby listing the evening's events. After the Elliott Wedding Reception was listed the Flynn Dance Party. We had used Cooper's last name and dance from the book title *Danger Dance: Passion Moon* as an inside joke. Only the people who worked on the project would know the meaning.

I must have been the last to arrive. Everyone was well into the party mood. Kaulder was there with a very young redhead who didn't leave his side and laughed a little too loud.

I'd just gotten a drink from the bar when Bex made an announcement from the front of the room.

"Could I have everyone's attention? Our dinner will be delayed for a little more than an hour. During that time, we will be conducting a live phone and chat interview with the author Angela Stryker and narrator William Kaulder of the Cooper Flynn series."

Raucous clapping and a few whistles.

I lifted my glass to the assembly, and Kaulder did a slight bow.

"The interview will be located in a penthouse suite upstairs," Bex continued.

There were loud oohs and laughter.

"Maybe we should renegotiate our fee for the next book?" Jay, the audio director, yelled above the voices.

More laughter.

"Okay, okay," she chuckled, "I guess you won't miss us, so please, continue to enjoy yourselves."

Bex smiled her way through a cluster of people, moving toward me. "I'm going up to the suite now. See if you can pry Kaulder from that woman and meet me at suite 2312."

I made my way over to Kaulder. The redhead latched tighter onto his arm as I approached. He gave me one of his charming smiles.

He raised his drink to me. "Linda, this is Emma, or should I say Angela Stryker, our host?"

Linda smiled but didn't lessen her death grip on him.

"Good to meet you," I said, then turned my attention to Kaulder. "I wanted to know if you would like to ride in the elevator with me to the suite?"

"Oh, I've never seen a webcast before, could I come too?" Linda cooed.

Kaulder's eyes were pleading with me. "Would it be alright? I'm sure she would be quiet."

"Like a cute little mouse, I promise," Linda said, trying to look childlike.

I made a valiant effort not to do an eye-roll but smiled kindly. I know Bex instructed me to convince Kaulder to come alone, but this woman had melded into his side and wasn't budging. "That would be fine. But we should leave now."

My heart stayed somewhere south of my stomach as we whooshed our way up to the twenty-third floor. We disembarked onto a plush carpet that ran through the ultra-modern hallway. If the suite looked anything like the corridor, we were in for a treat. Bex must have pulled some serious strings because this was not coming out of my budget.

Kaulder pounded on the door with Linda still hanging on to his arm. I was afraid if we encountered a gentle breeze, it might knock her over, she was that unsteady. The door swung open, and my harried friend rushed forward, wrapping her arms around me, exhaling a huge sigh of relief.

"I got one of Jay's tech guys to help me with the set-up," she said as she pulled me through and motioned Kaulder and his lady friend inside. "But we don't have much time until we go live. We're set up in the next room."

Kaulder was trying to convince Linda not to come into the room. She was a bit tipsy. Maybe he thought she couldn't be quiet during the interview.

"Just pick up the phone and order more champagne, sweetheart," Kaulder said, trying to disentangle himself to follow us, but she latched onto him again, begging to be inside the room with us.

They were still talking when I followed Bex into a dining area. Three laptops and phone equipment sat on the table.

"I've tested the equipment, but you need to get miced."

I slipped on the headset and sat in front of a laptop as Bex took her place.

"Remember that your interview with Addy Finch will start ten minutes after this webcast. Before we sign off, I'll invite everyone on the line to dial-in to the special edition to *Addictions to Love*. We'll also provide the information in the chat box. I'm sure they're already aware of the next event. It's been pretty heavily advertised, with the promo spot you recorded and Addy announcing it every five seconds."

"How much time do we have before we begin?"

"About a minute."

We both looked at the door. Bex got up and poked her head out. She sat back down.

"He's coming."

Bex pushed a button on her laptop. The splash page that said the webcast would start shortly was replaced by the cover art of the Cooper series.

"Hello, Cooper fans and welcome to the Passion Moon event. This is Bex Winston, and I will be your host during the next thirty minutes. As you know, I will be talking to the author of the Cooper series, Angela Stryker." Bex mouthed at me to say hello.

"Hi, everyone. This is Angela. I'm so glad to be here with you to talk about the new book and the release of the audio series."

Just then the door banged opened. I jumped at the sudden interruption, angry that Kaulder could be so careless. I pulled my gaze from the screen to see a man filling up the entryway in a steel gray suit, his dark hair swept back away from his face and bound, his mood intense. He ignored me and focused all his attention on Bex, who didn't appear to be shocked that Austin Santoro had entered the room.

"What the...?" I said.

Bex pressed a button on her laptop. "We're on mute. Give me a minute, and don't say anything while I'm talking. I'll say something about having problems with the feed, then I'll mute it again."

The chat portion on my screen exploded as people typed that they couldn't hear us.

"Sorry about that," Bex said smoothly. "We're having technical problems. Give us a minute to fix the audio glitch. In the meantime, type your questions in the chat box."

Austin slipped into the empty chair and put on the headset.

"Why are you here?" I demanded. "And where's Kaulder?"

He looked at me, his dark eyes narrowed. "I'm here. You're looking at Kaulder."

"Okay, now that's settled," Bex said, her hand nervously hovering over the button. "I guess we can open the phone lines."

"Bex, you knew about this?"

She nodded and glanced at her laptop. "I've got to continue the interview; I need to unmute and open the lines."

I pulled off my headset and pushed away from the table. "I can't do this."

"Don't do that," Austin warned. "You've got about 5,000 people on this call and counting. If you leave, you're damaging your brand, not to mention that my fan base is on the call as well. You can keep it together for thirty minutes while we chat with these nice fans. After, I'll explain everything if you still want to listen."

I glanced at my laptop. I hadn't noticed the attendee counter on the screen. It had just clicked over to 5,553 and wasn't showing signs of slowing. I had a cult following, but this kind of interest in the book was more than I had ever experienced.

I huffed and replaced my headset. I gave Austin and Bex the best *I'm going to kill you both and bury your bodies where no one will find them* look I could manage. Bex shuddered; Austin just grinned.

Bex pressed the button to unmute. "Thank you for your patience," she said, watching Austin and me having a staring contest. "It seems we've fixed the issue. I also want to introduce William Kaulder, the narrator of several books on the New York Times bestseller list and the voice of Cooper Flynn."

"It's great to be here this evening," Austin said leaning onto his forearms, watching his laptop.

When he spoke, his voice was deeper, richer, like the Kaulder that came through my earbuds. Austin had voiced William Kaulder like another character. That's why I didn't recognize his voice when he spoke to me.

Austin watched me as he continued. "I can't wait to talk to you and answer your questions about one of the best characters I've had the pleasure to voice."

"Let's go to our first caller," said Bex, "You're on live with us. What's your name, and where are you calling from?"

"Hi, this is Meghan from San Jose. This question is for William. I'm here with about fifty of your loyal fans listening at my house. I wanted to say, and I know I speak for all of us, we are so glad that you've agreed to do this interview. We just wanted to know why there are no photos of you? And why aren't you more accessible to your fans?"

Jeez, this was going to be the William Kaulder Show. I looked at my screen; there were some questions about the books, but it was mostly about Kaulder.

Just then, a drunk redhead burst into the room. "Willy," she said using her outdoor voice, "I told the staff here to bring two bottles of Clicquot champagne to suite 2312. I called five minutes ago. They aren't here yet. You'd think the service at The Lorelei would be as good as the Fairmont."

"What?" Meghan wailed with joy. "You're at the Lorelei? We're only a few blocks away." We heard a crowd screaming in the background.

"Oops, sorry. I guess I wasn't a quiet little mouse." Linda staggered out.

Bex hit the mute button.

Attendees were blasting out our location in the chat section.

Bex got up. "I'm going to call Jay downstairs to warn him." She found her cell and punched in his number.

Austin's phone rang. He pulled off his headset and reached into his suit jacket for his cell. He stood and walked to the corner of the room engaged in a heated conversation with someone.

I closed my laptop. The information in the chat box was moving at an alarming rate; it was too dizzying to watch.

"That was my manager," Austin said. "She was on the call and wanted to know what happened. She also said my social media is blowing up. She wants us to get out of the hotel now."

Bex looked up from her phone discussion. "Jay says people are already walking into the room demanding to see Kaulder. They even mentioned Angela."

"That was quick," I said.

Austin slipped his phone back into his jacket. "Everyone has a cell. You can assemble a flash mob in a few minutes."

"There's security in the hotel. It should be alright," I said, feeling more uncomfortable.

"Remember I told you I've been mobbed before because they think I'm that wrestler. Normal security for the hotel could be overwhelmed if they're not prepared."

"What do we do?"

"We walk out in plain sight." He turned to Bex. "Bex, would you ask the hotel to have one of the limo drivers meet us at the back entrance? Tell him it's for the wrestler and his girlfriend."

Bex nodded and left the room.

Austin started stripping off his suit coat and tie. He released his hair, opened a few of his buttons, and pulled his shirt out of its waistband. I stood there, staring like an idiot, wondering if he was going to strip again. He caught my gaze.

"You need to look like a wrestler's girlfriend." We both looked at my jacket.

"Come on, let's see what that dress looks like without it."

I shrugged out of the garment. The clasps on the straps had fallen opened, my breasts barely contained.

Austin's mouth fell open. "Yeah, yes, you'll do," he stammered. "But drop the one strap off your shoulder, get your hair out of that tight bun, and muss it up."

When we finished, we looked like a couple after a night of debauchery.

"The limo driver will be at the south entrance of the building," Bex called out from the other room.

We walked into the living room. The man I'd thought was Kaulder got to his feet with an unsteady Linda next to him. "What do you want us to do?" the fake Kaulder asked.

"Don't worry, Uncle, it wasn't your fault. Just pretend to be William Kaulder for a while longer. Linda can be Angela Stryker," Austin said.

"Goody," said Linda, "I can play Angela. Is she a naughty nurse?"

The champagne Linda order must have arrived. Austin picked up an open bottle, grabbed my hand, and pulled me through the door out into the hallway.

There was no one in the hall, but when we got to the elevators, we could hear a clamor as the car rose. "Let's just hope all the wrestling fans are at the Tank watching this guy wrestle."

"What?" I whispered.

"The UWF is here tonight at the Shark Tank."

I stepped away from him. "But he's a family man. I don't want to get him in trouble with his wife or that adorable daughter. I'm not going to--"

"Look, he's got about 20,000 witnesses that he wasn't in this hotel. I think his reputation is safe."

He threw his arm around me and pulled me to him. He kissed me as the doors opened, leaning into me and swaying a bit. We heard comments like "Get a room!" "Do you really think we'll see Kaulder?" and "That guy looks familiar."

Austin continued kissing me while we moved to the elevator. He took my breath away. All these weeks I'd forgotten how much I had missed him. Austin stopped the kiss, turned me around, dropped his hand to my bottom and nudged me into the elevator. I took a step, and he smacked me on the ass. The sound reverberated down the hall. He joined me inside and the doors closed.

"Was that necessary?" I was rubbing my behind. It didn't hurt, but he didn't know that.

He chuckled. "Sorry, I'm used to getting into my characters."

"Why did you kiss me?"

He stretched his shoulders, giving me a look I'd never seen before. "Because I'm a wrestler, and I'm used to kissing hot women."

I blinked back at this new persona leering at me. Lucky for him there was no time to protest. The elevator doors opened again to let in passengers. We moved to the back of the car. He had his arm around me as we imitated a drunk couple. We were on the twenty-third floor and must have stopped at each level on the way down. It had me practically jumping out of my skin each time new arrivals entered the lift.

If anyone stared at us too long, Austin would lean into me, the champagne bottle resting carelessly near my back as he swayed into his kiss. Sometimes he'd change it up and whisper sexy suggestions in my ear that I know had me flushing red. But I had to respond as part of the performance, so I cooed and giggled at his bawdy proposals.

A guy, seeing our kissing display, tried to shame us, protesting loudly that we were immoral. Austin took his time to finish his unhurried kiss while the man threw judgments at us. Austin finally stopped, placed his hand under my chin to angle it up, and winked. I wasn't faking the dazed look I knew I had on my face or my weak knees from our public make-out session. He drew me in, my cheek on his chest, and I was grateful for the support.

The man decided to launch into another diatribe until Austin gave him a fierce scowl. The man's hands flew up as if to fend off a blow, but Austin's arms remained around me. The man shrank back in terror, bumping into the side of the elevator. He turned away from us, intently examining his shoes until the doors opened and he bolted through. The rest of the passengers kept quiet and ignored us.

CHAPTER 28

Three Moons

We'd escaped William Kaulder's well-organized fans, but Austin planted himself next to me in the back seat of the limo and insisted we talk the moment the door locked shut. I tossed him a 'hell no' look that made him scoot to his side of the car.

I was rewarded with Austin's unblinking stare until I agreed to a conversation. It was under the condition that it happen at my house, and the driver had to wait outside while he gave me his feeble excuses. It would end with him walking into the night and out of my life.

I switched on lights as I moved through the kitchen. I didn't want to be as close to him as my small kitchen table, so I continued into the living room. I perched on the edge of the lounge chair, too keyed up to settle back, while Austin shifted his bulk onto my low mid-century couch. The large coffee table between us gave me the space I needed, but I still couldn't avoid the dark unblinking scrutiny.

"I don't have time for a staring contest. Your driver is waiting. Let's get this over with." I threw up my hands. "There's so much for you to explain, I don't know where to start."

Austin fell silent, studying his hands as they clenched and released. "I know I hurt you, I never meant--"

"Well, you did," I snapped back. I glanced to my right, fighting the urge to hurl the lamp from the side table at his head. I rejected the idea. He wasn't worth the cost of broken furniture. "The man I thought was William Kaulder," I said, pulling my attention away from a heavy bowl that was closer to hand, "is your uncle?"

"Yes, and Linda is his wife. She can be a handful sometimes. I was going to tell you at the cocktail party who I was, but I got held up by traffic again. Uncle Luis was never going to do the interview."

"Bex, Jay, and his crew all knew who you were?"

"I'd worked with Jay before on other books. I met Bex after you and I had our first meeting at the Waterline; she and Magda are friends."

I don't know what would have been a bigger disaster, Uncle Luis talking about a book he had never narrated or his wife giving everyone our location.

"I tried to approach you as Kaulder," explained Austin, "but we were told you wanted a fresh voice for Cooper."

"We? Who is we?"

"Magda is also my agent."

That made sense. His sister was trying to protect his heart and his business interests.

"I wanted to hedge my bet, so I decided to use my real name and demos of my early stuff."

"What if I had chosen Kaulder instead of Austin the unknown in the beginning?"

He shrugged. "If you had chosen Kaulder, I would have told you who I was. I figured you would understand because you wrote under a pen name."

I was drumming my fingers on the armrest.

"Look, you didn't make a decision right away. I was a new voice, and I had to convince you. That's why I did those phone demos. I was surprised when you answered me back as Molly."

"What? Those performances weren't about me speaking as Molly?"

"No, but you got into it, so I continued. I know it was wrong, but I liked Molly talking to me, even if it was to Cooper.

Guilty, I was getting off talking to that hot smart-ass Cooper.

"It was after reading the series that I became obsessed. I wanted to know everything about Molly. I searched out book reviews, blog posts, fan sites, anything that could tell me more. Those demos were the closest I could get to speaking to the woman who fascinated me. I thought you were her, hiding behind a pen name to write your memoirs. I blurred the lines trying to make you Molly."

"Memoirs?" I spat back. "She's a freakin' time-walker. Did you think I could walk time?"

He glanced down; shoulders hunched. "Yes, no, maybe? I was trying to get to know Molly, but it was at the duck pond when things changed."

"But you said I was Molly."

"We talked about this the day I met you on the road. I did. I think there is some of you in her. But no; you're not Molly Dixon."

"Who is G?"

He flinched, as if I had actually thrown something at him. "That would be Gina, my ex-girlfriend. She left my house just before you arrived the night you came over. She's been trying to get us back together, asking me to come over to fix things. That's why I had tools in my truck the day I repaired your door. She was the real reason I was late for our lunch at the Waterline."

He shifted his bulk, not appearing to be happy with my interrogation. Well-too-bloody-bad, if this was the last time I'd see him, then I would have all my questions answered.

"Gina heard me talking to you on the phone and figured out who you were. We broke up over Molly and my personality change. I knew I couldn't let her continue to hope for a reunion. I made it clear we were never getting back together. That's when she stormed out."

"That must be a record for you to have two women pissed off at you in the same night."

"I confronted her about the message on my phone, and she confessed she had seen you driving towards the house when she was leaving." He glanced at the kitchen. "Do you mind? I'd like a glass of water."

I opened the refrigerator to get a bottled water. I closed the door, and Austin was standing on the other side. I jumped. How could a man that large be so quiet? I handed him the bottle. He turned, leaning against the counter.

"What did Magda mean when she said you would be the best person to voice Cooper?"

"Cooper is Parker, right?" He twisted the cap off the bottle and took a long drink.

"Yes, it's a fair assessment." I didn't plan to, but I had used my brother-in-law as a prototype for Cooper.

"I'm the best person to do the voice because I was like Parker before the accident. How did you describe him? Cocksure, arrogant? If anyone knows the mind of that character, it would be me. Gina left because I changed. She wanted a brash construction guy, not a damaged sullen narrator." He looked at the drink in his hand. "You know, that night we were together meant something."

"That you were able to nail Molly Dixon?"

Anger flared in his face. He slammed the bottle down on the counter. "I asked you to stay that night, not Molly. I launched into the book because I figured you wouldn't leave if Cooper talked to you."

Why was he mad? I was the offended party. "I asked you to make love to me as Austin. Wasn't that enough to convince you I wanted to be with you?"

His eyes filled with regret. "I couldn't believe that you would want someone like me. That's why I offered to stay in character. You were living with Parker and wrote a series of books based on him. I didn't think I was the kind of man you wanted."

The pressure was mounting behind my eyes. It was too much truth to face. I'd wanted him badly enough to offer myself to him. I hadn't felt like that for anyone since Luke. I hated him for waking these dormant feelings in me and hated him because his passion wasn't for me. "I think I understand everything," throwing enough attitude in my voice to lower the temperature. I was more than done. He needed to be gone and for this episode to be a forgotten memory. "Thank you for coming. Your driver will wonder what's happened to you." I turned to walk him out.

"You said you loved me," he called after me.

I stopped. "Molly must have whispered that to you in your dreams; I never said--"

"No, it was you. You said, 'I love William Kaulder.' That happens to be me."

"You misunderstood."

"Didn't you engage in some fantasy of your own?"

I won't face him. I can't look into those eyes.

"You couldn't wait to find out everything you could about Kaulder. You asked me how I met him during our interview. Uncle Luis said that when he was introduced, you were so starry-eyed, he could have invited you to one of the bedrooms and you would have followed him."

I closed my eyes and shook my head.

He moved closer, too close. "No, I don't think I misunderstood. I understand what it's like to fall in love with someone you don't know. Cultivating an image in your mind until just the mention of her name starts you longing for her, but it doesn't compare to a woman in your arms, the one who wants you to love her. I want that again."

My laugh was bitter. "You don't even know me."

His hands were on my shoulders, turning me to face him.

"Molly healed me. Through all the pain and fear during my recovery, she was a constant. I needed to believe she existed somewhere outside of my imagination. No, you're not her... you're real. What did you say? Muscle, blood and bone?"

I turned again, placing my hand on the knob, Austin still behind me. His palm rested on the door just above my head. I breathed in his heat and spice that moved seductively around me.

"You said you wanted me. I didn't misunderstand that. I have the nail marks on my back to prove it."

"Let me open the door."

He pulled his hand away, still standing too close to me. "What do I have to do to crack that ice around your heart and drag you away from who, Cooper? Parker? Or do I have to fight Luke? Listen to me. I don't care how you screw up my words or meanings. I've wanted you the moment I saw you. I did everything I could to make you want me. I would have been Cooper if that's what it took, if that's what you want now."

I turned, leaning against the door frame, facing him. Cooper and Molly were here too, hovering. I could see them enticing me, begging me to be safe with them in the world I created. Maybe my ghostly companions were right, and it was too much of a gamble. I didn't need to have my heart torched and the ashes thrown in my face again. But I was tired of holding my life together with routines or living in my books to keep the pain away. The hard truth was that I needed to belong to someone, and I needed someone to belong to me.

I focused. Austin hadn't moved. He had planted himself in front of me with his chin tilted up, defiant like the night we'd made love.

He was determined to change my mind. "I'll wait for you, Emma. I'll wait until you can trust that I won't leave you."

He was quoting my words back to me. It was Cooper's promise to Molly. The words struck deep at my fears. Was I going to live on memories and paper heroes, or was I strong enough to take a chance? I wanted him and even if this went wrong, I'd survive him, like I'd survived before.

My hands clenched into fists, the nails biting into my palms. I closed my eyes and drew in a breath. At the moment of an exhale, the ghosts faded away to nothing, and it was just Austin.

I reached out for him. "You don't have to drag me away from anyone. I choose you." His face was lit by surprise. He almost stumbled into me to press his body to mine. His arms around me, his lips brushing my hair, my face on his chest.

"I'm sorry I hurt you. Can we start over?"

"Like the first time we met so you can try to drown me again?"

"I'm serious. I've screwed up every meeting I had with you. I knew there would be no more chances after tonight. Tell me that you want me."

"I need you."

"Not Cooper?"

"No."

"Not the wrestler?"

I looked up at him. "It doesn't matter how many men you offer; I only want you, Austin Santoro, not someone like you."

His fingers pushed an errant curl from my face. He smiled as if he had won a prize. "I have something for you."

I grinned. "Really?"

"I bought this for your birthday. It wasn't appropriate to give it to you then, but I think it's something that's more fitting now. Close your eyes."

I squeezed my eyes shut. A box fell to the ground, then something cold slipped over my head.

"Open your eyes."

My fingers held a silver chain with five charms. Three phases of the moon, a phoenix, and I examined the fifth charm. I'd discussed this piece with the silversmith but hadn't commissioned her to do the work. The design was exquisite. Austin's likeness reminded me of an old Roman coin. I touched the cool metal and drew my finger over his profile. In that moment, the old mechanical fortune teller

Madame Rafaela's prediction flashed in my mind. *You will know love is real when you see the metal of their true self.*

I looked up at Austin. He appeared to be worried about my reaction to the gift. "How did you know about this?"

"When Bex invited me to your surprise birthday party, I wanted to give you something special. She told me about your day in San Francisco and the silversmith. We saw the woman at her jewelry stall. I was only going to buy the moon phases, but both women suggested I purchase all the charms. The medallion wasn't on the chain the night of your party. He touched the silver token. "It didn't feel right. But when you agreed to marry Parker, I didn't leave it with Magda's gift. I decided to give it to you tonight. I hoped you would accept it even if it was only the moons you wanted to keep."

"Did the silversmith create your likeness from memory?"

"That was the interesting part. She took several pictures of me and insisted I take one with her for a comparison?" He shrugged. "She invited us back anytime for extra charms."

I laughed. I'd have to watch that woman. I stood on tiptoes, and kissed him. "Thank you for the beautiful gift. Now I'll have you close to me even when you're not here." He gave me a squeeze.

I glanced at the clock on the frig behind him, surprised at the time. We had talked longer than I realized. "It's late, but we can go out to celebrate Passion Moon; the limo is still outside."

Austin looked at me, considering. Although we'd tidied up in the car, we still looked like a couple that had been carousing for most of the night. But that wouldn't take long to put right.

I brushed my hand over his hard bicep. The muscle tensed under the cotton shirt at my touch. "What should we do?"

He caught my hands and placed them around his waist. I leaned in, my head on his chest, and inhaled his heady scent. His unhurried hands drifted to my hips. His right hand moved over the fabric in slow, lazy circles, his labor so sensual I had to stifle the urge to grind against him. The slow rubbing gave way, and he feathered the fabric of my dress up. I shivered from the rush of cool air when the material bunched at my hip, exposing the length of my leg. He was stroking bare skin, burning me where he touched, and I wanted to purr.

His fingers passed higher up my hip to find my panties, his palm smoothly slipping under the thin blue lace. I was actually about to swoon when his hands roamed. I tilted my chin up. He watched me with lusty eyes the color of darkest chocolate, my memory gliding to the night we made love and how delicious it was to mount him.

Austin caught the desire on my face and ran a light finger across my cheek. "I know," he said, curling his lips into a villainous grin, "how to celebrate. He swept me up, cradling me in his arms. "Let's ride."

The End

About the Author

Pax loves binging on fantasy romances, hanging out in her kitchen with friends and going on road trips when she can get away.

Editing endless business documents for work or ghosting an occasional article was her only writing experience. She made the decision to write fiction about two years ago when she got a wild notion to pen a contemporary romance.

Her stories are set in Silicon Valley, but the characters aren't tech moguls, nerdy engineers or venture capitalists, at least not this book. Anyone who is a part of this unique community knows there are other stories to tell about this valley.

Pax is a California native. She lives and works in Silicon Valley.

Someone like You is her first novel.

Before you go...

Thank you for reading *Someone Like You*. If you enjoyed this book, please leave a review on Amazon or Goodreads and help other readers discover my work.

The story continues for Emma and Austin in *Owe me Something*, book two of the **Sweet and Sultry Series.**

Read the first story in the **Love at Work Series**
Trinal is a free download at paxsinclair.com.

Trinal (erotic novella)
Love Contract
Work Spouse

Check the release dates of upcoming books, read excerpts, download a free ebook, or join my mailing list at paxsinclair.com.

Visit me
paxsinclair.com
Goodreads
Amazon Author Central

Trinal

(Erotic Novella)

A Free ebook
Download your copy now!

Shelby was named the youngest Director of Communications for one of the biggest social media companies in Silicon Valley. Young, beautiful and the mistress to a rich powerful man; why is she drawn to a hot brash reporter that could change everything?

The question is always the same. What are you willing to gamble, steal or throw away, for love?"

A triangle romance and the first of the *Love at Work* novella series. This book is a standalone. Contemporary steamy romance.

www.ingramcontent.com/pod-product-compliance
Lightning Source LLC
Chambersburg PA
CBHW050400260626
47156CB00003B/813